As prow

The Calico Cat

By
Amanda James

Jane,

Hope you enjoy
the journey with
Lottie!

Best wishes
Mandy xx

Also By Amanda James

Another Mother

Praise For Amanda James

"This is a great read and I would highly recommend it to readers who like a book that turns from a contemporary read into an amazing dark psychological suspense filled read." **Yvonne Bastian – Me And My Books**

"The book was enjoyable, surprising and comprised of layers of storyline that were weaved together to form an enjoyable read." **Susan Corcoran – Booksaremycwtches**

"Another Mother is an intense family drama that will get into your head and under your skin." **Michelle Ryles – The Book Magnet**

"A gripping, slightly chilling, very entertaining read." **Nicki Murphy – Nicki's Book Blog**

"This story will hit you hard. It will mess with your head towards the end and have your heart racing to find out the outcome, very fast paced." **Gemma Myers – Between The Pages Book Club**

"This books has some fascinating characters and I loved the writing style – it is a very good psychological thriller." **Donna Maguire – Donnas Book Blog**

"Readers looking for a page turning, spring time binge read, should add Another Mother to their list of must reads." **Christen Moore – Murder And Moore**

For my brother Martin who was the first to point out that my protagonist Lottie has more than a passing resemblance to me. I would love to be more like her, but I'm not quite brave enough.

I am however, a tenacious, some might say pigheaded person, and I learned that in the early days from you Martin. You taught me many things, and sometimes it felt like it was just me and you against the world. Thank you for being my big brother. Love always, San.

Chapter One

A Good While Ago

When I was eleven years old, I asked my mother if I could have a calico cat. Perhaps it wasn't the best time to ask as she was late for work, hobbling around the kitchen, one foot in a wellington boot, the other in a court shoe. She looked at me as if I'd asked her to explain the origin of the universe, pre-Big Bang and without the inclusion of God. A furrow creased her forehead and clouds of irritation chased across her eyes. I thought she was going to say no to the cat request, but instead she said, 'Have you seen my other shoe?' and kicked the wellington off. It landed in a corner and spat mud up the cream wall.

Under her breath I heard her mutter *the worst word* – the word that on no account should be uttered by me, then she stepped out into the hall huffing and sighing. I squashed cornflakes into a paste under my spoon and said, 'So can we get one?' I was disgruntled by her hypocrisy. Children were supposed to learn by example. That's what my parents always said.

I was learning that my parents said a lot of things that they didn't really mean.

My mother's voice came from a cupboard under the stairs, 'Get what?'

I leaned forward and spoke to her backside as she knelt, excavating various items of footwear into the hallway like some ferocious shoe mole. 'A CALICO CAT.'

I didn't mean my voice to sound as shouty as it did. I think it was because she was half in the cupboard and I knew I had to raise my voice to be heard, but growing annoyance at her disinterest gave it extra volume.

1

The excavation stopped. She appeared in the doorway. Her dark hair, normally in a tornado-proof neat bob, was splayed out at one side, her face red from the exertion, and I guessed by the look in her eyes, anger too. 'A calico cat,' she said in an ironed-out flat kind of way. 'A calico cat is the very *last* thing on my mind this morning.'

I asked her what the very *first* thing on her mind was.

The ironed-out flatness found animation.

'For God's sake, Lottie, look!' She glared at me and pointed a finger at her feet. They seemed mismatched; not a pair. The neat court shoe on her right foot looked wrong, juxtaposed as it was against the stockinged and muddy left foot.

I was reminded of a doll I'd had years ago that had two different legs. It had been stuck down the back of a radiator for ages and one of its plastic legs had warped into some crab-like appendage, so I'd pulled the leg off a similar doll I didn't like as much and fixed it onto the radiator casualty with a screw and Sellotape.

My mother lifted the muddy foot and pointed again, just in case I hadn't been paying attention the first time. 'I have mud all over my tights, I am late for work, and I'll be even later when I've been upstairs to put a clean pair on, I still can't find my shoe. And why do I have muddy tights?' She stopped, took a breath, her grey eyes made of sparklers.

I realised after a second or two that this wasn't a rhetorical question. 'Because you went out over the fields and got muddy?'

'Yes. And why did I do that?'

I shrugged and took a mouthful of cornflakes. I knew the answer, but I really couldn't be bothered playing her 'stating the obvious' game.

'Because I had to take Alfie for his walk. Alfie, I'll remind you, is our dog, the dog that *everyone* wanted apart from me, but *no one* can be bothered to walk, apart from me. And now you sit there asking for a calico cat!' She threw her hands up in exasperation and went back to the cupboard.

I thought perhaps she was getting a bit what Dad called overwrought. I decided I wouldn't say that to her though, because when Dad did, she became even more so. I finished my cornflakes and, as I took the dish to the sink, I noticed the toe of the court shoe sticking up from behind Alfie's basket.

'Mother, is this what you're looking for?' I stood in the hallway with the shoe balanced on the raised palm of one hand, the other behind my back. I consciously mirrored a remembered image from a Cinderella picture book, in which the prince's servant balanced a shoe on a gold cushion. I didn't have a cushion though, gold or otherwise, so a hand would have to do.

'Why do you insist on calling me Mother? You know I prefer Mum.' The ranty tone had gone and the ironed-out flat was back. She shifted her weight to her haunches and looked up at me. Her smile reflected a combination of inner relief and borderline mania. 'Yes, that's the shoe! Oh, you're a life saver, Lottie!'

'Why do you insist on calling me Lottie? You know I prefer Charlotte.' I wished I could have said something else, given the fact that I was back in favour, but that's the thing with eleven-year-olds, they speak before they think. Or maybe it's just me. I do tend to say what I think, even now I am twenty-eight. It's one of my strengths. However, I did let the edges of my mouth twitch into a brief smile to temper the words.

Mother sighed and looked at her wrist. 'Damn it, I forgot to put on my watch. What time is it, Lot – Charlotte? Have a glance at the kitchen clock while I dash upstairs.'

'Twenty past eight,' I shouted after her, 'and do you think we could talk more about the calico cat later?'

A disembodied voice drifted back a few moments later. 'What exactly *is* a calico cat?'

'They're black, white, ginger and… that's it, I think. I saw one in a film yesterday when you were at the shops with Auntie Hillary. It lived on a ranch in Montana.'

'You mean a tortoiseshell and white cat. Perhaps the Americans call them calico, but that's what we know them as,' Mother said as she hurried back downstairs.

I thought about the shell of a tortoise and decided it looked nothing like the coat of a calico cat. 'Well, *I* don't know them as that. I much prefer calico, not that it describes the colour – well, at least I don't think it does. I'll have to look it up. I just like the word – *and* the cat of course. I think calico suits—'

'Anything to be different, that's you.' Mother shrugged into her coat and picked up her briefcase and car keys. 'Right, Penny's mum will be here in a few minutes to take you to school. Make sure you brush your teeth and lock the door.'

Her lips brushed my cheek and I rubbed my finger at the sticky smudge of pink gloss. I wished she wouldn't kiss me after applying the stuff. 'So, can we get a calico cat, perhaps in a few months or so?' I knew what the answer would be as soon as she'd mentioned Alfie, but I was nothing if not persistent. My gran had always said that if you don't ask, you don't get.

'No. Absolutely not.' She checked her reflection in the hall mirror, combed the wayward bob into order, blew me a kiss and left.

I looked in the mirror to make sure that the blown kiss hadn't magically left another sticky smudge. It hadn't. I loosed my hair from the ridiculously neat plait that Mother had created for me earlier and gave it a good ruffle through with my fingers.

Anything to be different, she'd said, as if it was a bad thing. I thought it was the complete opposite.

Right at that second, I experienced a turning point in my young life, a cat-a-lyst if you will. Of course, at eleven years old, I couldn't put it into those words. I just felt determined. Being different was good, I liked it and I wouldn't change myself for anyone. Not ever.

I took my tie off, shoved it in my blazer pocket and opened the top button of my shirt, looked in the mirror again – I liked the defiance afire in my green eyes. They were a similar shade to those of the calico cat. Calico cats were different. They weren't just ginger, or black, or Siamese, but a mishmash of different colours. One day, I promised myself, I'd get one.

Chapter Two

Two Weeks Ago

Just in case you are interested in hearing more about my life, here's what happened recently. Two weeks ago, after six years teaching history in my local secondary school, I walked out of the classroom and just kept on walking. It was one of those moments, like the one I had seventeen years ago when I'd taken my tie off and decided I'd had a turning point.

A turning point?

I'm never sure how we know what one of those really is. Perhaps we have lots during our life but don't recognise all of them. It could be that we just like the idea of labelling particular moments which seemed to make a big difference to our lives. Probably life just goes on in the same way at the time really, because, of course, we only slap those labels on after the event – in retrospect. I know I said that when I was eleven I 'experienced' a turning point, but maybe I didn't realise it until later, when I looked back.

Two weeks ago was definitely a turning point though, because I physically turned and left the classroom, the building and teaching in general. I hadn't thought about it beforehand, hadn't known I was going to do it. Planning didn't come into it at all.

Halfway through teaching a lesson which asked the question: 'Was Custer solely to blame for the Battle of the Little Bighorn?' I told the class of fifteen-year-olds to look at a Power Point depicting a huge and colourful battle scene on the whiteboard at the front of the classroom. I started asking them questions about it and then my eye was taken by a petal of pink blossom stuck to the outside of the classroom window. That petal was shortly followed by more and yet more, as if from the heavens an unseen hand was scattering confetti.

I realise now, of course, that the spindly branches of cherry blossom trees lining the playground were having a hard time against a fierce and wet north wind, but at the time it seemed like a sign.

A turning point.

I longed to be out there in the wind, feeling the freshness of its kiss, the damp blossom sticking to my cheeks. I wanted to run to the wild ocean, immerse myself in nature, listen to the roar of the waves, fill my lungs and roar back.

One of the students spoke. I can't remember what was said or even who said it, but the voice drew me back to the classroom and twenty-five faces bobbed in front of me. Teaching wasn't enough. It was like looking at an open can of peas.

Not that the kid's faces were particularly round or green, of course, though Jamie Hurley's *was* sometimes, due to his gastric problems, but my job represented the mundane, the ordinary, the 'I care so little about what I am eating I'll just open a can of over-processed and chemically enhanced green vegetables' everyday type of life. The type of life I had decided I wouldn't live under any circumstances, the type of life that crushed your soul and swallowed your dreams, the type of life that killed you little by little and you wouldn't realise it until it was too late.

It wasn't the fault of the children; they were just as trapped as I was. They were mostly lovely and far from pea-like the majority of the time, apart from Jamie, as I've said, and I did love my subject, but the box ticking, target meeting, mechanical Ofsted-following sham that teaching had become was not for me. And in that blossom-filled, can-opening moment, I knew I had to get out, do something different, *be* someone different.

After I'd stopped walking, I went back to my flat and had a drink. I am lucky enough to live by the ocean in Newquay, and my apartment looks right over the Atlantic. Well, the person (me) inside the apartment looks, of course, not the apartment itself. I bought it with some money my gran left to me when she died eighteen months ago. I still have quite a lot of money in the bank following the sale of her big old house, also left to me.

Mother wasn't best pleased of course – she'd only been left a few ornaments and bits of jewellery. I went around to see her a little while after the will had been read, and she said she thought Grandma had been quite mean, as she *was* her only child, after all. I said that wasn't the most important thing here and explained that Gran and I were kindred spirits and saw the world through different eyes – 'artistic and in-touch-with-nature' eyes.

This didn't help my mother's mood. She turned her face into a Halloween mask, her words sharp and pointy, and sent them stabbing through the air at me. She said that artistic and in-touch-with-nature eyes didn't pay the bills, unless you were really talented or really lucky, and furthermore I should be grateful that I had a sensible honest to goodness teaching job. I begged to differ and pointed out that Gran had obviously been talented *and* lucky, because where did she think the proceeds of her bountiful will had come from, if not Gran's painting career?

Mother had pulled her neck back and pursed her lips so tightly that the lines around her mouth showed up like tiny furrows on a frosty field. Then she stabbed again. She would have me know that part of that money was from the proceeds of Granddad's hard graft at the bank for forty-odd years, hard graft, mark me, that he'd done to support his wife's ridiculous and fanciful notion that she was an artist.

I had said that it wasn't ridiculous or fanciful, it was the truth, and, furthermore, she was just angry because she'd been left out of the will. Mother's Halloween mask had melted back into her normal face and she began to cry. I decided I couldn't cope with the reproach swimming in her eyes and left. That had been a week before my second turning point, so after I had finished my drink and looked from my picture window at the ocean trying to drown a few surfers, I decided I'd give her a call and tell her what had just happened.

I lay on my bed, tried to close my ears to the things she didn't say, and instead listened to her false cheery words bouncing down the line, like a ball on a karaoke screen.

'Darling! So glad you phoned. Dad and I were just saying the other day that it wasn't a good idea to part like we did and not try to fix it. You are a good girl though. I told him you'd phone before long. You always know when you've made a mistake. Now, why don't you pop round on Sunday for dinner? I could invite Helen and her son Jon. You two got on so well last time, didn't you?'

No. No, we didn't. We might have done if we hadn't been thrust into a cringeworthingly (yes, I know it isn't a word) obvious matchmaking situation. Though thinking about it again, I don't think I could ever get past the caterpillar moustache. It looked oddly out of place clinging to the top lip of a twenty-seven-year-old guy. It would look much more suitable on the face of a man in his fifties, possibly employed as an extra in Poirot.

Apparently unnerved by my silence, Mother said, 'You *did* like him, didn't you?'

'Not especially. The thing is, Mother, I have walked out of my sensible honest to goodness teaching job...' The next bit was as much as a surprise to me as it was to her. 'And I've decided to be an artist, just like Gwendoline.'

'What? You have to be kidding me.'

'No. No, I don't actually,' I said, my head spinning from the excitement and shock of deciding to change career – just like that, in a few seconds, out of the blue. I thought about all the different blues on a paint palette, until a shriek and a tumble of choky sounding words assaulted my ears.

'But that is the most... *the most* ridiculous thing I have ever heard...' Next, Mother's voice sounded as if it was coming from the bottom of a well and I could tell she'd done that thing she does, clamping the phone to her chest but not covering the receiver properly. 'Keith! Lottie's gone and chucked her bloody career out the window!'

I sighed and looked at a crack in the ceiling. I wished I could shove Mother in it for a while and seal it with filler, just until she'd learned to think before she opened her mouth. The crack was too small though, like my mother's logical reasoning and imaginative powers.

'*You* have the cheek to sigh down the phone at *me* after what you've done?' Her choky voice narrowed to a squeak.

'I haven't killed anyone (yet), Mother, just made the decision to follow in Gwendoline's footsteps.'

'Gwendoline again? Since when did you call your gran Gwendoline? That's you all over, trying to shock, push the boundaries. And I'll tell you this for nothing…'

That's a relief. I certainly wouldn't want to pay for anything she had to say…

'You haven't a modicum of her considerable talent. Those night school classes you've been going to haven't made much impact to be honest.'

Now that was taking the biscuit. 'Thanks, Mother. You said you *adored* the seascape I did recently when you came over.'

'I said it to humour you. I wouldn't have if I'd known you were going to chuck your job in to do it!'

I could almost see her standing by the large Victorian fireplace in their large Victorian house, with her large Victorian work ethic (gifted by her father) rattling round her tiny brain, pushing her pulse rate into overdrive. She would probably be flapping her hand and hissing at Dad to come and listen to our conversation, which would be no good whatsoever, because he'd be hidden behind the newspaper, or pretending to be deaf while watching the telly.

'I really think you should learn to be more honest, Mother. You always taught me to be when I was little. You also need to stop contradicting yourself.'

'Contradicting myself. What the hell are you on about now?'

It wasn't lost on me that she'd let the honesty bit go. She couldn't really do otherwise, could she? 'Well, you said last week that Gwendoline had no talent and that Granddad had to support her fanciful and ridiculous notion of being an artist. Then, just now, you said I haven't a modicum of her *considerable* talent. Which is it?'

'Look, I haven't time for all this now. What I said isn't the important thing here…' *Now that, we could agree on.*

'The important thing is that you cannot leave a perfectly good job that you've been to university for, trained for, to be some kind of… of bohemian drop out!'

I laughed then. Not my normal, trained, polite and socially acceptable laugh that usually found its way past my vocal cords, but a raucous donkey bray of a laugh that caused my mother to use the worst word and slam the phone down. I looked at the crack in the ceiling and laughed and brayed and hee-hawed, until tears coursed down my cheeks and dampened my pillow. Then I got up, poured another glass of wine and looked out at the ocean. And do you know, all of a sudden, I felt so much better?

If I'm honest, before speaking to Mother, there had been a little frowny faced figure of worry, singing and dancing not too far away at the back of my mind. The song lyrics implied I had been rash, stupid and childish to just walk out on my job like that, and the dance steps thumped so loudly I thought I might be getting a headache. The reaction of Mother had swept the little figure out into the ether and reassured me that I had done the right thing. If she hated what I'd done, it had to be good.

Chapter Three

Today – Nearly Afternoon

So, I guess you're still interested, because otherwise you wouldn't still be reading this, would you? I'll assume that you're with me from this point forward. Okay, so this morning I got up and looked at the new white canvas on my new easel, next to my new acrylic paints by the picture window, and worried that the canvas would remain virgin white, blank, untouched for all eternity.

In the last few days or so – okay, it might be ten if you include today – I seem to be having a bit of trouble picking up a brush and applying it to the canvas. Not physically, there isn't anything wrong with my hand or anything, but I have chosen to paint the Atlantic Ocean right there in front of me. The trouble is, it keeps moving, as oceans are wont to do, and the light keeps changing when clouds chase each other across the face of the sun, and now and then a variety of sea birds swoop in and out of the scene, like they're doing it on purpose, to unnerve me.

This kind of thing is expected, and it normally doesn't bother me – has no impact on my artistic ability – but since I'd had my second turning point, I'd been in trouble with the school and the education department. Although expected, that kind of thing does tend to bother me, but I wish it didn't.

The morning after, I of course had remained absent from school. The head teacher phoned and asked if I could confirm that I had walked out on Year Ten at two fifteen yesterday afternoon. I answered in the affirmative. He then asked if I wanted to be referred to Occupational Health in order to get counselling, or did I just want to come in for a chat? I said I wanted neither, thank you very much and would just like to be left alone.

Then Mr Kershaw (please call me Tom) did that thing he does when he's unsure (not very often) and cleared his throat once or twice to give himself thinking time. He said he wouldn't be doing his job properly if he just left me alone, and was very concerned about me, and did I know that counselling is nothing to be scared or ashamed of? As I probably knew, some members of staff in Humanities had availed themselves of it, had taken a little time away whilst having it, and come back renewed and inspired teachers again.

I thought about the ones he meant and wanted to say he was kidding himself. I'd recently found Brenda Stacey hiding in the Geography store room with the lights off, her back to the wall, hugging her knees with one arm and a vodka bottle with the other. She looked neither renewed nor inspired. I promised her I wouldn't tell and volunteered to do her detention duty, so she could go home early. I'm nice like that sometimes.

Anyway, I didn't say he was kidding himself. Instead I replied that counselling wasn't new to me as I'd been made to have it when I was a teenager, and it had done far more harm than good. I walked to the window while I listened to Tom clear his throat a few times, his discomfort palpable across the line as I watched the waves. I felt like they were dragging me under, so I looked away. Tom was warbling on about the best thing I could do, and the first and foremosts, so I put the phone down. It rang again almost immediately. I unplugged it.

Then of course I've had to contend with letters from the education department talking about pensions and loss of earnings. Tom had sent letters too, because every time he'd phoned afterwards I'd put the phone down. I had to fill in a form to confirm I had no intention of returning to work and send off lots of other bits of paper that I can't even remember what they were about now. It has all meant that my stomach is upset, has been upset for about a week, and the damned canvas is still blank because of it all.

I think the main thing that unsettled me about Tom's call was all that talk about counselling. It brought lots of unwelcome memories stomping into my brain like an army of stormtroopers. Not the ones from *Star Wars*, they don't stomp really, do they? They tend to just charge about corridors in ill-fitting masks firing weapons. No, I mean the Nazi ones. They did the goose-stepping stomping and looked much fiercer than the ones from *Star Wars*. Probably because you could see their faces and they were real live people who did horrific and despicable things, not made-up characters in a film.

So anyway, these memories are now living with me and will not go away. No matter how much I try to squash them, lock them away in rooms of my brain I don't visit much, they still manage to pick the lock and goose step across the view of the ocean and leave dirty but invisible footprints on the canvas.

I close my eyes and try the deep-breathing exercise that I saw on telly yesterday. A woman in a pink and yellow leotard said it helped you to get in touch with who you were and allowed a sense of peace to wash away troubles. I am not sure who I am, really (who is?), but after a few deep in-through-the-nose and out-through-the-mouth breaths, I must admit I do feel calmer. Whether that is the same as having your troubles washed away with peace, I have no clue.

One of the deep breaths has brought with it the salt ocean air from the open window, and another, the ghost of a cinnamon and lemon candle I had burning last night. Yes. I am definitely feeling calmer. My determination levels are being replenished too – I can feel them rising up like mercury in a thermometer, until a sudden rush pushes the stormtroopers into a vacant room and barricades them inside.

I exhale and decide that there *will* be paint on the canvas this afternoon. I get up off my sorry arse, walk over to the easel, and there's a flurry of excitement in my chest. It might not be the best work I will ever do, but I will bloody do it. Even if I just sketch in the background, it will be better than the white square that has glared at me accusingly for the past ten days.

I pick up the brushes, select a 'sketching in the background' type one, and then the doorbell rings. Shit. If this is Mother I will just refuse her access. If I allow her inside I know she will destroy this new mood with a few words. Even watching her mouth forming those words will ruin everything.

I look through the spy hole in the door and see Caleb, a colleague from school. What the hell does he want? And is he carrying a bunch of flowers? I'm not a sodding invalid for God's sake.

'Caleb?' I say, opening the door a fraction of a centimetre.

'Charlotte, how are you?'

I open the door a little more and look at his sympathetic eyes (bluer than forget-me-nots according to Anna, also a work colleague and friend of sorts. Anna tends to read too many sickly romance novels), his windswept dark curly hair, a half smile on his face as if he is unsure whether or not to allow the other side of his mouth to go the whole hog. Perhaps he wonders if a full smile will detract from the overall sympathetic look he's trying for.

'I'm good, thanks.' I don't allow either side of my mouth to smile.

We both look at the flowers in his hand, a mixture of white lilies, red tulips and something yellow that I don't recognise, and he thrusts them towards me. 'Sorry they're a bit battered, it's windy out.'

I don't take the flowers. 'People always say that, don't they? Windy out. It would hardly be windy in, now would it?' Sometimes what I mean to say and what comes out are poles apart. In fact, more than sometimes. The thing is, those flowers are annoying me. Caleb's whole sympathetic, sheepish, apologetic stance is annoying me. Why the fuck is he actually here?

'Yes, unless you had a window open,' he says and tries a full smile.

I stare at him and he shifts from one foot to the other, his cheeks get pink, he stops smiling and lowers the flowers. 'So why did you come round?' I say, deciding to just play it straight. 'And how did you know where I live?'

He raises an eyebrow and then opens his arms expansively, scattering petals along the corridor. 'I wanted to come and see you, have a chat after... after... You know, like friends do? And Anna gave me your address.'

Anna had no bloody right, and friends, are we? I'd call us acquaintances. Yes, he's a nice enough bloke, we chat at lunchtimes and stuff, but friends? Not really. Friends go out for drinks and to each other's houses. I only have a few friends and I don't see them too often because they get on my nerves after a while.

'You said you wanted to come and see me after. After what?' I ask, fold my arms and watch his face intently. I'm good at detecting bullshit.

'You leaving teaching...' he shrugs, and his mouth makes a series of shapes as if it's searching for the right words... 'in *that* way.'

'*That* way. You mean the walking out of class in the middle of a lesson with not so much as a by your leave and never going back kind of way?' One side of my mouth turns up of its own accord.

Caleb laughs and looks more relaxed and less like a sheepish sheep. Then his words come out in a rush. 'Yes, I guess. Look if you're busy or rather I didn't come in, I quite understand. Just take the flowers and I'll pop off.'

Do I want him to 'pop off', whatever that means? My imagination presents Caleb as a bottle of fizzy water, his head the screw top. Then it shakes him, and his head pops off. I expect that you might think that's a very odd thought. You and me both.

I should want him to leave really – I'm busy, or about to be busy with my painting. But I think that would be impolite and he is being quite kind, isn't he? I stand to one side and wave him through. As he passes, I catch a whiff of flowers and fresh sea air on clean skin.

Caleb puts the flowers on my table and turns in a circle looking everywhere at once. 'Oh, my goodness, what a fantastic place you have,' he says and walks to the picture window. 'And this view is to die for.'

I have never understood that phrase. If you were dead, how could you enjoy whatever it was that you'd died for – in this case a view? To be polite, I say, 'Thanks, it is stunning. I wouldn't want to live anywhere else in the world.'

'I don't blame you.' He points at the canvas. 'I didn't know you were an artist.'

I want to say that, as he could see, I hadn't yet managed it. But my new determination levels said I shouldn't. 'I've been dabbling for a few months, and that's what I've decided to do as my new career. My grandma was a successful artist and I am following in her footsteps.'

Caleb's face is lit by a huge smile. 'That's fantastic! The flowers were to say congratulations for being brave and just walking out like you did, but a new career on top of that. My hat is off.' He takes off an imaginary hat and bows.

'Congratulatory flowers, eh?' I feel my spirits rise higher than my determination levels. 'It's amazing how a person can misinterpret "saying it with flowers". I thought you'd brought them to say, "Oh dear, it's a shame you lost your marbles and have become insane."'

Caleb shakes his head so vigorously that I worry that it might pop off. 'No way! I've always admired the way you speak your mind when everyone else doesn't, and you're unafraid to be completely different to anyone else, even when it's easier to run with the pack.'

He looks at me and his eyes are shining with passion. He runs both hands though his hair and begins to pace. 'When I heard that you'd walked out I knew you were okay, that you'd just followed your heart, even though others were saying you'd had a breakdown or something.' Caleb stops pacing and looks at me intently. 'Remember that time you told me that sometimes you felt trapped, like a tiny cog in a very big machine?'

'I can't say as I do, though I have said that kind of thing often'

'And then you said that one day you'd just walk out and keep walking.'

'Did I?' This was news to me. I had often thought it but wasn't aware that I'd actually spoken it out loud – and not to Caleb.

'Yes. You also said we only had one life and we should live it before it's too late.'

'Oh yes, I do say that quite often too—'

'Well I think you're bloody marvellous, and brave, and—' he does that shaping thing with his mouth again '—and different.' He throws his hands in the air and laughs, a little self-consciously I think.

The main thing I take from his little speech isn't that, though. The main thing is the fact that he has said I'm different. As you might have gathered, I have trying to be different since I was eleven, and Caleb has seen my difference and appears to admire it. Most people actively try to bury their differences and become like everyone else for fear of ridicule. They want to belong. They want to 'fit in'. They don't like to be singled out, have their differences scrutinised, put on microscope slides or in Petri dishes and poked by society. I on the other hand, rejoice in it. I don't want to belong if it means having to wrestle your individuality into a small space, paint it grey and make it... normal.

Caleb is grinning at me like the dog I saw on the beach yesterday. A big wide unselfconscious happy grin that stretches his face, a smile that invites the lips of others to copy it even though they might not want to. I realised mine are no exception.

We do stretchy grins at each other for what seems like two minutes, but it's probably only a matter of seconds, and then I say, 'Would you like to stay for lunch?'

Chapter Four

This Afternoon

Upset stomachs and salmon salads might not be perfect partners, but there isn't much else on offer. A growl from my abdomen is ambiguous in tone. Am I just hungry? I think I might be, because the churny anxious bubble I've had in there for the past few days seems to be absent. From the kitchen area I look out at Caleb on the balcony drinking a glass of wine and think the churny bubble might have gone because of all the nice things he said.

He turns and smiles, raises his glass, sweeps his arm across the view and mouths 'fantastic' at me. I nod and bob down behind the counter to stuff a hunk of bread and butter in my mouth. God, that is delicious. I chew it and quickly swallow it down. My stomach is grateful and asks for another. Luckily, I have another hunk in my hand. Hang on. What am I doing hiding away behind the dammed counter?

With bulging cheeks, I stand and butter more bread. I expect I look like a hamster or squirrel preparing for winter, but don't care. I'm a little annoyed with myself that I bowed to social pressure just then. What the hell does it matter if Caleb sees me literally stuffing my face? I can hear Mother's answer. She would say because it's bad manners, piggy, and definitely unladylike. Unladylike? Now there's a word that's just wrong on so many levels. She used it all the time in my teens when I stuffed my face, wiped my nose on my sleeve, broke wind, swore – the list was endless, or at least very long. The thing is, Mother was a bit of a rebel when she was a teenager; that's like this bread, hard to swallow, I know, but...

'Need any help?' Caleb is standing in front of me trying not to look at my spherical cheeks stretched to capacity. I didn't notice him come back in, too busy thinking, as usual.

I realise that I can't speak and an attempt to do so has scattered soggy crumbs on the work surface. I point at my cheeks as if that were necessary and then point at the lettuce and nod at the colander. He gets it straight away and my smile releases more breadcrumbs. I know that my cheeks are turning pink, not because I'm being piggy or the word that is wrong on so many levels, but spit-soaked crumbs on a work surface… well, it's a matter of poor hygiene, isn't it? I grab a cloth from the sink to scoop up the fallout of my ravenous appetite and notice, from the corner of my eye, Caleb chopping a lettuce and trying to hide a smile.

The bread has finally reached its destination helped by a gulp of white wine and I mask a burp by closing the fridge door too hard. What the hell is wrong with me? I consider trying a full-on ear-splitting belch to rectify my conformity to social etiquette, but I don't have enough air, and to do that would be a bit juvenile, I suppose.

'How are you getting on with the lettuce?' I hear myself ask in a bouncy karaoke manner. I frown and become worried that my mother has cast some evil spell over me – perhaps she's taken over my mind by inserting a clone of her thoughts and behaviours through my ear while I slept last night.

'All done. Anything else?'

'You could set the table. Where'd you like to eat – in here or on the balcony?'

'It's lovely and sunny but still a bit windy…'

'Out?' I say and am rewarded with another dog grin.

I assemble the salad, stick the salmon under the grill and watch Caleb set the table inside, but next to the window. I remember that Anna had added other descriptions of him apart from the forget-me-not blue eyes. She'd said his butt was as firm and round as peach and his thighs were to die for. Yes, that stupid phrase again. She'd said other stuff that I can't remember now, because I'd dismissed it along with her fluttery eyelashes and pouty lips whenever Caleb had been in the vicinity.

Why do we think as a society it's okay to describe people as if they are pieces of meat? Surely our personalities and souls are more important than physical attributes? Caleb had taken the trouble to find out where I live, buy congratulatory flowers and tell me that he thought I was brave and different. He leans across the table to place the salad bowl and I notice that his jeans are quite tight around his bottom. I look away.

I place my knife and fork together in the centre of my plate and pat my stomach, which is now copying the hamster cheek look. It doesn't have two spherical lumps of course, that would scare the shit out of me. No, just the one distended mound. The bread basket has two pieces left in there, but I shouldn't, really. I would say that my eyes are bigger than my belly, but that would be physically impossible today. Well, on any other day too, but you know what I mean.

'That was absolutely gorgeous. Thanks, Charlotte,' Caleb says and pushes his plate to one side.

'You are most welcome. Particularly since you arrived I've found I now have my appetite back. I pat my mound. 'Back in a big way.'

'You hardly need to worry about your figure.' He stops when he sees my frown. 'You've been off your food?' He tries again, eyeing my midriff – and did he just glance at my breasts? Because if that's why he's here, he can think again.

'Yes, I guess it's been all the crap swilling around my impromptu departure from the job.' I lean back in my chair and put my feet on the table and my breasts at a distance. I don't want to be stand-offish, but I don't want to encourage any untoward ideas. Untoward ideas? My mother must *actually* be in my head. I clear my throat, something I learned from Tom. 'I'm much better now though, and that's thanks to you, I suppose.'

'Really?' Caleb leans forward and puts his elbows on the table and a smile on his face. 'Why's that?'

'Because you said that I was brave and different from others, stuff like that.'

'You are. I wish I could be more like you, have the guts to just follow my heart. Who do you take after?'

'Take after?'

'Yes. Do you take after your parents? Did they encourage you to be… well, unusual, an individual?'

A donkey bray of a laugh builds, and I take a drink to drown it. If I allow it free rein I think it might never stop. 'No. I don't take after my parents. Well, my dad is okay, but he's no match for Mother.' I look at Caleb's open face, his head on one side looking interested. Perhaps he noted the ice in my voice when I said her name. In my throat I feel an ocean of words rising, but I don't want to let them spill out. 'Anyhow, I won't bore you with it all. I'm sure you have better things to do with your Saturday afternoon.'

'I don't actually, and I'm sure it won't be boring.'

How can he possibly know that it won't be boring? It isn't to me, but it might be to him. Other people's backgrounds and life stories don't really mean an awful lot to anyone but those people, do they? Not really. Of course, you can empathise and sympathise if necessary, but it's not your life, so you can't know what it was *actually* like for them. I said this to Anna once when we went out for a drink. She was halfway through her life story and then she shut up about it. I think she's oversensitive. While I look at the floor in silence, unsure what to say or how to say it, Caleb gets up and looks at the view.

'How do you fancy a walk along the headland? We could talk about our parents and growing up, or whatever we like really, and then we could have a drink in the Fort or somewhere after?'

I tell him I think that sounds like a good idea. I haven't been out of the apartment for over a week except to get necessities. I change into my walking boots because we've had a lot of rain lately and I know it will be muddy on the paths, and shrug into my parka which should protect me from the strong March winds. I love the fluffy pretend fur around the hood; it makes me feel like a Wookie. I tell Caleb this and he laughs and calls me Chewbacca. I look in the hall mirror and wish my hair was auburn instead of dark brown because it would add to the overall Wookiness.

Down the road, we stop and look over the railing at Whipsiderry beach. The wind is flapping my hood against my cheeks and bashing white waves against the rocks far below. Caleb pulls his woolly grey hat down over his ears more and says something that the wind doesn't want me to hear. He tries again and adds a few finger points and does wavy arms for effect,

'I said I think the tide's coming in, so we'd better not go down there!'

He points to the steep and windy steps leading down to the rapidly disappearing patch of sand. I nod and say, 'Do you know why this beach is called Whipsiderry?' I say it in a tone that obviously implies I do know.

'Not a local. I'm a Truro lad, just work here.'

I don't tell him that I'm not a local either and that I only found out by looking it up when I moved here. 'It's derived from the mining terms, Whips and Derrick. They used to mine iron ore here years ago.' I do wavy arms at a huge rock sticking up from the sand that he says looks like a giant's nose, and then sweep it across the wider area. 'Also, when the tide's out, there are lots of caves and rock pools to explore.' I know this from first-hand experience.

'That's interesting. I'd like to have a look one day when the tide's out.'

'Yeah. And the rock you called the giant's nose is really called Black Humphrey Rock, after the well-known smuggler, and some say wrecker.' I wonder if I sound like a guide book. I hope not.

'Interesting! You seem to know an awful lot about this area,' he says, leading the way back onto the path towards Porth.

'I know a fair bit,' I say, pulling my hood closer to my face because the west wind insists on searching underneath it. 'I do love history, of course, and the only big regrets I have about walking out are not teaching it anymore and of course leaving the Year Eleven kids in the lurch not long before their exams.'

Caleb nods. 'Yes, I did think you might. Let me ponder on it a bit.' He runs ahead and then turns and kicks a large pebble towards me. I kick it back and we have a game of pebble football all the way down to the little bridge that spans the cliff path at Porth. I kick the pebble too hard and it lands in the turbulent waves below.

'Oh no, I was enjoying that,' I say, looking over the bridge until a particularly large wave spits a spray of foam across the bridge of my nose.

'There are plenty more pebbles, come on,' he says and jogs off the bridge and up the incline towards the grassy promontory of the ancient Trevelgue Head.

My favourite cave is living up to my own name for it today – Dragon Cave. It's part of the head and ejects a huge spray of water when the waves bash up inside it. On days like this when the Atlantic takes it by storm, the spray looks more like an exhalation of smoke and a mighty hiss comes with it. I tell Caleb my name for the cave and explain it's because the sight and sound of it is just like I imagine a dragon's breath to be.

'Oh yes, that suits it perfectly,' he says, and takes a picture with his phone. I'm glad he understands and hasn't said there's no such thing as dragons or something similar. Of course, I know that dragons don't exist, but I like to imagine that they do from time to time, don't you? Especially when I'm up here surrounded by the rawness of nature, and the thumping of the waves against the rocks echoes that of my heart against my ribs.

'This would be a wonderful place to paint,' I say. 'Not on a day like this, of course.'

'It would, and you should.' Caleb takes another photo back towards the beach and adds, 'I've pondered on the leaving the kids in the lurch problem. You could spread the word that you'd help them revise on one of the beaches round here. You wouldn't be allowed in the school I don't think, after your dramatic departure and leaving of the profession.'

I like the sound of that – but would it work? 'Wouldn't I need parental permission?'

Caleb looks up to the left and strokes his chin. 'Hm. Not if they're just a bunch of classmates getting together on the beach after school. But if you wanted to be extra sure, you could get them to bring a letter?'

'Excellent!' I shout and do a little dance. Caleb joins in.

We walk back towards the beach and then on to the town and talk about nothing of any consequence, until Caleb says, 'You don't have to talk about your past if you'd rather not.'

Surprised, I say, 'I don't mind. I've just not thought about it since we've been out.' That is true. My head has been past- and trouble-free ever since we set out from my apartment.

'Have you enjoyed being out?'

'I have.'

'So have I.' He pulls the collar of his jacket up and nods out to the horizon where a crowd of dark clouds is gathering over the scene like thugs in a playground. 'But let's get inside before we get drenched and have a drink and that chat, eh?'

'Okay, you asked for it,' I say as I follow him through the door of the pub.

Chapter Five

In the Pub

The Fort Inn is a very lively family pub in the tourist season, so I tend to only visit outside late spring and summer. It has one of the most spectacular views of the ocean, harbour and the coastline and the food is locally sourced and plentiful. Caleb grabs a menu and we sit in a raised seating area at a round table. He runs his finger down the list making appreciative noises, but I can't tear my eyes from the view, even though we've spent the best part of three hours outside. Perhaps I am addicted to the Atlantic and should go to AAA meetings. Addicted to Atlantic Anonymous.

Caleb decides on steak and I go for honey-glazed lemon chicken, and then we look at our drinks and the view in what I hope is a companionable silence but worry that it isn't. An uncomfortable silence feels more accurate. Why, I don't know. I shift in my seat and trace a finger through the condensation on my cyder glass and draw a smiley face.

'Ever the artist, eh?' Caleb smiles and takes a swallow of his beer, the froth of which leaves a moustache on his top lip.

I watch him lick it off and think that the uncomfortable silence is probably just inside me. You know when you feel a bit jittery and kind of outside yourself? You might not; it might be something specific to me. But I think I know how to get rid of it.

'Tom Kershaw phoned after I walked out and talked about me having counselling,' I say while drawing a hat on the smiley face. 'That brought an awful lot of unhappy memories from my teenage years to the fore because I had counselling then. Mother insisted that I went. Dad wasn't so sure at first, but went along with her in the end, always does. He means well, but he's weak really, when it comes to Mother, anyway.'

Caleb turns and looks at me. I can see that his eyes want to be sympathetic but that he senses I might not like it, so he glances away and selects a casual voice. 'Why did you have counselling?'

I tell him about the calico cat day and the quiet rebellion that came after it, the actively seeking to be different bit and the subsequent attempts to squash that difference by my mother, and later my teachers at school.

'Why did the calico cat conversation trigger the change, do you think?' Caleb says as our food arrives, and we make space for the waitress to put plates in front of us.

I pick up an onion ring, blow on it and then crunch into it. 'I couldn't really say. I think it was a cat-a-lyst.' My wink makes him laugh and then I continue. 'I suppose it's because I wanted to be like Mother. In her youth she was a bit of a rebel. Her hero was David Bowie and she and her best friend used to walk around the place wearing zigzag make-up and black T-shirts with WE ARE THE DEAD emblazoned across the back. They did it to get on their parents' nerves, of course, but mainly to be different. She told me all this when she'd had too much wine after a works Christmas party.'

'Really? I bet she was devastated to hear of his death.'

'No. No, she wasn't, and that's her all over. I was more upset than she was, because after she'd told me that he was her hero, I listened to all his albums, watched videos and documentaries about him and totally identified with his desire to be apart from the crowd.' I pick up a chip and stab it at Caleb to emphasise my next sentence. 'But Mother is a fake. She never sticks to her principles, hopes or dreams... and her hero,' I bite the chip in half, 'someone who shaped her teenage years, is just reduced to a "Oh dear, that's a shock. Now I'm glad you phoned as I need to remind you to get a card for Cousin Matthew..." banal throwaway comment.'

Caleb swallows a mouthful of steak. 'What? Is that all she said?'

'Yes. I phoned her to ask if she knew he'd died and she didn't.'

'I assume it could be just part of growing older.'

Caleb assumes too much. 'No, it isn't. She's always been the same, and besides, I know people of her generation that went down to London to stand vigil and share their grief at the loss of such an icon. Mother stayed in and cleaned the cooker.'

He nods but I'm not convinced that he gets it.

'When I was about fourteen, my quiet rebellion got a bit noisy. I had this English teacher, Mr Baldwin, who was crap, but he thought he was Robin Williams in *Dead Poets* or something. He used to make lame jokes and tried to be our mates, but just came across as a tosser – you know the type.'

'Oh, I do,' Caleb says and wipes sauce from his chin. 'I think we have a few in our business studies department.' He takes a drink and then his eyes grow round. 'God, I hope the kids don't think I'm a tosser.'

A laugh waits in my throat and I want to tease him, but I'm not sure it will work as I'm in the middle of telling him about my rebellion, and I don't want my serious words to come out and find themselves misunderstood as levity. 'Of course, they don't. Loads of them have said you're a cool teacher and one or two have even said you're a legend.'

'Really?' he says and laughs. I nod and smile. The last bit wasn't true, but it has made him blush and go all sparkly, so it's worth a bit of a fib.

'Anyway, I decided that this teacher needed taking down a peg or two.' I smiled. 'That was one of my gran's sayings. So, I started to question him now and then just to test that he knew the answers to things. He did mostly, but you could tell he was very uncomfortable about being put on the spot. I could see him trying not to notice my hand up and pick one of the other, quieter kids, but I wouldn't have it.'

'I'm bloody glad you weren't in my class,' Caleb says with a grin.

'That would be impossible, wouldn't it, unless I had a time machine and could have travelled into the future? Us being of a similar age and all.' I watch him shake his head and wonder if he's older or younger than me.

'You know what I mean.'

'Yes, of course I do, just being facetious. So how old are you exactly?'

'I am *exactly* thirty and two months... not sure how many days, minutes or seconds.'

'Oh, so I'm two years your junior.'

'But how many minutes and seconds? You like to be exact,' Caleb says and drains his glass.

'Facetiousness must be catching.'

'Is that a word?'

'No idea. It should be though.' I take a few quick mouthfuls of chicken before the whole thing goes cold and say, 'One day it all came to a head when Mr Baldwin got the class to analyse some war poems by Wilfred Owen. Now, Owen was, and still is my all-time favourite and I'd already read quite a few. I can't remember which poem Baldwin was warbling on about, but he was chatting a load of old pants. I told him as much and offered my considered interpretation.' I pause and remember the tension of an expectant silence in the classroom.

'He didn't know what to say. He sat on the edge of the desk and opened and closed his mouth a few times like a landed fish struggling for air. Eventually he said I was being outrageously rude and that if I continued he'd put me in detention. I told him that it wasn't my fault if he was intellectually challenged and some of the class sucked in air, and a few expelled it in huge guffaws.'

Caleb leans forward, excitement in his eyes. 'Blimey! What did old Baldwin do then?'

'He told me to go next door to Mrs Hadley's class and tell her why I'd been sent out. I replied that I'd tell her he was an inadequate wanker who had delusions of grandeur.'

'Really?' Caleb says, and a bark of laughter escapes him.

'Really,' I say, and the bravado of that moment is relived just as if it had been yesterday. My heart rate quickens, and giddiness settles in my chest. 'So, I leave the class and do just that. Next thing I'm sent home at the end of the day with a letter telling my parents that I have been suspended. They go bananas, of course, especially Mother, and from then on, my school rebellion goes from strength to strength. I had already rebelled at home, but that's another story.'

'My goodness, what a maverick!'

I smile and glance at my plate. Dinner is beginning to look less appetising by the minute and I realise it must be eaten. 'Shall we have another drink?'

'Yes, I'll go.'

The food has my sole attention for the next ten minutes while he talks about his parents and, forgive me if I sound rude, ordinary and uneventful past. Maybe I'm being too harsh – see what you think. His mum works in a hairdresser's and his dad in a bakery, they've done the same job for over thirty years. He has an older brother and a younger sister who are both in the police now. When they were growing up they went to Spain, to the same resort, or the Isle of Wight camping… every year. Caleb never rebelled or did anything to upset his parents and he loves them both dearly. He has never fallen out with his siblings either and they meet up regularly for a drink or a meal.

I can almost hear you thinking that I'm just jealous of this 'ordinary and uneventful past' because mine wasn't, though you can't make a totally informed judgement because you don't know the full story yet. I suppose you might also think I'm right, but so what? Most people's lives are ordinary and uneventful, and, in the end, Caleb seems to be a nice, well-adjusted young man with parents who love him. And isn't that the most important thing after all?

To be perfectly honest, I'm not really sure, because I'm not really 'up' on love. I think I love my dad, but it could just be fondness and a sense that he's always around and will be there if I need him. I feel comforted by his presence in the world. I think you can guess my feelings on Mother... though they are complicated, but my feelings for Gwendoline were the closest thing to love I've known – or at least what I imagine love to be.

I know without doubt I have never experienced romantic love, whatever that is. Men I slept with during my university years and after have all left me cold. The term 'boyfriend' sounds so childish to me, and my attitude to that, and relationships in general, has meant that these men have been the ones to end it. 'It' for them was a series of dates, sex (some called it making love) and a view to a future long-term something or other. 'It' for me was a release of sexual energy – a physical human need, like eating, drinking and sleeping.

One man I was with recently got a bit shirty, said I acted more like a man than a woman because I wasn't emotional enough. I told him to fuck off out of my apartment before I pushed him off the balcony, and was that showing enough emotion for him?

Caleb finishes his meal, leans back in his seat and rests his muddy left boot across his right knee. I can see a painting... muted light with a few diners daubed here and there against a predominantly green and dun surrounding, a smudge of blue outside and Caleb as the subject. Yes, just perfect. *Man with Muddy Boots* by Lottie Morgan. It might surprise you to know that I prefer Lottie but got so used to correcting people for shortening my name without permission that I'm now stuck with Charlotte.

Caleb looks at me over the top of his pint. 'So that's my life and sorry, I completely interrupted yours, please carry on,' he says and takes a big swallow of beer.

The moment has passed for today, I tell him. It's just that I don't feel like getting into all the heavy counselling and stuff and can we leave it for another time? If he wants to hear it, of course. Caleb says of course he would like to hear it, and then the conversation turns to painting, Gwendoline and so forth.

It is true about the counselling, but I kept something back, too. You see there is something in my past that took my, some might say, 'natural' little seeds of wanting to be different on the calico cat day, and genetically modified them into a bloody great oak tree. A bloody great oak tree with furious roots that tore at the earth, and branches that shook gnarled fists at the sky.

When I was thirteen, a big fat secret that my parents had kept hidden for twenty-three years stepped out into the light. A secret that was so devastatingly important that it shaped my future behaviour and affected the rest of my life. Of course, I haven't breathed a word of this so far, but I'll tell you about it very soon.

We run out of conversation and decide that we'll call it a day, just as the door opens and a gust of chill salt air blows in pulling behind it a group of six men in their thirties, dressed to the nines, carrying a seventh between them like a human battering ram. They rush forward and pretend to bash the unfortunate man's head against a table in front of us, until he yells, 'Oi, you fuckers, that's enough, now!'

The others roar with laughter and shove him into a chair. 'Stop whingeing and enjoy yourself! It's not every day you have a stag do, is it? Now whose round is it?' booms a large bullet-headed man in a purple shirt.

The groom-to-be jabs a finger in Bullet Head's purple belly. 'Yours, you tight wad! And be polite at the bar, we don't want to be chucked out of another pub tonight!'

Bullet Head hawks phlegm into his mouth and threatens to spit it at groom-to-be, but then he just laughs and swallows it. Nice. He leaves for the bar. Caleb and I stand to put our coats on while the men make themselves comfortable round the table, expelling into the calm atmosphere of the room a testosterone cloud of raucous laughter, table thumping and expletives.

Just as we're about to walk past, one of the men bellows, 'Yeah, well these bloody refugees should just stay where they are and stop moaning about their life instead of coming over here and demanding fucking housing, jobs and that. What about our own people? This little fucking island ain't got enough to go round for us lot, never mind those sponging twats!'

Caleb sees my expression, blows heavily down his nose and takes my arm to guide me past, but I shake him off and look down at the man that has just spoken. A fire of fury lights in my belly and it's a wonder he can't see sparks flying from my eyes. The man folds his arms across his ample belly and looks at me with wary eyes swimming in alcohol fumes, red rimmed. Eyes that soak up the hatred screaming from newspaper headlines and spewed from TV screens every day, while the brain behind the eyes has neither the analytic skills nor the intellect to challenge it... or perhaps even the desire to.

'Got a problem with me, darlin'?'

Caleb takes my arm again and I shrug him off again. Does he think I'm unable to think for myself? If I'd wanted to walk past, keep my head down, ignore this contemptuous lump now looking me up and down as if he'd like to eat me, I would have. 'I'm not your darlin' and yes, I do have a problem with you. Well, with what you said, to be specific,' I say, and fold my arms across my breasts.

'So, *you* eavesdrop on a private conversation and *I'm* the problem?' He points a podgy finger at his chest.

'You were yelling so much I think that the whole of Newquay could hear you.' There's more raucous laughter and table thumping from his friends.

'I'm not ashamed of speaking my mind. These bloody immigrants should stay in their own fucking country. We'll end up tipping into the sea out there if we keep letting 'em in!' He flings his hand at the view of the darkening sky and navy Atlantic.

'How did you choose which country to be born into? Did you look at a map, or what?' I say, my voice cold, flat.

'Eh?' He runs a hand across his close-cropped dark hair and knits his bushy brows together. Then he walks right into my trap, must be more stupid than I think. 'Nobody can choose where they're born.'

'Yes, that's right! It's a matter of pure luck. And I know I'm grateful every day that I was lucky enough to be born here, when I see pictures of those poor people running from murder, rape, poverty, slavery, so desperate that they risk their lives and their children's lives to try and get just a little bit of what some of us take for granted. I'm sure you've heard people say we have only one life and should make the most of it? Well that's all they're trying to do.'

There's no laughter or table thumping, just a tense silence. The man shakes his head and belches. 'Yes, but it's not our bloody fault, is it? Their governments have buggered their own countries up, made 'em poor. Then there's all these different bloody religions all scrapping. Why should we have to pick up the pieces?'

I do wonder if further response is going to help. It's like talking to a tabloid, but then what did I expect when I started on this? Caleb's face is a mask of concern, but I know I must continue. Raw emotion trumps rational thought, and anyway, if even one of these men agrees with something I say then it's worth it.

A deep breath. 'If you knew your history you would find that past governments and the ruling classes of this "little fucking island", as you call it, dominated, exploited and ruined many of these areas that people are fleeing from, or at least had influence there. So why the hell shouldn't they ask for something in return, you moron!'

A nervous titter escapes from one of the men. Bullet Head returns with a chattering tray of drinks and everything seems to slow down, a freeze frame buzzing with electrically charged air. Then the one I am addressing slams his fist on the table. 'If you were a man I'd fucking deck you, bitch!'

I thrust my neck forward and unfold my arms. 'If you were a man I'd be worried!"

The man springs to his feet, Caleb steps in front of me and then two men step between them and hold on to their friend's arms. 'Leave it, Jay, we've all had a drink and we're out to have a good time, not get in a bloody scrap,' one of them says.

Jay glares at me and Caleb and says, 'Yeah, until this mad bint starts shouting her mouth off. Take your bird home and teach her some manners.'

I say, 'Oh right, a sexist shithead, too? That figures!'

Jay strains against the hold of his friends – a raging bull in a pen. And Caleb grabs my arm more forcefully this time and drags me outside.

We walk in silence for a few seconds and then he stops under a street lamp, glances behind him and lets go of my arm. 'Jesus, Charlotte, you really know how to end an evening with a bang!' he says, his voice shaky, his eyes alive with a mixture of anger and I think perhaps… a shot of admiration?

'Well, I can't just let scum like that shout filth in my earshot and do nothing,' I say, and realise there's an unspoken narrative threaded through my words which says, 'Unlike you, Caleb'.

'Oh, believe me, if he was on his own I would have said something, but there were seven of them, Charlotte. I would have been torn apart.' He folds his arms and sets his jaw as if he expects an argument. Part of me wants to carry the remnants of my anger into the cold March evening air between us, warm it with fire. The other part of me realises this will be foolish and that Caleb is absolutely right. It was different for me because of my gender. Humour might be a good idea right now.

'You said if he was on his own you'd have said something. Well, that's hardly likely – he'd have to be talking to himself, wouldn't he?' I smile and push him with my shoulder playfully as I walk past.

'You think you're a smart arse, don't you, Charlotte?' he says, and though I don't look back, I know he's grinning because it's there in his voice.

'Yes, actually,' I send back.

'I agree. You were brilliant in there, so proud of you.'

I stop and turn to look at him and lots of words fight to get out but none of them can. They are jumbled and incoherent and my heart is beating fast. In the end I say, 'Can you call me Lottie? I prefer it.'

Chapter Six

The Tent Shopping Day

It's two months later and my canvas has lost its virginity. Several canvases have been deflowered, actually, giving themselves wantonly to seascapes, ruined castles, windswept moorland complete with a few sheep and half a calico cat. I don't mean that half a calico cat is on the windswept moorland with the sheep; no, she is on a separate canvas, my current work in progress. I kind of like the paintings but I'm not really happy with them… they aren't fantastic, if I'm honest.

Caleb and I see each other about twice a week and we kiss and hold hands. I know, I sound like a twelve-year-old, but it is all quite sweet and rather lovely. He wanted to take it further after about three weeks, and so did I, but something made me say no. It felt wrong somehow, and I don't know why. I think I'm worried that everything will change if we sleep together and this special friendship we have will become something else, something unknown, and I'm not ready for that. Luckily Caleb understands and says he will be happy to carry on just as we are. I know it's difficult for him, though, and it's becoming more so for me. I also know that he won't want to wait forever, and neither will I.

The revision sessions with Year Eleven have been going really well. Sometimes just a handful turn up on the beach in town, sometimes it's an armful. I am so pleased that they have learned so much over the two years, it makes me feel like I've been useful, a building block in their education tower. I see learning as vertical. It can be horizontal too, I guess, because of the breadth of learning, but overall, the more you learn, the taller you become. I hope the students remember me fondly in years to come. I would hate to be a Mr Baldwin anecdote, saved for reunions and grandchildren.

The calico cat's one green eye watches me from the easel next to the window and it feels like she's imploring me to give her a second one. An eye, not a window. That would look odd, even for a surrealist painting. Though thinking about it, it might work. The eyes are the window to the soul, don't they say?

I think about the concept of cats having souls as I make a third cup of coffee. There have been debates about that, whether animals have souls, though why, I don't know. How on earth could you prove or disprove it? What is a soul anyway? Does it live in your head, heart, brain, belly – where? Is it your conscience, guide, the essence of you? If yes, what does that mean? Does it have a colour, shape, substance?

Are you still following my thread? Do you think as much as me, or in the same way as me? Sometimes I wonder if my thought patterns are odder than most. I think the man in the pub that I argued with must have very different thought patterns to me. But is that because of his upbringing, his life experiences? If he had a similar background and upbringing to me would he think like me? Is it all nurture with a sprinkle of nature? What makes us unique, if indeed we are we unique? What makes us, us?

My dad once told me that I think too much and ask too many questions. I think as a general rule people don't think or question enough. This leaves their brain more susceptible to the relentless dumbing-down process of the media and the desire of an individual to escape from the pressures of everyday life by drinking alcohol and watching mind-numbing 'reality' shows, soaps or perhaps endless sport. Antonio Gramsci had a great theory about that – he called it hegemony and other modern social theorists have developed it. Look it up, it's fascinating.

The coffee is rich and hot and makes my head buzz. Painting might not be a good idea at the moment, because the frame of mind I'm in (can minds be framed? Mine would make an interesting painting) could see me paint a window instead of the calico cat's right eye. It might be fun today, but I know I'd hate it tomorrow.

It is mid-morning on a Saturday, and outside my apartment window the May sunshine paints bold yellow sparkling strokes across the cerulean Atlantic, and on the bouncing figures of passers-by on the street. Have you noticed that people tend to put more of a bounce in their step when it's a lovely day, as if their feet are invisibly connected to the heartbeat of nature and thump along in time? They might be late for an appointment, or going somewhere they'd rather not be going, but at least they feel alive and part of the world. However, when it's hard to tell night from day on dark winter afternoons, the heartbeat of nature is laboured and distant, and passers-by huddle along, their gaze to the ground, disconnected, apart... anchorless.

Mother has called round a few times and we have gone out for lunch. She's able to do that because she works only part time at the estate agents nowadays. On these occasions she has behaved herself perfectly – that worries me. Experience tells me that she's probably going to try to make me do something I don't want to do, but I'll feel obliged as she's being so nice. If it's something little I might consider it, otherwise she can whistle. That's another one of Gwendoline's and I never really know what it means. Of course, I know how to use it in context, but why should a person being made to whistle be a problem to them? There are worse things.

Dad is still full time in car sales but hopes to go part time in a few years. He said the other day on the phone, 'I'm fifty-five, and ten more years of trying to sell heaps of metal to poor saps who can't afford them will be the death of me.' I asked him why he didn't just leave and do something else and he laughed. It was the kind of laugh that has something to say. Not a joyful, carefree laugh, but one that was weary and laced with irony. A laugh that said, *we can't all be like you, Charlotte; some of us are living in the real world.*

You might think that was an awful lot for one laugh to say, but I heard it. I told him that the real world isn't a place I care to visit much, which puzzled him, as he hadn't actually spoken those words out loud.

Two things are happening today. One I am very much looking forward to, the other I could do without. Caleb is coming round at two-ish and we're going to Truro because he wants to buy a tent, and I've decided then I'll tell him about my big fat secret over coffee, and Mother is phoning in a moment to have a chat about 'something important'. Guess which one I'm not looking forward to? Yes, you're right, though the big fat secret bit of the happening that I'm looking forward to might not be plain sailing. We'll see.

'Hi, Mother, yes I'm fine. No, I haven't tried the turnip chutney you brought over yet. No real reason, just haven't got round to it. I'm sure it is good for me, yes...'

Oh dear. She does talk a lot of twaddle. Sorry, this must be very boring for you, but there's no point in listening to her side of the conversation really... unless you'd like to? Okay then. I'll ask her something now or we'll never get to the point.

'So you said you had something important to talk to me about?'

'Yes. I've been thinking. Well, me and your dad have been thinking...' *You have been thinking and talking and he has been listening, you mean.* '... that you should probably try to do something with those paintings. I thought they were really rather good when I came round last week.'

'You've changed your tune. You said I had no talent not so long ago.'

'Ah, but I was angry and it all came out wrong.' *That's as near as I'll get to an apology.* 'Anyway, I was thinking that if painting is to be your new career as you say, then it has to be organised properly.'

'Organised? I think I know how to mix paint, pick up a brush, etcetera.'

'You know that's not what I mean. No, I was thinking that perhaps you should use some of your gran's money to open a studio with a shop attached. They have a few of those round and about here. There was one come vacant last week actually, just put it up in the agency yesterday.'

Oh, I see what she's up to, and what her recent perfect lunches have been about. She wants me to move back to Tintagel so she can try and control my every waking moment. No bloody way.

'I had been thinking along those lines, too,' I say. *This is true actually, but I've done nothing about it yet because I have no head for business.* 'But I want to stay around here, thanks.'

'There's no suitable premises in your area, I've looked.'

I hate the sound of her voice now. It's changed, lost its wheedly lightness and is closed down, hard, taken on an 'I know better than you' tone. 'There's no rush is there? I have plenty of time to find the perfect place. I might even set up in a beach hut,' I say and try to hide a giggle. I can picture her face, perfectly plucked brows pulling together over the bridge of her nose as her forehead furrows, while her mouth draws tighter than a duck's arse.

'Oh please, a beach hut?'

'Yes, a beach hut.'

'Look, I don't know whether you're pulling my leg or not – I can't see your face – but I was thinking you'd do really well in this lovely little shop on the high street. You've lived here all your life and know the place inside out. It will be the height of tourist season soon and you'll quickly build up custom, and you'll get interest from our old friends and neighbours and—'

'I haven't lived in Tintagel for years, Mother. I have made a new life here and you might not have noticed, but it isn't so easy to just set up business and—'

'Yes, but me and Dad will help. It will be wonderful. Dad can decorate it and I can make some flyers for you—'

'You need to stop reading those chick-lit books, Mother. The ones with titles like *The Best Little Pink Art Studio in Fluffy Chocolate Town by the Sea* – happy endings guaranteed, or your money back.'

'I don't read chick lit, I read women's fiction.'

'I've always found that an odd description. Does that mean that if a man opens a women's fiction book, all the words will slide off the page in a swoon, or flutter a fan and scamper away in horror? Or perhaps the book will explode to ensure no manly eye can read what he's not supposed to?'

'Can we have a sensible conversation, please?'

'We are. I mean, can you tell me why we don't have a section in bookshops called men's fiction? Or does the genre "women's fiction" imply that we are only allowed to read those and no other, possibly because our pea brains can't contend with ideas outside love, marriage, pink shoes and chocolate? It's like *Woman's Hour* on the radio. Are all the other radio hours dedicated to men?' I am being half serious, but mainly exercising my right to drive Mother barmy.

'So, would you like me to have a look round the premises I mentioned?'

Is she mad? Hasn't she been listening to one bloody word?

I suck in air and hold it, then I let it out around a few quick breathy sentences. 'No, Mother, I wouldn't. I have no intention of moving back up to Tintagel, much as I adore the place,' (just a shame you live there) 'I have a life here.'

'You say that now, but I think you'll come round. Dad and I—'

My nails grip the leather pad of the settee cushion so hard I fear they will puncture it. 'Oh, shit – is that the time! Sorry, Mother, I must go, I'm meeting a friend. Bye, speak soon. Love to Dad!'

The call at an end, I slump sideways on the settee and pull the cushion over my face in an effort to smother a scream. But why am I doing that? I'd feel much better if I just gave my anger and frustration release. My mouth opens, I fill my lungs and send a primeval roar bouncing off the four white walls, until I'm out of air and the tendons in my neck strain like girders and my face feels like a furnace. I imagine what I must look like and start to laugh. God, I feel better for that.

The cheval mirror in my bedroom says that I might have overdone the eyeliner. Before you ask, it didn't actually speak, no, that would be very weird, and I would probably have run screaming from the room.

I lean in and run a damp finger under both eyes: yes, that's better. My finger isn't, though. It's covered in black eyeliner and mascara and I was in the middle of buttoning up my floaty jade summer dress. Nothing to be done about that now.

I walk to the bathroom and, true to its description, the floaty dress floats off my shoulders and settles around my hips, so by the time I reach the bathroom door I'm grabbing at the material with my left hand and flicking my right hip out to the side repeatedly to stop it sliding further. On telly the other night there was a crab on the ocean floor doing a mating dance, displaying movements which bore more than a passing resemblance to mine at this very moment. Perhaps my libido is trying to tell me something. I stick my finger under the running water and scrub at the black stain. It reminds me of how the consequences of the big fat secret put a stain on my teenage years. I heave a sigh and leave the bathroom.

Caleb's car is a bit show-offy, sporty, black and very fast. It has a soft top which is down at the moment, it being such a lovely day, and he's sitting behind the wheel waving and grinning as I walk down the path from my apartment. He looks fresh and spring-like in his turquoise shirt and his dark curls are even curlier because of the drive here in the breeze. I don't normally like show-offy cars, but his has a certain character, and often show-offy cars have show-offy owners, whereas Caleb isn't. He's a kind, thoughtful man with forget-me-not blue eyes, a quick wit and a crazy sense of humour. Not as crazy as mine, I'll grant you, mine is odder, literalist, and all round different.

'You look lovely, Lottie. The dress matches your eyes,' he says. I lower myself into the car and the breeze lifts the hem of the floaty dress and exposes my knickers as I do.

I tug it down and slam the door. 'Thanks, not sure it's the dress for such a breezy day, though.'

'It's not as breezy as this in Truro… shame, really,' he says with a wink.

I treat him to my best withering stare and notice that his gaze skips briefly over my black-and-white sneakers and the corner of his mouth forms a smirk. He thinks I haven't seen it as he checks the mirror and pulls away from the kerb.

'What's up? Never seen a girl in a floaty dress *and* baseball boots before?' I say in a mock hurt tone.

Caleb glances at me and I keep my face straight. 'Um… no, actually, but I was thinking they make a pretty cool combination.'

'Good. Right answer,' I say and laugh. 'It's all part of being an individual and not conforming to the idea of wearing things that are supposed to "go together". I don't do it for the sake of it though.' *Though sometimes I wonder if I do.* 'I do it because I like the way it looks. I do enjoy colouring outside the lines, as I call it.'

'What a great description! I like that you do as you please. Some people would worry that they would get looked at. I know my sister wouldn't dare wear that combination, well, not out in town, anyway.'

There was something about the tone of his last six words that made me wonder if he did actually admire my choice, or whether he thought his sister was right. I look out of the window at the bright colours most people have on display – their weekend early-summer best – and I wish they would always dress like that. I also decide that Caleb probably *did* mean what he said. After all, I am an acquired taste, but he doesn't seem to want to eat anything else at the moment.

Truro is one of my most favourite cities in the whole of the UK. It has all the shops you'd get in a characterless modern city centre (I won't give examples of these cities because it wouldn't be very nice for the people living in them), but all the old-world charm and historical character of some of the little Cornish towns, too. The weight of ages is present in the cobbled streets and waterfront, but nowhere more so than in the lofty cathedral. I discovered once that there had been a place of worship on the site since the twelfth century, and the ancient church was incorporated into the main cathedral that was built in the 1800s.

Now as you may remember, Caleb wanted to buy a tent. I have no idea when he intends to go camping, but he wants my opinion before he buys one. I did explain to him that I have as much knowledge about tents as I do cricket, but he practically begged, so here we are in the outdoorsy, mountain climby, campy type place, looking at a big blue square tent with a pretend plastic window.

Caleb frowns, strokes the stubble on his chin and says, 'Do you like this one, Lottie, or would you prefer that orange dome one over there?' He points at it.

The orange dome looks like a giant hand has shoved an enormous satsuma into the ground and drawn a zip on it. 'Not especially. But then I can't really get excited about tents. Where will you be camping?'

'That's the thing.' He cocks his head to one side and looks at me like a thoughtful sparrow. Yes, sparrows can look thoughtful, I've watched them. 'I was hoping you'd come with me in the summer holidays... I thought we could walk the South West Coast Path from Newquay towards Land's End and see where we'd end up after about two weeks.'

I say the first thing in my head – I'm a bit flabbergasted. 'Eh? What, carrying that massive blue tent? We'd probably get as far as the Atlantic Hotel and collapse!'

Thoughtful sparrow becomes grinning dog. 'Tents are really light nowadays. Besides, we could stay in B&Bs part of the way if we got too knackered.'

All the time he's been talking I've been thinking that we would be in the tent together for two weeks, and though it was big, it wasn't *that* big. I'd have to insist on separate sleeping bags of course. 'And we'd camp rough, near the path?'

'It's called wild camping. Not strictly allowed unless you get the permission of the landowner, but if we camp at sunset and then set off early the next morning, nobody really minds.'

'You've done this before, then?'

'No. Read about it.'

Only reading about it doesn't inspire confidence and I walk around the tent imagining an irate farmer yelling 'GERROFF MY LAND' and setting the dogs on us. I also imagine what I'd feel like after even a few days of wild camping. My temper would probably be wild too, due to uncomfortable sleeping, the stink of unwashed bodies (mine and Caleb's, not random folk's), and the endless cooking of canned food and lack of fresh veg. We'd probably actually get scurvy and die. I lift the flap of the door, peer inside at the uninspiring interior and walk back to Caleb.

'Well?' he asks, an expression on his face borrowed from a hopeful schoolboy.

Don't get me wrong. I can *absolutely* see the attraction of the walk. I have seen programmes about it on telly, that Baldrick guy did some of the walk, not all of it, obviously, because as far as I recall, it is over six hundred miles. It's an artist's dream. Panoramic views as far as the eye can see of craggy coastal rocks under swathes of green headland, surrounded by a huge blue ocean, more types of seabird than you could shake a stick at (not that I'd want to do that – it would be most unkind), white cushions of sea campion, blue sheep's-bit, pink and purple thrift, yellow vetch and many others wild flowers the names of which Gwendoline taught me but I've now forgotten.

I ponder for a few more moments and then say, 'So you want to go on a walking holiday because your surname is Walker? What would you do if it was Crapper?' This earns me a withering look. This silliness has given me time to test the real words to my answer in my head. 'Yes, okay, I think I'd like to come along, but I won't stay in the tent. I'd rather opt for the B&Bs.'

If Caleb was wearing a crest it would have fallen. I watch his face for a second or two and then the clouds pass over, and he struggles to find middle ground between a pout and a smile. 'Okay, if that's what you'd prefer. The main thing is that we get to walk some of the most spectacular coastline in the UK… and,' a pink tinge splashes his cheekbones, 'we'll get to know each other a little better, too.'

That would be nice, but I won't say this. I don't want to make him think the holiday is going to be something it won't be. Whatever that something is, I can't articulate, anyway. It's the unknown thing I mentioned before. What I do say is, 'Okay, I'll come. Now let's go for a coffee and I'll tell you my big fat secret.'

Chapter Seven

The Big Fat Secret

It's one of those mellow afternoons, you know, the ones that are made out of sunshine and the heat on your skin makes you behave a like a bumble bee? You take a lazy buzz along the winding streets, inhale the aroma of coffee and pastries as you pass open café doors, sniff fruit and flowers on the outdoor stalls, and then eventually settle on some bar stool and drink deep of the nectar on offer.

Okay, yes, I said we'd go for coffee, but Caleb had other ideas. He said he knew the very place, and so here we are inside a rather lovely restored Georgian townhouse which is now a wine bar and restaurant called Bustopher Jones. Its logo is a monocled fat cat in a top hat and tails, holding a cigar in one paw and a walking cane in the other. Apparently, it is a cat from *Cats* the musical, which Caleb has seen but I haven't.

Caleb hands me a cocktail menu. 'I thought this would be the ideal place, you liking cats and all.'

'I don't like all cats, just calico ones, really.'

'Well, I couldn't find a place here in Truro called the Calico Cat,' Caleb says in a pretend upset manner. 'What's so good about them, anyway?'

'I didn't say they were so good. I like them because they're different, or I did when I was eleven. I don't think I'd seen one before I saw that particular cat on the old film. I've since discovered that apparently not many people actively seek them out as pets because they're a bit messy to look at. They're neither one thing or the other. Not black, white, Siamese, ginger, Maine Coon or tabby. Most people like order – things in boxes, pigeonholes, compartments. They like their cats symmetrical, neat. I don't.'

Caleb leans his elbows on the bar and stares at the menu some more. He says, 'Why have you never got yourself a calico cat?'

My eye is caught by a cocktail called an Old Cuban which has lots of interesting ingredients including Prosecco. I plump for that and say, 'Only for the simple reason that I have never owned a house with a garden. When I do, then such a cat will be very high on my list.'

'A nice ambition to have,' he says and decides he'll have the Bustopher Jones Espresso Martini. I look at the ingredients and suggest that he has nothing else alcoholic after this, or driving will be out of the question.

He says he wouldn't dream of it and points to a chalkboard listing hot chocolate and coffee of various intriguing types. Caleb also says that perhaps we might have an early something to eat here later if we like. I am non-committal because my churny stomach is sending little prickly messages of anxiety to my brain. The little prickly messages are concerned that I don't quite know where to start with the big fat secret, and worried that I might make it sound more dramatic than it is. Then I reassess and realise that it *is* dramatic, well at least the consequences of it are/were… you see – I can't even decide on the tense. I suspect I could use both as the consequences/fallout are/is still with me today, though not as demanding and forceful as when I was a teenager, and the consequences/fallout are/is most definitely under my control.

Can I see you raising your eyebrows in surprise because you're guessing that one of the consequences was, let's say, my less-than-planned departure from teaching? The guess would be correct, but no need for the raised eyebrows. I am extremely pleased how that worked out, and the situation was never beyond my control. If I'd have wanted to return to teaching I would have, simple as that. Or as many people tend to say nowadays, 'simple as.' Another similar phrase is 'end of'. Not end of story, just 'end of'. Perhaps soon we'll start to miss bits off all our sentences, until through the process of evolution we'll have to use sign language because all our words will have disappeared. End of.

We are now sitting on comfy leather wrap-around chairs at a private corner table – well, as private as it can be, given we're in a bar. I couldn't let my secret out perched on a bar stool. All that emotion wouldn't be able to cope shoved up against clinking classes and too loud laughter. The little prickly messages aren't as anxious now, either. That might be because we've changed seats, or because the cocktail is smoothing their spikes.

Into a tiny breath of a gap left by Caleb in a conversation we're having about the walking holiday, I say, 'So the big fat secret wasn't really mine. It belonged to my parents. The secret was that they'd had a baby boy when they were sixteen and then had him adopted. He knocked on our door when he was twenty-three and I'd just turned thirteen.'

My heart rattles about a bit and I suck in a breath, but apart from that, I don't feel too bad at all. Caleb on the other hand looks like someone has shoved two fingers up his nose and tried to pull his brain down. His brows are up, his eyes are round, his mouth is open, and he makes a noise in his throat that sounds like a cough but is probably 'God'.

'Sorry, you weren't expecting that, were you?' I say and swirl a blue plastic stick around some ice in my glass while he has chance to gather his thoughts.

'No… not really, and not just like that, in the middle of a discussion about the holiday.'

My fingers stir the stick faster and irritation pulls my eyes to the table. What did he mean – not just like that? What did he want – a fanfare, an announcement by the town crier? What? Does he think it's easy for me to spill this shit? In fact, why am I bothering? Then I remember it's because we're friends and it's nice to share stuff with friends, so they can 'get to know you a little better', that's why. He's mumbling something, and I look up.

'Sorry, what?'

'I said that it must have been a hell of a shock for you and I'm here to listen,' he says and puts his hand over mine on the table. It feels warm and heavy and big and encourages me to give him a break.

'Okay,' I say and take a mouthful of Old Cuban's minty bubbles that kick the back of my throat as they slip down. 'So, this is what happened. My parents were boyfriend and girlfriend since the age of fourteen, and Mother found herself with child at fifteen. She gave birth to a baby boy the day after her sixteenth birthday and was persuaded by my dad's parents and her own dad to give him up for adoption. Gwendoline was the only one who said they'd work something out, even though Gerald, my granddad, was adamant they wouldn't.'

'Did your mother tell you all this?' Caleb says.

'Yes, in theatrical fanciful instalments after James, that's my brother, tracked them down, but Gwendoline told me most of it. Hers was the unadulterated, sugar-free version.'

'So, James didn't make contact beforehand, just turned up?' Caleb finished his drink in what I think is a very quick time considering the alcoholic content. This could indicate that my big fat secret is too fatty for his system to absorb and he needs an injection of booze to help it go down. Or it might just be that he likes the taste.

'Yes, he just turned up one Wednesday teatime. I was doing my homework at the kitchen table and my mother went to answer the door. I heard a muffled cry from the hallway and poked my head round the kitchen door to see what was going on. From behind, my mother looked a bit like a manikin, all angly arms and elbows silhouetted against the porch light, then she slumped against the wall and I watched her shoulders shake up and down. Her sobs came out some time afterwards, as if there was some kind of time lag.'

My words dry up and I'm back in that scene. The smell of toad-in-the-hole drifts from the kitchen, Mother sobs and James is outside, one foot on our step, the other on the driveway, his hand hovering over Mother's shoulder like a trembling bird afraid of alighting. He looks like a younger version of Dad, only his face is pale and crumpled. Dad's face has never been crumpled. Well, hardly ever. The only time I saw him cry was when Alfie had to be put to sleep a few years ago.

'What happened next? You don't have to go on if it's too upsetting,' Caleb says and pats my hand.

I'm not a fan of hand patting; it always feels patronising somehow, even though it's not meant to be. 'No, I'm perfectly okay, just thinking.' I remove my hand in case he's inclined to do more patting and fold my arms. 'Mother shouted Dad and he ran in from the living room, startled by the tears in her voice. Then Mother flung herself into his arms and sobbed something into his ear that I couldn't catch. I came out into the hall and stood behind them all. Dad looked at James and unpeeled himself from Mother. He stepped out and hugged James so tight that he coughed.'

'Hello, there. Can I get you more drinks at all?'

The waiter's voice startles us, and we look at each other and pull 'shall we?' faces.

Caleb asks for a hot chocolate and I ask for the same again. Even as I do, it occurs to me that it might not be wise. Lunch was at least five hours ago, and a warm buzzy cloud is settling behind my eyes already. Impulsively I ask Caleb to order food too and say that anything he chooses will be perfect. I have never asked anyone to choose food for me before. The thought would normally horrify me; I like to be in control. Never mind, there's a first time for everything, isn't there?

Food ordered, Caleb says, 'So what did they say to you? Did James know that he had a sister?'

'They didn't say anything to me at the time. And no, he didn't know, apparently. When James had finished being hugged by Dad he waved at me. My parents turned around and Mother gasped as if I was a fucking apparition or something. I asked who James was and she said, "Never you mind," and told me to go to my room and stay there until I was called.' Though I speak quietly there is a rage building inside me that is noisy and strong and indignant, and I want to smash my fist on the table.

Caleb articulates how I feel by saying, 'What? She shut you out? For fuck's sake – what was she thinking?'

'I have no idea. Dad looked a bit unsure but kept his trap shut as usual. I ran upstairs but peeped through the spindles on the landing. I saw them all go into the living room and I crept onto the stairs – halfway down so I could try and hear, but if one of them came out I'd have time to run back up before they saw me. I didn't hear an awful lot though, just snatched words. I seem to remember *adopted, search, emotional,* and lots of *oh my God*s, and Mother sobbing, of course, she's good at that. When he'd gone we just ate a slightly burnt and cold toad-in-the-hole, while my parents covered the mammoth in the room with a plethora of small talk in helium-high voices.'

'No wonder you don't get on with your mother. How could she be so thoughtless? Didn't she realise that you would want to be included, want to know what had just happened?' Caleb says through a tight mouth.

'I don't think she really cared. She had her son back. A son that made her proud, a son that had almost completed a medical degree, a son that had spent his life wondering about her, a son that she'd abandoned and didn't really deserve, and I'd been sent to punish her. She thanked God she'd been reunited with James – it made having such a pain in the arse for a daughter more bearable.'

'WHAT!' Caleb says just as our drinks arrive. The waiter hovers, unsure. 'She told you that?'

I smile at the waiter; he does his job and skedaddles. I smile at Caleb too to let him know that I appreciate his anger on my behalf. 'No. I overheard her talking to Dad the next day. They thought I was at a friend's, but I came back early and listened at the French windows, peered through a gap in the blinds. They were outside, gardening. After I'd heard her say what I just told you, Dad said something like, "Oh come on, Jen, that's unfair. Yes, Lottie can be headstrong and yes, odd sometimes. But we still love her, don't we?" Mother pushed her floppy gardening hat back from her forehead and looked at the sky. Then she said, "Yes I suppose so. But not like I love James. James is my salvation, Lottie is my penance."'

'Jeez. Is she religious or something?'

'No. Just a dramatic, self-centred, Grade A bitch.'

The word 'bitch' hangs in the air between us like thick smoke on a windless day. Society would frown upon that word being applied to one's mother. A part of me frowns, too, but there is no escaping it. The way she behaved back then, and to a large extent now, means that she deserves the title.

'You say Gwendoline told you all about what happened?'

'Yes. As I said, Gwendoline said they'd all manage somehow, but my grandfather Gerald said it would be better if they had James adopted. Mother was always one for an easy way out. Of course, she was devastated, loved the boy, but she was easily swayed, apparently. Gwendoline said that she just didn't try hard enough and put it all behind her quicker than was good for her.'

Caleb sighs and nods, and I'm not sure he understands – but why would he? Like I said before, you can't know other people's lives, not really. I say, 'I think she just flits from one thing to another, she's no staying power, or real fight, you know? Like she was when Bowie died. She barely acknowledged it, as if it was irrelevant, she'd moved on, forgotten how she felt when she was a teenager. Mother is and was shallow and self-seeking. Dad was pressured by his parents and they were in cahoots with Gerald.'

Our food arrives then, and we eat in silence for a few moments apart from the obligatory mms and nods to indicate that it's good. Caleb says, 'What did your parents eventually tell you about James?'

'A few weeks later Mother told me who he was and that it had nearly killed her when they wrenched him from her young arms. She said she was overjoyed that he'd found her, that he'd ignored the advice about contacting birth mothers by letter, because he'd just wanted to see her face. That's because he'd known instinctively that she'd want the same, that he was deeply connected to her, had always been, even though they had been apart for twenty-three years.'

'Did she ask how you felt about it all?'

'No. She just drip-fed me information, flung her arms about dramatically while doing so, and cried prettily during performances. Mother seemed to think that I should share in her joy at her long-lost son's return and was most put out when I was less than enthusiastic. I asked Dad about how it all happened, but he just lowered his newspaper and said, "Ask your mother, she's dealing with this one." Then he raised the paper again and no more was said.'

'Unbelievable. Why did they send you for counselling, then?'

'I refused to see James, said I liked the way it was before he came into our lives, and Mother went crazy. She said all the stuff directly to me that I'd overheard and more. Hateful stuff, wounding stuff. I was a nasty little bitch, hadn't the brains of my brother, wanted everything my own way, hard to love…'

I stop and pretend to have trouble swallowing a piece of seafood pie. It isn't the seafood pie. All of a sudden, I don't want to tell Caleb the reason why I'd been sent to counselling. It makes me feel unsettled. Perhaps some secrets shouldn't be shared, aired, dragged up from the bottom of an emotional well and spewed out for all to see. 'I think it's safe to say that my behaviour after she said those vile things got a bit erratic,' I say into my glass and take a large swallow.

'The rudeness to Mr Baldwin?'

'Yes, but… look, do you mind if we don't dig it all up? I had counselling… I had anger management issues and unpredictable behaviour issues, let's leave it there.' My words have sharp edges and I don't mean them to.

Caleb looks away and says quietly, 'Sure, of course. Sorry.'

I don't want him to feel sorry. It's not his fault that I can't tell him the reason, is it? 'Don't be sorry. Anyway, the counselling made things worse – made me feel like I was some kind of alien living in a world of nice, normal humans. Yes, I like to be different, but alien was pushing it a bit. From the time I underwent counselling, I never called Mother *Mum* ever again. As I said before, around the time of the calico cat day, I sometimes used to annoy her by calling her Mother for the sake of it, but normally called her Mum. To call her Mum now might be desirable on occasion, but impossible. It would be giving her more than she deserves.'

'Yes, *Mum* is more affectionate, warm, isn't it? I call my mother *Mum* or even *Ma* sometimes,' Caleb says and grins. Then he hides the grin quickly as if it's something unseemly. 'Oh sorry. That was really insensitive, wasn't it?'

'No, it's nice. I don't want you to change *your* behaviour because of what *I* went through.' That makes me sound like I have been in an accident, or had a terrible illness or something, an attack, a victim. I am *so* not a victim.

He nods and blinks sympathy from his eyes. 'What did James say when you eventually met? Do you like him?'

'Doctor James Vincent, Consultant Dermatologist and I have never met.'

'Never?' Caleb has stopped chewing; his knife and fork poised in mid-air makes him resemble a praying mantis – a very surprised, tortilla-eating one.

'That's what I said. I refused to be around when he visited. I barricaded myself in my room or ran out. In the end my parents met him elsewhere. Oh, I'm sure he's nice enough, and none of it was his fault, but I know I couldn't meet him. I'd be reminded of how my parents feel about him and how they feel about me. That's not a good basis on which to build a relationship.'

Caleb swallows his mouthful and says, 'Has he never tried to contact you over the years?'

'He did phone me once. Mother had reluctantly given him my mobile number. I think it must have been about ten years ago now. She told him there was no point and she was right. The conversation didn't last long. I said it was nothing personal, but I couldn't meet him. James encouraged me to explain how the whole situation made me feel. I said it made me feel like I was the old piece of broken crockery shoved at the back of a cupboard and kept for sentimental reasons, while he was the revered best dinner service brought out on special occasions.'

Caleb stares at me intently across the table until I feel like he's reaching into my mind. Then I see his eyes fill with tears and heat rises up my neck. I don't know what to do about it – I'm not good with tears unless they're mine, and I certainly don't allow those out much.

He says, 'Oh, my poor Lottie. How you must have suffered.'

There is something about his manner and words that make me think I've strayed onto the set of a period drama. I don't know what to do or say, but I know that laughter is on its way into my throat. What would you do? I guess you would force the laughter back down, say, 'Please don't get upset, I'm okay, really.' You might even reach out and pat his hand once or twice. I, however, make my excuses and flee to the lavatory where I can laugh in peace.

Caleb looks more like himself when I return, and we agree to leave my past alone for the remainder of the evening. We talk about lots of different things, and, as we do, in a different compartment of my brain, I simultaneously assess the success of the big fat secret reveal. Overall, I think it has gone quite well. Caleb must now be able to add more information to his 'getting to know me better' collection, and my heart tells me we have grown the closer for it. Yes, Caleb is definitely a friend. He's certainly the best friend I have ever had.

Chapter Eight

A Great Idea

An old 1960s song has somehow got itself lodged in his consciousness. It was there at 3 a.m. when he went for a pee and it's still there now. Caleb stretches out under his duvet and yawns into the pillow. Sod off, pretty flamingo, la, la la. Why would anyone liken a woman to a flamingo? They look awkward; they have a huge beak and tiny beady eyes. Lottie for one would tell him to sod off if he called her a pretty flamingo. That's par for the course with her though; any kind of compliment earns him a frown rather than a smile.

Like the song, Lottie is always lodged in his head these days. He throws off the duvet and looks through the curtains. Another glorious day and a Sunday, too. He wonders if Lottie has made a start on the other eye of the calico cat yet. She said she wanted an early start on it and that he shouldn't come over because she wanted to spend the day painting.

It occurs to him as he runs the shower that she might actually just want time alone after the trauma of yesterday. God, what bastards her parents were, or her mother at least. Mind you, the dad isn't blameless; he should have the bloody guts to stand up to his wife. He soaps his body and thinks about James. It would be nice if some bridges could be built between him and his sister. If Caleb had been James, he wouldn't have just left it at one phone call. Aren't doctors supposed to understand when someone needs help, care and attention? Being told that your sister feels like a piece of broken crockery should have been a big clue to her state of mind. A kernel of an idea hisses into his ear with a jet of water. No. He shakes his head. That's not going to work.

Caleb rubs his chest briskly and then drops the towel. He wishes he could do the same with the kernel that has grown inside his mind. It isn't any of his business, really, is it? But the fact is that it's getting bigger, more insistent, nagging at him until he has to admit that it is a shaping up to be a great idea.

Heavitree Hospital, Exeter, is a series of red-brick blocks and has many windows. It looks quite welcoming as hospitals go, but a nervous twist in Caleb's stomach suggests that he's been a bit hasty. What had seemed like a great idea in a sun-drenched breakfast kitchen yesterday morning feels a bit empty the next afternoon as he stands at the entrance to the hospital. Once across the threshold he'd be in someone else's life, and in someone else's business. He might not be thanked for that intrusion and the great idea could all crumble about his ears. He has a quick discussion with himself. Stay or go? It would be cowardly to give up before he's started. A glance behind and he steps through the doors.

'But is Mr Vincent expecting you?' a bespectacled eagle of a receptionist says. She looks like she wants to peck both his eyes out and rip his gizzard to shreds with her talons. Medical receptionists often give him that impression. Something about protecting the very important medical staff from all and sundry, he supposes.

'No, but I think he'll see me once he knows why I'm here.'

'Not without an appointment, I'm afraid.'

She doesn't look afraid, she looks smug. Caleb can hear others behind forming a queue, shuffling feet and coughing unnecessarily to tell him they are waiting. He leans forward within pecking distance and says in a low voice, 'It's a personal matter to do with his sister.' He puts a letter on the desk between them and pushes it forward with a forefinger. 'I wrote that just in case Mr Vincent wasn't on duty today. I'm willing to wait while he reads it.'

The receptionist pushes it back with a talon. 'I can't deal with Mr Vincent's personal business, and if you don't mind, there's a queue of people who do have appointments.'

He figures there are two choices: walk away and forget the whole thing or bend the truth a bit. The fact that he's come this far, in terms of initiative and distance – an hour and a half up the M5 after a full teaching day, and the fact that this woman needs to be taken down a peg or two, to use Gwendoline's term – swings it.

He squares his shoulders and says, 'It is a very serious matter, and I'm sure Mr Vincent would be most upset to have missed the opportunity to be reunited with his sister.' He looks directly into her narrowed eyes. 'Before it's too late.'

The eyes widen briefly, and the talon pulls the letter towards her. She heaves a sigh. 'Okay, Mr… er?'

'Walker, Caleb Walker.'

'Mr Walker, please take a seat over there. I have no idea how long it will be – Mr Vincent does have quite a few people still to see today – or if indeed he will want to speak to you, but—'

Caleb raises his palm to halt her words. 'That's fine. I can wait as long as it takes. Thank you for your understanding at this very sad time.' He turns quickly before she catches his smirk and makes his way to a row of blue padded chairs.

The same green cat-like eyes as Lottie's regard him across the desk. They sit in a pale face full of concern, a face that is symmetrically handsome and remarkably unlined for a man nearing his forties. His hair is more tawny than Lottie's chestnut brown though, and he runs one hand through it as he says, 'I'm confused now, Mr Walker. My receptionist tells me you seemed to imply that Charlotte was very ill. Yet this letter says only that you want to discuss the possibility of a reunion.'

'I must confess that I might have given that impression, yes. I saw no other way of getting to meet you.' Caleb hears a rill in his voice as if it's just breaking. *Great.*

The green eyes narrow and James sits back in his chair. 'So, Charlotte asked you to come?'

'No. She has no idea I am here and I'm not so sure she'd be very pleased if she did.' Caleb is all of a sudden sure she wouldn't be, and he begins to question the merits of the whole thing.

'How did you find me?'

'I Googled you. It wasn't hard, really.'

James looks out of the window; he seems to scan the clouds and then looks at his watch. 'I have another patient and then we can meet at the Globe pub down the road in about forty-five minutes, if you like?'

'Thank you. I won't keep you for long,' Caleb says and tries a smile that he hopes looks more confident than he feels.

It looks as though his journey hasn't been wasted, but what exactly James is thinking is anyone's guess. Caleb has told him everything that Lottie revealed about her past and now James is at the bar waiting to be served, his face undecided between anger and bewilderment.

'There's no wonder she behaved in the way she did, then,' James says as he sets an orange juice in front of Caleb and takes a pull on his pint. 'Now that I know her version, it all makes more sense. I'm so bloody furious at the way she was treated by Mum and Dad, and I'll certainly want to have words with them about it. I know Mum is bit of a drama queen and certainly bossy, but this…' His gaze becomes distant as if he's looking into the past. 'This is vile.'

Shit. Caleb hadn't thought of others being involved. If James told his parents about it, then Lottie would get to know, and then Caleb would certainly be for the high jump. How foolish of him not to have thought it through. He'd assumed it would just be kept between the two of them, until they'd worked out a way to get Lottie to agree to meet up with James.

Caleb's hand closes around the cool of the glass. That's what he needs to be. Cool. His thinking needs to be cool, calm, in straight lines and no-nonsense, because if he doesn't take control, everything will go suddenly and irretrievably tits up.

'I'm not sure that would be helpful at this stage, James. I thought we could come up with a plan to make Lottie see that meeting her big brother would be the first step to healing all the hurt and trauma of the past.' Yes, that sounded cool, ordered, calm and reasonable.

'I would love to meet my sister, Caleb, but given our past history I'm not sure she would want to meet me. I don't like doing things in secret, either. After all, I was one big secret until she was thirteen, kept from her by her parents. So, if you and I plot behind her back she might see it as another betrayal by someone else she cares about.'

'It wouldn't be plotting or a betrayal, more like a nice surprise,' Caleb says, but even to his own ears it sounds a bit Disney.

'I think that might be naive if you don't mind me saying so. Charlotte, or Lottie as she now seems to prefer, had a very, *very* difficult time of it. Now I realise the full extent of why... poor kid. Those feelings and memories don't just get swept away like they never happened, you know.'

Caleb hears a superior tone in the other man's voice that he doesn't like. It goes with his expensive suit and messy hair that's actually been cut by an expert. Okay, maybe his 'nice surprise' comment was a bit crass, but he's not totally insensitive.

'I do realise that, and the counselling your parents made her have made things a lot worse. She felt like she was an alien or something.'

James sighs and shakes his head. 'Even though their actions, or Mum's at least, triggered Lottie's behaviour, I don't see that they had a lot of choice. Psychotic episodes don't just right themselves without help, normally.'

Caleb shifted his weight on the chair. He didn't like the flutter of panic inside him that James's last sentence had prompted. 'Psychotic episodes? Yes, she might have problems with anger management, but calling your teacher a tosser hardly adds up to psychotic, does it?'

'Ah. I see that you don't know the full story, and I'm not sure if I should be the one to tell it,' James says, drawing his hand down his mouth and chin as if he's trying to create a barrier to further comment.

'But if we're to put things right for Lottie, I have to know.'

'Then why didn't she tell you all of it?'

'I don't know,' Caleb says almost to himself. James makes him feel small and unsure, yet nobody is closer to Lottie now than Caleb, at least he doesn't think so, and that makes him resent the knowledge about her that James holds stored out of reach in his head.

'Look, if I tell you, it might change the way you feel about her and that wouldn't be fair.' James puts his head on one side, allows a half smile. 'You *are* more than friends, am I right?'

None of your bloody business. Caleb remembers about being cool and says, 'We are good friends, and yes, I do care very much about her.'

'Then I suggest you ask her, not me.'

'But if you tell me, it will help us work out a way forward won't it? How can I be the only one ignorant of her past if I'm to try to help her heal it?'

'I'm sorry. I can't be the one. How would that look if we were to get her to agree to meet up and she found out I'd told you things about her behind her back?'

Caleb has to concede that James is right. Perhaps Lottie hadn't told him everything because she was scared that he'd judge her, look at her differently. 'Okay. But tell me one thing at least. Did she… do any harm to anyone?' Damn it, where did that come from? It makes him sound weaselly and weak.

'Yes, but not in the way you mean, judging from your expression. Nobody died.'

James takes a swallow of beer and wipes his mouth on the back of his hand. His eyes have become cautious, veiled.

Caleb isn't surprised. He probably thinks that Caleb is looking for a way out now that he knows Lottie has once done something serious. 'Whatever she did, I will be there for her. She's not that frightened and rejected little girl anymore. She's got through whatever it was and now I think a little closure would be useful.' God, he hates that word *closure*. It's bandied about far too much, but he has to admit it's appropriate.

James's wary eyes look less than convinced but says, 'Okay, if you think it would help Lottie to meet me, then we'll try and come up with something. I won't mention anything to my parents, of course. I have your number and,' he takes a card from his wallet pushes it across the table, 'you have mine.' He leans forward and looks Caleb straight in the eye. 'But I'll give you a bit of advice. Take this slow and don't push her. I'm on the end of a phone if you need advice.'

Caleb nods and feels a bit more positive. 'I will, and I really hope you two can forge some kind of relationship in the future.'

James finishes his drink and stands. 'I really hope so too, Caleb,' he says and shakes his hand, and Caleb is relieved to see real warmth in the other man's eyes. 'It will give me some closure, too. I have wanted to make things right between us for years but feared all was lost. Thanks for giving me hope.'

As Caleb watches James walk away, the enormity of his task settles across his shoulders like a lead cloak. It squashes his fledgling positivity and there is a nagging headache gearing up at the back of his eyes. This great idea might not be so great after all. Not only has he undertaken a responsibility to help Lottie, he now has James's expectations to hold up as well. Marvellous.

Chapter Nine

Half a Cat

So, it's nearly the end of the penultimate week of July, and I have half a cat on the canvas. I would have had a whole one, but I've been far too busy planning this walking holiday. I'm not normally a big planner but I want to make sure that the basics are taken care of so Caleb and I can enjoy ourselves. We go tomorrow, and I am so looking forward to it. The B&Bs are booked, well, for the first week, anyway, and yes, before you ask, separate rooms. I thought I wouldn't book two weeks, because we might decide the whole thing is a bad idea and want to come home. If we don't, then I'm sure we'll find accommodation somewhere.

I look at the half-cat and think I will probably get back to it when I've done the laundry. It's funny, because even though I have been busy planning and researching the holiday, the best walks to take and the like, I have managed to paint the Dragon Cave. It just needs a few finishing touches to the waves and the light playing across a gull's wing, but then that's it. So perhaps I'm avoiding the cat? But why? I turn away. I can tell by the look in its green eye that it's really pissed off with me. But then what do I expect? I would feel the same if I had been left half finished, incomplete, not whole, or is it unwhole? Is there such a word?

Oh, yes, I almost forgot – I have been busy with other stuff too. You will be pleased to know that I have been viewing possible premises for an art studio/shop over the last few weeks. There's a little place on a side street in Newquay that might do, though it is a bit out of the way and next to dry cleaners. Not that there's anything wrong with dry cleaners, it's just… oh, I don't know – too practical, boring, I suppose. Art isn't practical, it's to do with feelings and emotions and existential love of the world and one's place in it.

I don't often say 'one's'; I think it sounds stuffy and pretentious. It's the kind of word someone would use on a late-night programme about philosophy or art (intellectually inaccessible to most people). It's the only word that feels right in certain sentences, though. But I expect you might feel differently.

The other premises are at a little place called Mawgan Porth, about ten minutes up the coast a bit, the location of one of my most favourite beaches. It's really near the beach and not much bigger than one room – an offshoot, really, but that's all I need. The rent isn't peanuts, but I can afford it, as you know, thanks to Gwendoline. Caleb says he's going to help with the business side of it, him being a business studies teacher and all.

He has been a great support in this new venture but has been behaving a bit oddly recently. For example, into conversations about a TV programme, or anything like that really, he'll drop questions about my past. I don't always answer them; I don't like being put on the spot. Examined. Besides, these questions feel planted and orchestrated, because they are so divorced from the context.

I walk over to the half-cat and turn her to face the sea. That might appease her until I can find the time to finish her. Anyway, I was talking about Caleb. Sometimes it's as if he's trying to make me feel better about my parents, and how they behaved during the time of the big fat secret reveal. He actually said the word 'healing' in reference to my past the other day. Now that made me furious. I don't need healing. I did once, but now I am healed. The counselling was supposed to do that, but as I said, it made things worse. You see, I healed myself, with Gwendoline's help, of course. Who does Caleb think he is? That first afternoon, and since, he's said he admired the way I am different, but sometimes it feels like he wants to change me.

Mother and I met for a jolly lunch last week. She is happy that I am looking into opening a shop and thinks it's her idea, of course. I did remind her of the beach hut conversation to illustrate that

I had been thinking about it for some time, but she swept crumbs from the table cloth, and with them, any verbal acknowledgement of my comments.

Instead, she said that if she were me she'd look at somewhere like St Ives rather than Mawgan Porth. After all, St Ives has hundreds of visitors year-round and I would earn a good living. I thanked her for the advice but explained that she isn't me (thank God, that would really be very confusing, because who would I be?), and that I am happy to see how business goes just in the summer and autumn months for now.

Mother thought that idea was folly because how would I survive in the long term? Gran's money won't last indefinitely, didn't I know? I said that was none of her concern, I was mostly setting up this new venture for the love of it and that I would reassess the situation if and when it arose. Experience told me that behind a sniff of derision and a furrowed mouth, a cutting remark waited, so I got there first. I said, 'There's two hundred thousand in my bank account, I own my flat outright, so I think I have a while yet before I start to panic, don't you?'

The mouth drew even tighter and she did that tucking her bob behind her ears thing – a display of irritation she'd had as long as I can remember. A blotchy rash crept up her neck, which indicated that she was angry, embarrassed or both, and she looked anywhere but at me. I could tell she was thinking of a polite answer, but it escaped her, and she changed the subject.

Sometimes I think I should cut her a bit of slack nowadays. After all, the James revelation, how it was done, and the counselling were a long time ago. We have muddled along, kind of, over the years. Most of the time though I don't think she should be given any slack. I mean, think about it, why would Gwendoline have left everything to me? If she'd have thought her daughter deserved it, surely the will would have been in her favour? No. Gran had the measure of Mother and Mother knows it. That's why she changed the subject, that's why she couldn't look into my eyes, because if she did, she would see right away that I knew it too.

Gran didn't leave anything to James, either. She had met him often and told me that he was a fine young man, well adjusted, full of humour, and luckily, he'd had wonderful and wealthy adoptive parents. Because he was more than financially secure, he was left out of the will, apart from a few sentimental bits.

I do miss her, every day. Once or twice she tried to get me to meet James and talked a good talk. I couldn't agree to it, though. I wish I could have, for her sake, if nothing else.

The biggest rucksack ever made stands bulging by the door and everything is crossed off my list. Caleb will be just about leaving the school gates now for the long six weeks holiday and I remember that feeling well. One of my colleagues once said it's the furthest away we'll ever be from starting the new term in September, and he for one was so happy he could hardly breathe. He had been at the school for twenty years, though.

Teachers get a bad press by and large, don't you think? When people talk about the excessive length of teachers' holidays, you'd think that they leave the classroom on the twenty-second of July, or thereabouts, and just laze about on a beach drinking cocktails until going back at the beginning of September. What about all the marking, planning, going into school during the holidays to do photocopying, ordering books and shit? Yes, other workers don't get as many holidays, but they damned well should! Teachers shouldn't get fewer, other workers should get more. We all need more holidays, I say! Phew, sorry about that rant, had to be done, though. If you think teachers have it easy, then try it. Enough said and end of.

The late afternoon sun slants through the blind and paints a yellow slice across the back of the canvas on the easel. This makes me sad and the reason for it is irrational. I feel it would be wrong of me to jaunt off on a two-week break while leaving half a calico cat staring mournfully out to sea, all alone and disembodied. Okay, half-bodied. How on earth can a painting stare, anyway? It's not alive, not a thinking, breathing entity, is it? I have a teddy that lives in my bedroom. I make sure that it has a blanket over its legs at night... I bet nobody else does this. I bet nobody else would feel sorry for half a calico cat painting either.

Even as I tell myself that it doesn't matter if my thoughts are a bit odd from time to time, and that of course I realise the cat won't be lonely and the teddy won't be cold, I hurry over to the easel and turn it round. Two hours later the cat has its right eye, the rest of its head and the outline of another cat in a tree nearby. There. It can't complain now, can it?

Chapter Ten

Fancy a Walk?

Well, I'm all ready. The biggest rucksack ever made is bulging even more after a sudden impulse to shove my teddy in, and I have made sure everything is in order. This involved cleaning the apartment thoroughly and changing the bed linen and towels. Mother always did this before we went on holiday as she said she couldn't bear the thought of a dirty house and slept-in sheets to come back to. This morning, I resisted following in her footsteps as long as I could, told myself that a clean house didn't matter, but strangely I found myself with a duster and polish in my hand… as if by magic.

Objectively I realise that it's a good idea. To come back to a home that needs no extra work, given that I will have tons of washing to do and I'll probably be road weary, is far preferable to the opposite. But because it's what Mother always does, there is resistance. Never mind, it's done and dusted now. I won't say pardon the pun, as what would be the point? People only say pardon the pun to draw attention, to make sure people 'get it'. I find this kind of thing all very odd.

The doorbell rings at just a smidgen (I adore that word) after eight thirty and my heart does a little hammer of excitement followed by a forward roll in my stomach. I do love holidays, you see. It's all the anticipation and expectation after weeks of planning and dreaming, isn't it? Then of course there's a little nag of worry waiting somewhere in your system (I didn't use 'one's' here, it didn't feel right) that says that it might not live up to all those expectations. The little nag of worry isn't allowed to say anything more though, because I fling the door open and say to fresh-faced Caleb, 'Hello, fancy a walk, my 'ansome?'

Three hours later on the top of a hill we break for a snack; we have walked five miles and are well within our scheduled ten. We decided that the first few days shouldn't be more than around ten miles until our feet got used to the hammer, though having said that, our longest day's walk will be just under fourteen miles. The object of this holiday is to enjoy our surroundings, immerse ourselves in nature, not to break the land-speed record for walkers.

At first, I didn't like the way Caleb had plotted, measured and calculated our steps. It should be all about following our feet with unfettered, bouncy, and carefree abandon. But in the end, I conceded it was necessary if we were to book B&Bs for the first week. It would be no good walking seven miles one day, deciding that it was enough and then realising we were actually another four or more from a bed for the night, would it?

Caleb rootles in the top of my rucksack for the flask of coffee I stashed in there and pulls out my teddy. He frowns and shakes the old brown-and-white floppy bear at me. 'What's this doing in the bag?'

'Do you have to shake him like that?'

'Sorry, I just didn't expect to find a toy rabbit in there.'

A rabbit? Is he blind? 'It's a teddy and I thought he might enjoy a break.' There's a glow of embarrassment on the way to my cheeks and it irritates me. Why should it be a problem?

'What's his name?' Caleb holds him up and smooths out the fur on his ears.

The irritation grows as I realise I never named him. That was remiss of me. Caleb stops smoothing and looks at me, a question in his eyes. 'Algernon,' I say, for some reason, and then a black-and-white bird hanging from the sky on invisible strings catches my eye. 'Algernon Oystercatcher.'

A bellowy half-snorty laugh explodes from Caleb, as if someone's ignited a firework of humour in his chest. I do like it when he does that; it makes me feel giggly inside. He says, 'Algernon Oystercatcher – you've just made that up!'

I hand him a banana and try to keep a straight face. 'Quite possibly, Caleb, but you'll never know, will you?'

On a bench with Algernon between us we eat bananas, apples and cheese for the next few minutes while in silent contemplation of the wondrous scenery all around us. Well, I do – I couldn't tell you exactly what's going on in Caleb's head, but he looks like he's enjoying the view. The sky is blue with not a proverbial, the grass is green and has that lovely springy-spongy texture underfoot, the ocean is vast – turquoise in the shallows and sapphire blue further out – and today it has put a calming and peaceful shhhh into its ancient song.

I eat a sliver of apple and wonder which I like best – the ocean at its angriest, roaring at the top of its voice as it storms the beach, smashing great salt fists against harbour walls and leaving a trail of destruction in its wake. Or when it's like this – serene, quiet and thoughtful. It would be silly to try and choose one over the other, wouldn't it? Both ends of the spectrum are wonderful and all the other ocean moods in between.

Sometimes it's not angry, just a bit grumpy and grey. Other times it pretends to be a bubble spa, caressing your feet with gentle foamy whirls to encourage you further, then when you're not looking, it sucks up a few waves and spits them up your jeans as you try to make a run for it. An ocean in a playful mood is one of my favourites.

Caleb wants to make a start on the sandwiches, but I say we should wait until later – it's only eleven thirty after all. He accepts this without a murmur. A snapshot of my mother sending her pointy words stabbing at my dad flashes in my head, so I pull out the sandwiches. 'Hey, have one if you're hungry. What difference does it make?' I say, hoping that my cheery tone isn't too karaoke bouncy.

He sends a grateful smile that makes me cringe, takes a sandwich and points out across the wide blue. 'According to the map,' he says, waving the guide book at me with his other hand, 'this bit of sticky-out headland we're sitting on is roughly halfway between Crantock beach, which we've just walked across, and Holywell Bay…'

I know this already but say nothing, to atone for the sandwich bullying – not that I bully sandwiches.

'And did you know that Poldark is filmed at Holywell, amongst many other stunning settings in this fair county?' Caleb takes a bite of sandwich and looks at me.

'I did, yes. I adore that programme.'

He looks away and makes a hmmn noise that vibrates through his sandwich.

'What's *hmmn* mean?'

Caleb swills the mouthful down with coffee and says, 'Are you sure it's not the guy that plays Poldark you adore? Most women do.'

'I'm not most women, am I?' I say and pick up Algernon, so he can see the view better. I do think that Aiden Turner is remarkably handsome, but I don't see why I should have to admit it, particularly if most women think the same.

'It also says here that there are lots of unusual wildflowers on this bit and when we get to Holywell we might see dolphins!' Caleb's voice holds a tremor of excitement.

For someone who has lived in Cornwall all his life he should realise that while dolphin sightings are not that common in these waters, they're not that rare either, particularly at this time of day. Surfers and fisherfolk normally get the best views. The guide book is probably aimed at tourists too, though I don't say any of this. I think that his enthusiasm is endearing and who knows? We might actually be lucky.

'My sketch pad is at the ready for those wildflowers, and maybe even a dolphin if we get up early enough on this holiday. Sunrise, dolphins and ocean, who could want for more?' I hug Algernon to my chest and inhale the scent of wildflowers, ozone and banana and exhale a heart swell of peace, calm and happiness.

Happiness is funny, isn't it? Elusive for some, taken for granted by others and unrecognised by many. We are encouraged to think that happiness comes wrapped around a new car, house, various expensive this, that or the others, or maybe it is hidden in the in arms of a lover – the Mr or Miss Right that we all must find.

This soulmate has to be everything we dreamed they would be, or if they're not, we pretend that they are and hide our disappointment. To go through life without our 'other halves' is to show the world that we have failed, that there's something wrong with us. Then, once we have found our soulmate and amassed our expensive this, that and the others, we need to make sure our success is passed on to future generations. Children are the cherry on the cake, the completion of our world – our happiness.

I worry that while many are in (often futile) pursuit of all the above, they might miss the delicate and wondrous beauty of a wildflower, a butterfly, the scent of the sea, a sun-warmed stone, the feel of wet sand under bare feet, the taste of fresh-baked bread. Does that make me sound pompous? Self-satisfied? I think it might, but I don't mean it to.

I certainly don't claim to have all the answers, and I know I am very lucky not to have to worry about the practical day to day, but I wish people would take their gaze from the monolith of 'happiness' more often, slow its relentless build and, instead, truly appreciate the daisy growing through the crack in its brickwork.

An hour and a half later and we can see the twin rocks in Holywell Bay sticking out of the ocean like the spines of an enormous sea monster. We are standing on a high dune to catch our breath and I say, 'Oh look, is that Poldark galloping across the sand over there?' I shield my eyes from the bright sunshine with one hand and pull my shirt away from my sweat-soaked skin with the other. I'm hot, sticky and thirsty and wish the breeze we'd had earlier hadn't gone off somewhere else. The rucksack feels as if someone's been adding house bricks to it when I wasn't looking.

'No, I think it's just a mirage.' Caleb hands me a warm bottle of water. The water tastes like plastic, but I gulp it down, nevertheless.

'Damn, it's hot,' I say in a southern American accent. 'Shall we go down to the beach and sit in the shade for a while, have lunch?'

Caleb consults the map and nods. 'Yes. I think that would be an excellent idea. In this heat, lugging these rucksacks, we need to take it easy, and it's only another hour or so from here to Perranporth.'

I slide down the dunes after him and imagine I'm a member of the Foreign Legion lost in the Sahara Desert. It's nice to fantasise like that, isn't it, particularly when you know that you're not lost and only about fifteen minutes from the nearest pub.

In the welcome shade of a huge rock that smells of seaweed, lunch done, and toes in the sand, we both decide we feel much better. Caleb even says he could probably walk another ten miles. I say nothing. His energy must have been short lasting, because he leans his head against the rucksack and closes his eyes while I sketch the spines of the sea monster.

Twenty minutes later I give up because the pencil lines will not behave. The drawing looks static and unappealing. I turn to ask Caleb's opinion, but his chest is moving in a gentle rise and fall, and his dark lashes flutter like the wings of a tiny bird. We have kissed a few times today; I didn't mention it, because it's not unusual and something we do quite a lot nowadays, but I want to kiss him awake, just to see the surprise in his eyes when I do. He does have very pretty eyes and—

'A lovely day for it, eh?' a man's voice says.

I turn back to the sea, and in my view stand a man and woman. I can't see their faces as the sun is behind them, but I can tell they are male and female from their outlines. I presume the man means my sketching.

'Yes, though I'm not pleased with it. It's a bit... flat, really, so I might leave it and come back to it another time,' I say, though can't think why I feel the need to answer in so much detail.

The woman kneels down in the sand next to me and I can now see that she's probably in her thirties and has red corkscrew hair and freckles. She has an open, smiley face, twinkly green eyes, and looks like the kind of person one would pick as an imaginary friend when one was a child, but an imaginary friend that has now grown into an adult. I never had an imaginary friend. I had an imaginary donkey, but that's another story.

She looks closely at the drawing and says, 'I disagree.' Her voice is light and melodic, and her smile makes me feel as if I have just found the courage to attempt something that I thought I couldn't. She points at the sea monster. 'You have captured the light on the rocks so well – imagine what it would look like as a painting.'

The man kneels and looks, too. He's about the same age as her, has blond crazy surf-dude hair and amber darty-about eyes. 'Wow! That's awesome! I agree with Neave about the light. And that wave there looks totally real,' he says in a voice that sounds as if he'd borrowed it from a lion. I don't mean he roared, that would be very scary; no, it's very deep and has a bit of a growl around the edges. He looks like a lion too, come to think of it. 'Will you paint it?'

'Yes, I think so,' I say, and wonder if the whole situation is a bit intrusive. I mean, here Caleb and I are, relaxing – he's actually asleep – and then these two bound out of nowhere and start asking questions about my work.

'Hello,' Caleb says in a half-sleepy, half-surprised tone.

The lion leaps over to him and shakes his hand. 'Hi, hope we didn't wake you. I'm Leo.'

I hide a smile. *Of course, how could it be anything else?*

'My wife Neave and I were just admiring this fine artist's work here.'

I like the way Leo didn't assume I was a wife or girlfriend like many would have. Refreshing. Caleb introduces himself and then me... as his girlfriend. It's natural that he would, I guess. I am a girl (well, a woman, but nobody says womanfriend, do they? Why, I don't know) and his friend, but even so, why did he feel the need to label me, our relationship, in that way? Was it because Leo had introduced a wife and so Caleb had to present me in a similar way?

Was it a macho thing? Or am I just over-thinking stuff, as usual? I expect you think I am, and you are probably right.

Granted leave to join us by Caleb, Neave and Leo are making themselves comfy and pulling energy drinks, nuts and fruit cake from their rucksacks. They work efficiently and in synchronisation, each knowing where an item is, and passing them back and forth as required without the need for words.

I remark on this, and Neave says through a tinkle of laughter, 'Ah, yes. That's because this is becoming as normal to us as breathing. We have been on the road for months, so we should know what we're doing. We have to be super organised to function properly.'

'Months?' I say. 'Must be a very long holiday.' I don't say that I would hate being 'super organised' and isn't a holiday supposed to be fun?

'Bless you, it's not a holiday!' Neave says and flaps a hand at me. I don't like people blessing me or flapping hands either. I'm about to say something grumpy when she continues, 'No. We're walking around the entire British Isles to raise some dosh for a good cause.'

Oh great. Now what do I say? It so annoys me that people have to do this.

'Well done, that is brilliant!' Caleb says, and asks them which charity.

'Yeah, thanks. I took a year's sabbatical from my job at uni to raise money for a premature baby unit in Bristol,' Leo says and slips his arm around Neave. 'We lost our prem twins two years ago now and want to give something back to the staff that work tirelessly in difficult conditions, didn't we, love?'

Neave smiles up at him. 'Yes, we did.' Then she casts her sparkly green gaze at my face. 'We've raised thirty grand for new equipment already and hope to reach at least eighty by the end of the walk.'

There is an unspoken expectation that I join in with Caleb in congratulating them, but I return to my sketching. Because of the heart-breaking reason for their walk, I don't speak my mind as I am wont to do; I think it's best to just keep quiet. Caleb leans in over my shoulder and says, 'That's a huge achievement, isn't it, Lottie?'

I smile and nod at them briefly, because it is. There's no denying that at all.

'We'll give you a donation, won't we, Lottie?' Caleb digs into the pocket of his rucksack and pulls out his wallet. A knot forms inside my gut and pulls tight. No, Lottie won't, and Lottie does not like that fact that Caleb thinks he can volunteer her for things without asking first.

Leo shakes his mane and waves Caleb's twenty-pound note away. 'Thanks so much, mate, but can you do it online? We have a fundraising cash thermometer and it's great to watch it rise – it encourages others to give, too.' I feel his amber eyes on me and wonder if that last bit was for my benefit. Leo hands Caleb a leaflet with information about the walk and how to donate.

'Do you guys have a favourite charity?' Neave asks, offering us pistachios. Caleb takes some and explains that he gives 'as and when' but feels guilty he doesn't do it more often. Then everyone looks at me until the knot threatens to choke off my blood supply. Okay, they asked for it.

'I don't give to charity very often. Sorry if that make me unpopular.'

Caleb frowns so hard that I think his eyes will disappear under the shelf of his brow. The other two look surprised and uncomfortable. Neave tosses her curls and looks out to sea; Leo coughs unnecessarily and dusts pistachio shells from his shorts.

'Why not?' Caleb asks, and folds his arms in a school teacherly way.

'Because there is already enough money to buy the state of the art equipment needed in that hospital and in every other, enough to make sure nobody is homeless and everyone is well fed, enough for education and new schools, enough to make sure every old person isn't left lonely and cold, enough, enough, enough,' I say, and realise my voice is loud and tremulous.

'But there isn't – that's why we're doing this.' Neave's voice has lost its melody, become discordant, bitter.

'How much do you think a Typhoon jet fighter costs on average? Go on, have a guess,' I say, and fold my arms against all three reproachful expressions.

'I know what you're going to say—'

'I doubt that.' I cut Caleb off. 'Eighty-seven million pounds each.' I repeat the amount and watch each of their faces for signs of shock. There are only downturned mouths and shifty eyes. 'The MOD has ordered one hundred and sixty of them. That's nearly fourteen billion pounds of tax payers' money on instruments of death instead of health and well-being. Now tell me again that there isn't any money.'

'So that's why you don't give to charity, because the government chooses to spend huge amounts of its budget on war?' Leo says, through a tight mouth.

'I do sometimes give, but I think it's necessary to have this discussion first, otherwise the powers that be just sit back and get let off the hook time and time again.' In my mind there are two pictures side by side. One is a picture of Leo and Neave in some hospital corridor clinging together to prevent each other being swept away by grief; the other is a jet fighter raining bombs and missiles on some unsuspecting target.

Neave looks at me and shakes her curls. 'Of course, what you say is true, and it's not as if we haven't joined demonstrations, written letters to MPs and lots of other stuff, but little gets done, so in the end *we* have to do something.' She throws her arms in the air and three wooden bangles clack together as they slide down her wrists. 'Ordinary people have to do something, or children die, people starve, people remain homeless, lonely and all the other things you said.'

'But you shouldn't have to!' I say and chuck my pencil down. Already I am unsure of how I feel and can't bear the sadness clouding the sparkle right out of Neave's eyes. I try to block more images. I don't want to think about her swollen belly, ripe for the harvest, and then hollowed out and clothed in black a few weeks afterwards.

'No. But we do,' Leo says, and I see his Adam's apple bob. 'We do.'

They all look down at me and I don't know what to say. I have words spinning around in my head but when they reach the springboard of my tongue they dissolve, and I swallow them. The sea shushes, and the breeze drags the plastic toggles of my rucksack back and forth against the rock, but there's no other sound. Neave starts to pack her things away and I stand up and look out towards the horizon.

A deep sigh leaves Caleb's chest as if he's been holding it there for ages and he says, 'What would you do if you had suffered their loss, Lottie?'

I look at him. His eyes are serious; he's embarrassed by me, ashamed of my words. There's a rush of blood to my cheeks and I feel like a naughty schoolgirl. Okay, perhaps I could have kept quiet just this once, given the circumstances, but then I wouldn't have been true to my beliefs, would I? I'd have bowed to social norms and values, conformed, nodded and congratulated them, while all the time the argument about the jet fighters would have screamed in my heart for release.

Leo turns away and hoists his rucksack; Neave places her small hand on his big shoulder and whispers something into his mane. Again, I can see them in the hospital corridor and something unlocks my words. I say in answer to Caleb, 'I would probably have done the same, Caleb, though I have no real idea how I would react, of course, never having experienced such an horrific loss.'

Neave turns to me and allows a small smile to lift one side of her mouth. 'It took a good while before I could even get out of bed, but now this walk has given me a real purpose – something to aim for.'

'I expect it has,' I say and take a deep breath. 'I really didn't mean to offend anyone.' I look at all three of them but especially

Leo and Neave. 'But I have to say how I feel, otherwise it's all fake. If I was raising money for anything, just before I asked for a donation I would say, "I shouldn't have to do this because…" and then I'd explain. At least then I'd have made someone think, even if it is for just a few seconds. There's not enough thinking done about important things, if you ask me. I hope you understand, and I really do wish you all the best with it.' I test a smile.

Leo nods, slips his arm around Neave and she says, 'Okay, we understand. And I will try that suggestion, Lottie, see how it goes.'

Neave steps forward and gives me a warm hug as tears push behind my eyes. This surprises me. As you know, I'm not great with tears and I *never* let mine out in company. I kneel down and pretend to save my pencils from blowing across the beach even though they are only wobbling to and fro on the sketch pad. Caleb hugs Neave and shakes hands with Leo and we all say bye. When I look up after a bit more tidying they're just about to be lost from view behind a line of rocks.

Caleb gathers his stuff together and asks if I'm ready to go. For the first time since we have become close I don't feel connected to him. It's as if a wire has come loose in our circuit and normal service is not being resumed. We walk in silence across the wide sandy beach towards Perranporth. It won't be me who breaks it, because didn't I explain the reasons for my reaction very honestly to Neave? If she understood where I was coming from, then so should he. I kick a pebble hard. Oh, I don't know. Perhaps I am in the wrong, what do you think?

A little while later, Caleb stops and looks at the map. From the beach I look towards the town and feel like we have been away from civilisation for ages, not just eight hours. In a way, I wish we were going to spend the night in the tent under the stars rather than the guest house. Being out in nature might reconnect us.

'According to this, the Seiner's Arms is just off the beach over there.' He does a wavy arm towards a big blue building on the edge of the beach.

'I kind of remembered that from when I was booking it. Nice that's it's so close to the beach, we might be able to see the stars tonight.' It's the first time I have spoken for ages and my voice sounds unsure of itself.

Caleb puts the map in his pocket and takes me in his arms. 'I have all the stars I need when I look in your eyes, darling.'

I frown. This isn't like him, to be so cheesy. Then in his face I see that he has one of his firework laughs building and my palm on his chest releases it. 'Oh, very funny,' I say. 'I thought you were going all stereotypically romantic on me for a minute.'

'Your face was a picture!' He laughs again and then looks serious. 'Lottie, I used the time during our quiet walk to have a think about the whole situation with Neave and Leo. At first you made me angry, disregarding their feelings just for the sake of your opinion. I thought you were bloody minded and uncaring.' Caleb sighs and shakes his head. 'But then the more I thought about it, the more I realised that you were right, and that it's because you do care and look at the wider picture that you had to say what you did. I admire you for that, Lottie. I just wish I was as strong as you, but I'm not.'

Then he kisses me and whispers into my ear. 'And it's true about the stars.'

Chapter Eleven

In the Money

The wind blows a few salt breaths in though my window the next morning and I am glad of it, because the breeze we had yesterday was half-hearted and ineffectual. Walking demands something more substantial when it comes to cooling hot feet and sweaty skin. I open the window further and look out along the length of the early morning beach. There are a handful of surfers astride their boards bobbing on the swell already, and splashes of purple and pink bursting from split seams in a cobalt sky.

I expect you're wondering what happened last night after Caleb and I talked on the beach. Well, I was happy that he said he realised I was right about the Leo and Neave thing and that we were reconnected; I didn't know what the hell to make of the starry eye comment though. Yes, when he'd said it first he was just doing it to get a reaction, but when he said that he'd meant it, my nervous laugh filled the small space between us and, feeling trapped, I broke free of his embrace and hurried up the beach. He laughed and followed after me and nothing more was said about it.

Perhaps I'm reading too much into it, but don't people say that kind of thing to each other when they are in love? Yes, I know that romantic love is a social construction, and that it is packaged and sold in a particular way to unsuspecting folk via various mediums but... I don't know. I think it was the look in his eyes that worried me, all kind of soulful and honest. I'm not ready for all that, not sure I ever will be. I certainly haven't asked for his love, nor do I want it. End of and simple as.

After breakfast we're on the move again. We have a packed lunch and two flasks of tea and coffee thanks to the B&B. Both of us are feeling refreshed and ready to go, which is lucky, because this time it's a twelve mile or so walk to Portreath. Caleb has made a few notes of what to look out for on the way. He's hoping to see kittiwakes, razorbills, guillemots and puffins from the sheer cliffs around St Agnes Head. I remind him that he didn't see dolphins yesterday so should be ready for disappointment. He seems unperturbed and bounds up the steep and rugged path like a mountain goat.

The wind that greeted me from the window this morning is thankfully still tagging along. I have to stop and put my hair into a tight ponytail though, otherwise I will be walking with a hair-blindfold over my eyes thanks to its efforts.

It's one of those fluffy cloud-scudding, yellow sun-filled, blue-sea-sky summer days. It's the type of day where the sun can pretend that it's actually not too hot, while all the time it's sneakily painting red welts on the backs of exposed necks and legs. Well, I'm wise to sneaky suns and have put fifty tons of sunscreen on. I bullied Caleb into doing the same and this time I didn't care that I sounded like my mother – it was a necessary evil.

'How about stopping for a coffee and a look out for those birds, now?' Caleb says as we walk onto the steeply curving crown of St Agnes Head.

I join him at the edge and face the ocean and the stunning view of the rugged coastline towards St Ives. Caleb tells me that the pair of rocks out to sea are called Cow and Calf and I say it's a poor description. He reads more of the guidebook and says legend has it that a child-eating giant hurled both rocks into sea. This appeals to me more, but I wonder out loud why he didn't eat adults. Caleb doesn't answer because he's already doing a pointy finger at something in the distance.

'See that there?' he says, excitement in his voice.

'What where? Give me clue.'

'That bird! And there's another!' He does more direct pointing. 'It's not far from that walker with the green rucksack – look just to the left of it!'

I see a black-and-white bird with red legs follow another in a nose dive off the edge of the cliff. 'Ah yes, a couple of oystercatchers, I do love those birds.'

'Eh? No, they were puffins! Never seen them in the wild before. Come on, let's try and spot them again.' Caleb begins a lopsided jog off the path and over the uneven ground, the heavy rucksack pulling him over to one side.

'Be careful, Caleb!' I say and run after him – the way he's going he'll be over the edge with the birds in a minute.

We stand and peer over the sheer cliff and can see a few ordinary gull-type birds riding the thermals in lazy circles, some perching on rocks far below. 'Can't see them. They must have gone underwater.' He pants, hoists the rucksack off, places his hands on his knees and tries to catch his breath.

'Yes, or they just flew round to the next beach. Oystercatchers don't dive, as far as I know.'

'They were puffins, I saw the red markings on their beaks.' Caleb stands upright, shields his eyes against the sun and scans the birds flying below us.

Now I am almost one hundred per cent sure that they were oystercatchers, but he looks too famous-fivey for me to say that. Instead I shield my eyes and look left to the next stretch of path and see a few brown towers jutting from the land like a collection of bad teeth. Excellent, just the thing for a young lad seeking adventure.

'Hey, Caleb, isn't that Wheal Coates Mine, that you mentioned the other day?'

He does the dog smile. 'Yeah, looks like it.' Puffins forgotten, he hoists the rucksack and sets off towards it. 'Come on, slowcoach!'

'What about that coffee first?'

The breeze catches his reply and chucks it back to me. 'Let's have it at the mine!'

I am unexpectedly moved by the hulking ruin of a tin mine. We find that it has claimed the lives of many miners over the years, and rumour has it that their ghosts roam the engine house. As the wind moans through the brickwork and we listen to the waves crashing against the rocks far below the floor of the building, I can almost allow my imagination to believe it.

'Did you know that these guys had to work under the sea in cramped tunnels, listening to the rocks and pebbles rolling in the waves above their heads?' Caleb says, reading the information board.

'I did know, but I can't begin to imagine what it must have been like for them. It makes me feel sick to think of it.'

'Me, too. And some of us feel that we're hard done to, having to work long hours and not many holidays. Makes you think when you read stuff like this.'

'Yes. It makes me think that we are so much better off today than they were. It also makes me think how much better off the super-rich are than us, because of their exploitation of the majority of the world's population, and that thousands of people in the developing world have to face working conditions not dissimilar to those men that died here a few hundred years ago. It's all relative, really.'

Caleb turns from the board and gives me a wry smile. 'There you go again, making me think.'

'Yes, it's good for you.' I hope the levity in my voice tempers the school teachery sentiment. 'Now are you ready to go again, or do you want more coffee?'

Caleb pulls his mouth into a side twist. 'I've been thinking that we might take a detour inland a bit to see the St Agnes Beacon. It will be a three-mile round trip and out of our way, but I think it will be worth it. You'll like it, being an historian and all.'

I notice that the famous-fivey look is creeping back into his eyes and decide that a three-mile detour will be okay, even though it's another five or so to our final destination afterwards. You only live once, right? Well, that's what they say, but how do we really know? I have heard some interesting stories about reincarnation and have an open-ish mind on that. I can't see a really good reason for it though, so my mind is more closed than open, but the jury, as they say, is out. It tends to be out a lot over the bigger questions as I get older. Perhaps the jurors are having a too much of an argument to ever come back in.

The beacon is another stunning sight, or rather the view from the top of the 629-foot hill is. A beacon would have been lit here to warn of invasion and was active during the Armada apparently. I didn't know this, even though I have read lots of local history. I pretend I did know when Caleb reads it out – why, I don't know. Okay, I do know. It's because I think I should have known it, and if I say I did, I can almost pretend it's true.

I slip the rucksack off and raise my arms up and out to the side as if I'm flying. The cooling wind wraps itself around my body as I turn in a circle and look at the wide canvas of greens and blues. The colours are framed by the gently curving line of the north coast as far as my eye can see.

'I wish I could fly,' I say to Caleb. 'Imagine what it would be like to just let the wind pick you up under the arms and carry you out over the ocean?'

'It would be awesome.' Caleb smiles at me, then sits on the grass and unwraps sandwiches.

I sit next to him and stare at the horizon, but I can't see where the join is between sea and sky. I take a deep breath and out comes, 'Growing up by the sea saved me, I think. Though there was a time after the big fat secret and during the counselling where I considered throwing myself off a cliff into it.' Saying that out loud hadn't been the plan and it's as much a surprise to me as it is to Caleb.

He looks at me, eyes sympathetic, cheeks full of sandwich, and puts his hand on my thigh. I am wearing shorts and my skin is hot under the sun, but his hand is hotter, though his touch makes me shiver, or to be more accurate, tingle. I shift slightly and push how I feel about that to the back of my mind, concentrating instead on the words waiting in my throat.

Before I have chance to order them, I say to the horizon, 'Yes, I once stood on a clifftop in Tintagel and thought how beautiful it would be to end my life right there. I could spread my arms like I did just now and walk right off the world. Then I thought about how much it would actually hurt if I wasn't successful, and realised that if I was thinking about that, then I probably wasn't ready.'

Caleb opens his mouth to say something, but a voice behind us gets there first. 'Afternoon, isn't this a stunning view?'

A portly man in a red T-shirt, and shorts baggy enough to store a couple of elephants in, steps into our aforementioned view, which is a little rude considering we've just climbed up a huge hill to see it. I pointedly crane my neck past his hairy calf and say, 'Yes, stunning.'

The man laughs, well chortles really. I love the word 'chortle', though I don't always love listening to one, but then again, that depends on who's doing the chortling. This man's chortle is pleasant and sounds like river water rushing through stones. Not little stones, the larger round ones – it's a deep chortle.

'Sorry, I'll get out of your way,' he says, stepping to one side. 'Would you mind very much if I ate my sandwiches with you?'

While I'm thinking about that, Caleb says, 'Of course. Be our guest.'

The man sits on the grass next to Caleb and introduces himself as Peter Halliday. He has thinning brown hair, looks to be in his fifties, has a cherubic round face and remarkably smooth skin. His eyes are round like his face, keen, navy, and I can tell by looking into them that he is intelligent, quick and probably very funny. You might think this is a lot to take in from just one glance but I'm good at it, and rarely wrong.

I tell him my name, take a bite of a cheese and tomato sandwich and listen while he and Caleb chat. It's not that I don't want to join in, but until there's something more to comment on than general chit-chat, I'll use the time to wonder why on earth I felt it necessary to tell Caleb about my suicidal thoughts back when I was fourteen. I had told him the big fat secret and some of what happened after, so why stir the hive again?

'You two on holiday, then?' Peter directed this question at me, so answers to my unpredictable psyche would have to wait.

I considered saying no, we live out on the path all year round and use caves for shelter but wasn't sure if it was chortling material or just 'out there'. That's another one, where exactly is 'out there'? Presenters say it a lot on TV, don't they? Okay everyone out there, here's the number to ring if you want to vote for Douglas the farting budgie to win Britain's Got Nothing to Offer. The 'out there' in the sentence I just used, though, means something weird, doesn't it? Perhaps there are two 'out theres' or even multiple ones, as in parallel 'out there' universes…

I realise Caleb is frowning at me and Peter is smiling politely. 'Sorry, Peter, I was miles away, you know, "out there"'. I sweep my arm in a flourishy way and a bit of cheese lands on Peter's walking boot. I pretend not to notice as he flicks it onto the grass. 'Yes, we are on holiday, initially for a week and then we'll see. Caleb is a teacher and I used to be, but now I'm an artist. I hope to open a shop and studio soon – well, with Caleb's help. What do you do?' Now, he certainly can't say that isn't a full answer, can he?

Peter puts a wide smile in his round face and I think it looks like a child's drawing of the moon. His face isn't silvery-white; it's ruddy, so perhaps it's a blood moon.

'I used to be a hotel manager at an upmarket place in St Ives, but my life changed beyond all recognition three months ago,' he says, and offers us a custard cream.

I accept and hold a bag of sherbet lemons out to him. Peter says he'll take one for later and I tell him to take two. I always say that to people. One, because I like to be generous and two, because I wonder if the sweet will feel lonely or abandoned, all by itself in a stranger's pocket, under used tissues and other people's odds and ends. No, don't worry… that was actually an 'out there' made-up comment… I think.

'Sounds exciting,' Caleb says through a mouthful of custard cream.

I correct him. 'Intriguing. I mean, until Peter has told us how his life has changed, how can we say if it's exciting or not? It could be awfully tragic and then we'd feel bad.'

Peter does the river-water chortle and nods at me. 'You have a very direct way of speaking, Lottie. I like that.'

'Thank you. I do pride myself on saying what I think – well as much as I can without hurting people,' I say, remembering the sparkle in Neave's eyes yesterday disappearing under the shadow of a jet fighter.

To Caleb he says, 'It is exciting, actually. I won the bloody Euro Millions lottery!'

Caleb and I stop chewing and look at each other, our faces frozen in surprise as if we are each other's mirror. Then we look at Peter and I say, 'My goodness, how much did you win?'

'Let's just say it was a lot. Huge,' he says in a voice that sounds like it can't believe what it just said.

I'm glad I swallowed my mouthful of sandwich because my jaw drops just like Caleb's and we both say at the same time, 'Huge?'

Peter's chortle comes out higher and raspier this time. 'Yes, and I still find it hard getting my head round it.' We are both still gawping at him with our mouths open. 'Your faces are a picture. Everyone looks like you two when I tell them, though.' Peter grins and takes a swig of water from his bottle.

There's a stunned silence that stretches a bit too long until Caleb says, 'So, what, you won it all by yourself?'

'Yes. I'd been doing it for a few years but hadn't told my wife because she moaned, said it was chucking money away.'

'I bet she didn't moan when you told her you'd won,' I say, and notice that there's a dark side creeping across his moon.

'She wasn't too pleased, as it happens, because I told her I was leaving. Verity had been having it off with various men over the twenty-five years we'd been married and thought I didn't know.' Peter's moon is almost totally eclipsed now, and I wish I'd never asked. But what else could I have done?

'Oh dear,' Caleb says.

'Indeed,' I say. And then we look at each other for inspiration.

'Yes. I was too in love with her all those years to say anything in case she left me. I thought it might stop, settle down after we had the children, but no. So, when I won all that money I decided that she could have the house and I'd leave. It's the children's home, after all. Well, I say children, they're nineteen and seventeen now. She had half the money in the divorce settlement of course, even though she didn't deserve it, but that's the law.'

'But that is so unfair!' I say, wishing his cheerful expression would come back.

'Yes, but it's all behind me now,' he says, granting my wish. 'I left my job, bought a new place overlooking the beach, gave lots away to good causes and started this walk. I feel so free!' Peter flings his arms up and laughs out loud.

Caleb's face brightens. 'Oh, I'm so glad. You deserve to be happy – many lottery winners aren't, are they?'

'No. And some just carry on in the same old jobs and lives. What the hell do they bother to enter for if they don't want change?' Peter says.

I nod – I have often thought this myself. 'What will you do in the long term?'

'I don't know. Travel perhaps, or perhaps not, whatever really.' Peter fixes his intelligent gaze on my face. 'The thing is, I can spend my time just finding out about who I am and what I want from life, just doing what makes me happy. My life was like a frayed old washing line with me pegged out on it by the balls, you know?'

I think I do, kind of. My imagination certainly does, and I have to smother a giggle.

'Verity did the pegging and I was helpless to do anything about it apart from hang there, miserable, impotent.' He looks out to sea for a few moments and then back at us. 'Now I have the chance to come out from behind the facade, the pain of pretending to be normal, happy when I wasn't. Say what I like, be who I want to be instead of some sham husband. Do you know what I mean?'

Caleb nods, but I can tell he's doing it to humour Peter. He doesn't really know, but I think I do.

'Yes, I do know what you mean. I decided that I wouldn't be like everyone else when I was a teenager – well, before that really, but certainly from the age of thirteen. I am true to myself and refuse to be moulded, put in anyone's box or pegged out on anyone's washing line, balls or no balls,' I say and give him a big grin, the kind of grin that you can feel spreading through your body and that shows all your teeth.

'I'm happy to hear it, Lottie. I must say it's refreshing to meet someone like you. That's something else I'm doing: collecting experiences and emotions, trying to remember them and how I felt at the time in order to build a new me. I'm open to lots of things now that were closed to me before. Instead of just existing and at the behest of Verity, I am at last alive.'

Peter's eyes moisten and before mine have a chance to copy them, I rummage in the rucksack for the coffee flask while Caleb says how pleased he is for Peter and so forth. This tearing up business is all very odd and has to stop. So, does the random spewing up chunks of my past into regular conversations. It isn't like me. It puts an anxious roll in my gut and makes my heart beat too fast.

'Where are you thinking of having your business, Lottie?' Peter says.

The word 'business' sounds like I want to make money and that's not what it's all about. I tell him this and add, 'My new venture is kind of what you were talking about, you know, doing what makes you happy, being the person you want to be, actually living life.'

Peter nods. 'I'm lucky enough to be able to do that because of the lottery win.' He tilts his moon to the side and does that slightly glazed stare at me that people do when they are considering something. 'If you need money I will gladly give you some. I have a good chunk left in the bank, the interest keeps growing, mad really—'

'No, no!' I say and flap my hand at him and wish I hadn't, because as you know I hate it when people do it to me. At least I haven't said bless you. 'That's so lovely of you, but I have enough – a little nest egg from my grandma's will.'

'Oh, I'm so glad. You must let me know when you're up and running, I'll pop by and have a look.' He jots down an email on the back of a paper bag and hands it to me.

'You can count on it,' I say and swallow a wiggle that's appeared in my voice. I notice Caleb notice it and he jumps up and starts clearing stuff away with more noise than is necessary.

He slaps Peter on the back. 'We certainly will, Peter. You're a really nice guy and I can't think of a better person to win the lottery.'

'Me neither,' I say and mean it.

The moon beams and Peter makes ready to leave.

Caleb does the twisty thing with his mouth that he does when he's had an idea but isn't sure if it's a good one. Then he says, 'There is a cause that you might like to give some of the interest to in the future, if you'd like.'

We watch him scribble details from a crumpled leaflet onto a bit of the paper bag that Peter used. I knew immediately after he'd said it that it was for Neave and Leo. Then Caleb explains all about how we met them yesterday and Peter says it would be his pleasure to give. Then Caleb looks right at me with his forget-me-nots and then back at Peter as he says, 'We shouldn't have to give to charity and Neave and Leo shouldn't have to walk round the UK to raise money, but they do. I mean, there's plenty for war and destruction, but it seems the pot is always empty when it's for the NHS and stuff.'

'Oh yes, that's the tragedy, isn't it?' Peter says, and I can tell he means it. He hoists his rucksack. 'Well, it's been great to meet you.' He shakes us both by the hand and his grip is warm and reassuring. 'And I will look forward to meeting you again very soon when you open the shop.'

We tell him that we enjoyed meeting him too and then we stand hand in hand and watch him stride away over the bouncy heather. Nearly twenty-four hours ago I had felt like a wire had come loose in our circuit. Now because of what Caleb had just said to Peter and the way he'd intuitively built a subtle screen with his noisy clearing away between Peter and my uncharacteristic emotion, our connection feels stronger than it has ever been. Unbreakable perhaps? Not sure, but I hope so.

Chapter Twelve

That Thing I Worried About

I look from my bedroom window at Cliff House (an adorable B&B right next to Portreath beach), just as another morning is creeping over the sand. It drops sparkly kisses into rock pools and gradually sharpens the edges of the purple headland until it turns green and stark against the pale blue sky. A pendant moon still dangles over the horizon, though its necklace of stars has long since faded.

Judging by the white horses galloping in on the waves it looks as if the wind is stronger than yesterday, but I don't want to open the window to check, as it's still early and I might wake Caleb. That surprised you, didn't it? It certainly surprised me last night.

That thing that I worried about happened not long after dinner as we kissed and embraced outside on the moonlit beach. We were both exhausted after the day's walk and decided we both needed an early night. But moonlight does something to a person and the longer he held me, the longer I wanted him to... and then I heard myself ask him up to my room.

Am I still worried? Yes and no. Yes, because as you know, I don't want the way we are with each other to change – our friendship is very special. No, because I loved what happened last night. Last night our connection deepened, in fact it was no longer a connection, we almost became the same person. I know that's impossible, but that's how it felt to me. Physically we couldn't get any closer, but it was as if our hearts and souls were one, too. It was very different from just the physical need thing I told you about before, you know, when I'd had unemotional sex with men. The night I spent with Caleb meant something. But I can't be doing with all that lovely-dovey romance nonsense though, and I'll tell him to stop it if he starts.

Caleb opens his lovely eyes and beckons me back to bed. I go to him and decide that I'm not too worried about that thing for now. Then after, we get ready, have breakfast and set off to Hayle. This leg of the walk is around twelve miles again and I'm looking forward to the short six miler from Hayle to St Ives tomorrow. Don't get me wrong, I'm loving every minute, but it will be nice just to pootle about St Ives for a bit and perhaps go for a swim.

First stop is Ralph's Cupboard, which is in fact not a cupboard at all but a collapsed sea cave, where yet another giant used to store his booty. He would get this from ships that he wrecked and then eat the sailors later. Waste not, want not, I say. The thing is about this cupboard is that you can only see it from the top of a very sheer cliff. I know I said earlier that I wished could fly, but that wish only manifests when I am atop cliffs that have absolutely no danger of sending me toppling onto to the jagged rocks and white sandy beach below. Well, unless I'm contemplating suicide, of course, which I did as a teenager, but not anymore.

'Wow, this view is spectacular!' Caleb's excitement is evident even in the shaky snatch the wind allows me to hear.

He is standing far too close to the edge. I am standing a good five feet back now having just peeped over and had that wiggly feeling in my stomach that you get when you realise how close you might be to death. 'Yes, come away now. I don't like you up being there!'

Caleb turns to look at me and pretends to wobble. 'Oh, no… I think I'm going to fall!'

'STOP IT!' I yell, and feel my stomach turn over. I know he's just fooling about, but what if he really did lose his footing? The thought of my world without Caleb in it makes me panicky and nauseous. This is a worry because I haven't experienced such a thing before. I watch Caleb walk towards me laughing at my panic, and even in worrying about his potential loss, I realise that

I am totally selfish. People in general are totally selfish, aren't they? Because when they worry about someone they care about dying, or even leaving for a long time, they say things like 'I'll miss you. I don't know how I will live without you.' So really, it's all about them, isn't it? It's about how they will be affected. But I guess that's normal. How else can we measure what matters? Then I remember that I don't like being normal and get very confused.

In Caleb's arms now, I rest my head on his chest and inhale the smell of him through his T-shirt. He is warm and comforting and I'm reassured by the fact that he's not in Ralph's Cupboard ready to be eaten by a giant.

'You'd miss me if I'd fallen over the cliff, wouldn't you?' he says, and his voice vibrates my ear still against his chest.

I step back and push him playfully on the arm. 'Not at all. Just didn't want the faff of phoning the coastguard and interrupting my holiday.' We both know I don't mean it, but I want to prune that lovely-dovey look budding in his eyes before it blossoms.

Lunch is two hours later just before we come to Godrevy Lighthouse. Caleb is yet again looking over the cliff, though this time there's a railing to prevent folk plummeting to their untimely deaths. I am placing my jacket on the ground as a makeshift cloth and putting out fruit and a couple of now coldish pasties that we bought just before leaving Portreath.

The flavour of a cold pasty is more intense than a hot one, I find, and just as my mouth is about to wrap itself around one, Caleb turns, flaps his hand at me and hisses something I can't catch.

'Speak up!' I say through a mouthful of pasty, because in the end I'd rather stuff my face rather than find out what he's on about. And he knows I don't like flappy hands.

He pulls a puzzled face and flaps again. I realise he can't hear what I said because of my pasty-filled mouth, so I shove the pasty back in its bag and drag my feet over to him in an exaggerated show of disgruntlement. When I'm about two feet away, he points at a sign that tells me this is Mutton Cove and that there are seals basking on the rocks below. It further informs us that if we make a noise or allow our dogs to bark we could scare them off.

I'm considering pointing out that we have no dogs when he grabs my arm and hisses in my ear. 'Look, there are three seals down there and now a baby one with its mum's just arrived.'

It takes a while for my eyes to distinguish between rocks and seals but then I see them and I'm glad I made the effort. Most have grey pelts sprinkled with brown bits like chocolate on a cappuccino, but some have more of a Horlicks effect going on. 'They are delightful,' I say in a low voice and lean my elbows against the railing alongside Caleb's.

We stand and watch for a while in silence and then he says, 'What the hell is that?' and points to our left past the first assembly of rocks and out into the turquoise shallows.

A round pale shape about six feet across (though it's hard to tell from this height) is moving slowly through the water, propelled by what looks to be a single fin. Whatever the creature is it looks like it could be ill or wounded – it's flopping its fin about and not getting very far doing it. 'It looks like a sea turtle that could be injured,' I venture.

'No idea, never seen anything like it in my life.' Caleb shades his eyes to try and get a better view.

A few other visitors have gathered, some with binoculars. Caleb asks one man if he can see what the creature is, and the man trains his bins on it. 'By 'eck. I reckon it's a sunfish, lad,' he says in a voice he's borrowed from Wallace, the character in *Wallace and Gromit*. On closer inspection I find that in profile he looks very much like him too.

I want to ask him if he likes Wensleydale cheese in the same accent, but gut instinct tells me that would be too 'out there' for an opener. 'A sunfish?' I say instead. 'Are they supposed to flop about like that?'

'Oh aye. That's what they do, they're not in any rush to get about. We should take a leaf from their book if you ask me.'

My imagination presents a picture of a sunfish trying to read a book with its floppy fin and I hide a smile. 'Are they quite rare? You seemed surprised to see one.'

'They're getting more common round this coast over recent years due to the sea temperature rising, but you certainly don't see them too often and not at all further up the country.' Wallace turns to look at me and gives me an even-toothed smile. 'Water's too cold up north, see?'

I nod and then he says goodbye and moves off, a silent and very well-behaved dog at his heels. 'Do you think that dog's called Gromit?' I whisper to Caleb.

Caleb smiles. 'Possibly.' Then he walks back to our picnic muttering, 'A sunfish. What a lovely surprise.'

I finish my pasty, look in the rucksack for a wet wipe and notice that Algernon has a disturbing orange stain on his backside. I pull him out and examine it. Looks like a squashed satsuma segment. The poor bear might have been happier at home on my bed after all, rather than stuffed upside down in a rucksack every day. Still, there is nothing to be done about that now and I guess he might enjoy the sea air. I scrub at the stain with a wet wipe and sit him on the grass next to us.

'I see we do have another visitor for lunch after all,' Caleb says, pretending to give Algernon a sip of coffee. I give him an enquiring look. 'Well, every day so far we've had very interesting lunch guests. I thought today would be an exception.'

'Oh yes, so we have,' I say, thinking of Peter, Neave and Leo and wonder where they are on the path at this very minute. What a shame we've had none today.' I pat the bear's head. 'Not that you're not exciting, old bear, it's just that you don't say much, do you?'

'You know, I've been thinking quite a bit about your brother, Lottie. You have loved meeting new people on this trip, so I think we could try and get him to come around after we get back—'

'What the hell has my brother got to do with new people?' I say perhaps a bit too stabbily, but the connection Caleb's made here is beyond comprehension, and totally random.

'He is new really – you haven't met him,' Caleb says in a soothing voice. It's the kind of voice one would use with an overwrought person or perhaps a child on the verge of a tantrum. This makes me very unsoothed. 'I think if you did meet, it would help the healing process, make the past a more friendly place to visit.'

What the fuck? That's the second time in the past few weeks that he's mentioned the healing process, and that last bit he said about the past makes me feel… actually it's beyond description. The expression he's trying on is overly sympathetic and my hands itch to slap it from his face. 'What's all this about healing and friendly visits to my past, Caleb? It's not the first time you've said stuff like this and I don't get it.' I congratulate myself on keeping the tone of my words cool and my anger locked in.

'I think it's because yesterday you mentioned the fact that you'd been suicidal.' Caleb puts his hand on mine, but I withdraw.

'You talked about healing before we came away,' I say, wishing I had been able to keep my bloody mouth shut about walking off clifftops and wanting to die.

'But I think you do still have issues, don't you? When you told me about your brother coming back and the way your mother behaved, you wouldn't tell me why you had to have counselling, well, not all of it. And if you'd come to terms with it all, you wouldn't have had a problem. Then yesterday you told me about the suicidal thoughts and—'

'Oh, for goodness sake, Caleb! You sound like a counsellor yourself now, talking about issues and coming to terms. Next you'll be banging on about bloody closure.'

'I hate that word,' he says and smirks.

I am not in a smirking mood. 'I hate it too, and I'm not over-fond of all this concern for my mental health, either.'

Caleb pulls his eyebrows into a furrow and does that pouty grumpy thing with his mouth which I normally find endearing, but at the moment irritates the hell out of me. 'I'm not suggesting there's anything wrong with your mental health, Lottie.'

'Really? Then what are you suggesting?'

'That you should meet your brother and tell me why you had to have counselling. I think it would help you put the past in perspective and make you feel better about the future.'

'What are you, a problem page personified?'

He looks away and tips the last dregs of coffee from the flask into his cup. 'I hope not. It's just that I care for you... care for you an awful lot, and I want you to be happy.'

'I am happy, thank you. In fact, I'm happier than I have been for some time.' I realise that this is true but that I hadn't known it until this minute. 'I've left my job, started out in a new direction, have a best friend in you, and the future looks pretty cool, if you ask me.'

'I'm glad to hear it,' Caleb says, then he leans in and I feel his soft lips on my cheek. 'I'd like to think we're more than best friends, too.'

There are a number of replies lining up for release but none of them sound right – they're all a bit spiky and reproachful. *What do you want me to say, that you're my boyfriend? That's a bit juvenile isn't it?* Or *I think being someone's best friend is a fine thing to be, what's the problem?* The rest of the replies are similar and won't make the situation we have found ourselves in any better, so I say, 'Yes, of course you are.'

I get up and walk over to the railings and watch the seals sunbathing. The sunfish has wobbled off and so have the other people. I can hear Caleb packing away behind me, whistling something cheery. I can tell it's a whistle that he's organised to try and make us feel as if we've not argued; that the afternoon is still as sunny, bright and hopeful as it ever was. But it isn't. It isn't, and it feels false. The sun looks too bright, as if it's trying too hard, the ocean too blue and the seals too cute, and my chest wall is pressing against my heart so hard that I wonder if it will stop beating.

Aware that part of this heavy feeling is because I'm leaning all my weight against the railing, I step back and grip it with my hands instead. It helps a little, but my heart still feels squeezed.

Caleb said that I was brave and different and bold and other stuff, but was he thinking that I needed help all that time? Am I some sort of project for him, a broken toy that needs mending?

Then I feel his hands on my shoulders and a kiss in my hair and I tell him what I'm thinking. I can't see the point in pretending that the afternoon isn't just a backdrop to a stage play. A play that's too sad for any audience.

He turns me around to face him and says, 'Of course you're not a project. I honestly think it would make you feel better if you told me everything, that's all.' Caleb's eyes hold mine and I find it hard to look away. Then he takes a deep breath and opens his mouth.

Quickly I turn back to the ocean because I am fairly sure he's going to say something romantic. I certainly don't want to think about that right now and once again my mouth takes over before my brain has time to properly decide what I'm going to say. 'I had counselling for many reasons, as I said that day in Bustopher Jones. I told you anger management, and unpredictable behaviour.'

Caleb joins me and grips the rail, mirroring my stance. He says nothing, just looks at the seals. Then he says, 'Yes. But don't feel pressured to tell me anything else. I'm sorry if I—'

'The night after my mother said all those cruel and hateful things to me when I said I wouldn't see James, and that I preferred our life before he came along, I crept into my parents' bedroom and cut off all her hair on one side with kitchen scissors as she slept. It was a Friday night and she'd had her usual two or three glasses of red, so she didn't wake up, nor did Dad. Before they'd gone to bed I'd taken all her best clothes from the wardrobe and hidden them.'

I hear Caleb clear his throat and sigh but I daren't look at him or I'll dry up, and he asked for this, didn't he?

I say to the sky, 'Anyway, after I'd cut her hair, I took the clothes out to the shed and poured paraffin on them. Then I set the shed on fire. They only woke up when they heard the sirens of the fire engines. Mrs Kelly next door had called them.'

'Bloody hell, Lottie.' Caleb speaks quietly, but the emotion in his voice hurts my ears.

'I think I chose the shed because Dad was the one that used it most. He had to shoulder some of the blame. After that, I found myself in counselling so fast it made my head spin, which as I said before made me feel like an alien. And the anger management bit actually made me more furious because I was made to feel like I was the one in the wrong – abnormal. That's when the self-harming and suicidal thoughts came in.'

A seal slips into the water and I wish I could too, as a sneaky glance shows me the look on Caleb's face. He recovers quickly, but not quickly enough, because the expression of shock and pity takes a sledgehammer to my confidence and self-assurance.

'My poor Lottie. What a terrible thing you went through,' he says and tries to pull me into his arms.

I back away. 'I saw that look on your face just now, Caleb. You think I must have been crazy to do those things. You wanted to know the truth, but now you wish you didn't know it.'

'Hey, that's not fair. It was a bit of a shock, that's true. But I can see why you went off the rails—'

'Went off the rails.' I laugh humourlessly. 'Damn right I did. They said I wasn't acting in a normal way, and I wasn't. Because the counsellors said that even though what Mother and Dad had done wasn't the best way to handle the situation, it didn't warrant my reaction. I'd had what they called a psychotic episode and needed help.' I throw my arms out to the sides and thrust my neck forward. 'Me. I was the one that needed help, not Mother!'

He tries to hold me again, but I walk back to the rucksacks letting my words flow behind me like a vapour trail.

'But you know what, Caleb? If normal is talking about your daughter as if she's worthless, if normal is saying your daughter isn't what she expected, like I was some kind of faulty mail-order fucking vacuum cleaner that she could send back, write a shite review about and get a refund on or something, then I didn't want to be normal. Still don't want to be normal.'

'Lottie, I'm on your side. I totally agree. You mother was so wrong to do what she did, and teenage years are tough at the best of times. It's a wonder you got through school in the end.' Caleb follows my lead and hoists his rucksack.

'I didn't. I was expelled after the Mr Baldwin incidents. The worse one I haven't told you about. One day after a lesson where we'd had another set-to, I tipped sausage, mash and gravy over his head in the dinner hall.' The memory of the sheer horror on Baldwin's face makes me laugh out loud and I feel a bit of tension leave my chest.

Caleb's eyes widen, and a sound leaves his mouth – a cross between a cough and a bark. 'Bloody hell. So how did you get your qualifications, go to uni?'

'Gwendoline paid for private tuition. If it wasn't for her, I really don't know where I would have ended up.' I set off down the path again before Caleb can see how much I miss my grandmother.

Just around the headland is Godrevy Point. We stand and look at the sweep of the coast to St Ives and the lighthouse on the little island, and I tell Caleb that it's the lighthouse that inspired Virginia Woolf's *To the Lighthouse*. I also tell him that I don't want to talk about my past any more today, just in case he's going to say something further. He says he completely understands, and that he's glad I told him what happened, and he slips his arm around my shoulder.

As we set off across Gwithian beach towards Hayle, I have to admit that I do feel a bit lighter inside. Caleb knows all there is to know about me now, and though he was shocked at first, he doesn't seem to think any less of me. If he did, that would just be too bad, because I've had a tough journey to become me, and I like who I am. Just like everyone else, he will have to take or leave me, because I won't be changing any time soon.

Chapter Thirteen

An Unexpected Turn

I never expected the fourth day of the holiday to begin in this way. As I said yesterday, I was looking forward to the short walk to St Ives for a spot of pootling around the town and possibly a swim. Now I don't feel at all like pootling or swimming. Today I feel like hiding under my duvet and pretending that last night didn't happen. I look at my rucksack on the bed and consider sweeping it onto the floor and doing just that, but then Algernon gives me an encouraging wave and I resist. Yes, I know Algernon is a stuffed bear, and can't wave, but he's stuck out of the bag at an angle and looks like he's waving, so I'll believe that he is. I need all the encouragement I can get this morning.

So okay, this is what happened last night. Caleb and I had dinner and then afterwards we decided we were so tired that we'd just go to bed. We still had the two rooms booked because we hadn't thought to phone ahead and cancel, and besides, I think that neither of us wanted to assume that sleeping together was now a 'thing', but he came to my room anyway.

We lay in each other's arms afterwards and everything felt wonderful, but just as I was drifting into sleep he said he knew he'd promised not to bring up my past again, but he thought that part of moving on must involve a meeting with my brother. I said in no uncertain terms that I wouldn't meet him, and would Caleb please stop talking about it all. Caleb said it was only important because he was the person Mother had measured me against all my life and that I needed to see he was not some perfect angel but just a man. I mentioned that he might be actually be a perfect angel and then how would I feel? Caleb said, and make sure you're paying attention because I can hardly believe what I'm going to tell you – Caleb said that he'd already met him, and he was just flesh and blood like everybody else.

Can you believe it? Caleb had *actually* gone up to Exeter to the hospital where my brother works and talked to him about me. Yes! And all without my knowledge or consent. I bet you're in shock, because I was and still am this morning. I mean, how *dare* he do something like that? To say that I feel betrayed is an understatement. In fact, I can't really put into words how I feel. My guts are as tangled as my bed sheets, and whenever I think of Caleb, I experience a combination of a kick in the head and a huge sense of loss.

The loss is because after he'd told me all this I threw him out of my room and told him I never wanted to see him again. He said he understood why I was angry and that after I had thought about it I'd see he was right, then he shoved my brother's business card in the rucksack. I mean, how arrogant was that? For one, he could never understand why I was angry because he'd not been where I'd been, lived my life, felt what I'd felt, had he? And for two, I will not be thinking about it and he'll never be right. How can it ever be right to go behind someone's back to do something that you know is expressly against their wishes? To betray someone's trust?

You might be thinking that he only did it because he wants the best for me, but how does he know what's best for me? I'm not some child that needs guidance and the wisdom of others to put them onto the right path. I am a fully-grown woman with a mind of her own and can find the path just fine *on my own*, thank you very much! Sorry to be shouty, it's not you I'm angry with; it's the whole bloody situation that Caleb created.

I walk to the window and look out into the narrow street. People in bright clothes are going about their business, laughing, meeting friends, having fun. The holiday season is in full flow, vibrant as a coat of many colours or the iridescence of a butterfly's wing. It is dark and cold in my head. Caleb is now out of my life for good. There will be no reprieve.

I remember now why I put people at arm's length, don't keep many friends. It's because I can't cope with them betraying me, letting my guard down so they can burrow into my soft places, rip into my flesh, pull my heart out still beating and trample all over it. Mother did that once and Caleb came very close.

He banged on my door this morning twice, but I ignored him. The third time I asked reception to please ask him to stop. Then he tried to phone and sent loads of texts, but I didn't answer and have blocked his number. I saw him leave about an hour ago and, when I asked, the owner of the B&B told me he'd asked for information about bus services.

I sit on the bed and hug the rucksack against my chest and consider returning home because the holiday has lost its appeal. I ask Algernon what he thinks, and he is non-committal, but then a seagull alights on the roof opposite and yells at me over and over. I see it as a sign that I need to carry on for my own peace of mind. I need to show myself that just because there has been a slight hiccup in my plan doesn't mean I should slink home and hide under a duvet in a darkened room. I have views to see with my in-touch-with-nature eyes, sketches to make and turning points to note. I think this moment right here as I sit on the bed might be a third turning point, because it feels like it is.

An unexpected turn of events has confirmed my suspicion that I can rely on nobody in this life apart from myself. This thought galvanises my resolve, hoists my rucksack onto my back and moves me out of the door. Already I'm happier, stronger and in control.

And as you know, that's just how I like things.

Chapter Fourteen

Louisa Truscott

Nothing much happened yesterday. I went to St Ives and wandered rather than pootled around the town. Just so you know, pootling has more of a purpose than wandering. Pootling means that you are hoping to find something unusual or desirable in the shops that you might want to buy, or a wonderful view that you didn't know about, or a place to eat that exceeds all your expectations. Wandering is more aimless. Having achieved my aim of arriving in the place, the rest of the time was spent aimlessly.

Swimming seemed more trouble than it was worth, given that the weather, like my plans, had taken an unexpected turn towards grumpy and unsettled. This doesn't make me grumpy, but I am a little unsettled, I suppose. And perhaps I'm being a bit over-dramatic in describing the weather. There were a few rainclouds hovering a little way off to the left of St Ives, but they never actually plucked up the courage to open up over the town, just contented themselves with worrying people on the beach.

It's much the same today, but the breeze has freshened itself up a bit, which I'm glad of, as I have over thirteen miles to walk to Pendeen. The map tells me that Zennor Head is around six miles away and I decide that will be my first stop. The guidebook mentions that the path is particularly arduous, but that doesn't worry me; I'm sure the views will be to die... spectacular.

Arduous, I find, is not the best description of the roller-coaster path I've been on for the last hour or so. My calf muscles are yelling at me to have a rest and I'm convinced I have a sixteen-stone man hitching a ride in my rucksack. But the views, oh the views...

As I walk along the seven-hundred-and-fifty-metre promontory head, its sheer cliffs flanked on either side by the Atlantic Ocean, the salt breeze in my hair and lungs, the wild coastal flowers and rugged beauty of the landscape all around me, I temporarily forget my discomfort and my unsettledness. A couple of seagulls hang in the air, just tipping their wings now and then to keep them on the thermal ride, and once again I wish I could fly. This reminds me of the day I told Caleb this and, stupidly, the rest, too. I must learn to keep information about myself that I don't want others to know inside, where it belongs. I know I told you that I pride myself on speaking my mind, but sometimes it's just a very bad idea, isn't it?

Pendour Cove, sometimes known as Mermaid's Cove is the next stop and my feet pick up a pace, even though they are begging for a rest. They know they'll get one while I have a snack, or possibly lunch, but that's not the whole reason I'm hurrying. Eagerness to see the cove where, legend has it, a young man fell in love with a mermaid, drives me, and in my mind, I already have my sketch pad unpacked and a pencil in my hand.

Turns out that the cove is so stunningly beautiful that I'm not sure I should even bother unpacking my sketch pad because there is no way that my talent, or anyone else's come to that, can capture it. The ocean is turquoise, the sand is white and a little horseshoe of land wraps itself around both in a show of affection, or is it protection? Hard to decide. For now, I'll sit and have a bite to eat and do the capturing with my eyes.

An hour later I have made a start on a sketch and, I must admit, it isn't half as bad as I imagined. I'm not sure what to do about the sky as it's still grumpy and my artistic hand isn't too good at those, so I look up at it and from the corner of my eye I see a tall, willowy woman with steel-grey streamers for hair coming closer along the path.

She looks self-assured and as if she belongs here. Perhaps she's a permanent fixture on the path, just in case walkers decide to take a photo to show friends what a confident walker in touch with her surroundings should look like. Maybe I should take a photo?

Then I imagine how I would feel if a random person did the same to me. I wouldn't like it.

I look back to the sky. Perhaps I'll take a photo of that instead and leave trying to draw it for now, because it won't keep still.

'Hello. May I have a look at your drawing?'

The woman with steel-grey streamers for hair is standing close by. She smells of oranges, muddy boots and wax jackets. Her voice is gentle, and I think she has made it so to show respect for my privacy. When Leo came upon me sketching the other day, he was boundy, excitable and had no concept of intrusion; this woman is more aware.

'Of course,' I say and hold the pad up to her. She sits down next to me and looks.

'Oh, I do like this,' she says and looks at my face as if she's trying to read something in it. Her turquoise eyes reflect the water and the lines on her sunburned skin tell me she is a way past sixty. She has a smiley mouth. Even when it's not smiling I can tell that it's used to doing it. Often.

'Thank you. I was going to draw the sky but it's a bit changeable. The truth is, I'm not too good at skies, yet. I need more practice.'

'Skies can be tricky. We like to hold them in our eye, but they are too wide and beautiful – bits of it have a habit of escaping.' The woman smiles. The smile grows so wide and warm that it makes dimples in her cheeks and sunlight glint in her eyes.

'You're a painter, too?'

'Only as a hobby over the years, and I once sculpted. I still dabble occasionally, but my little business takes up most of my time.'

'Oh, what kind of business?' I say, wondering if I should be minding my own.

'Let's introduce ourselves first, shall we?' She sticks out a hand with a tattoo of an olive tree on it. Its branches grow up her index, middle and third fingers. 'My name's Louisa Truscott.'

I take the olive tree and say, 'Pleased to meet you, Louisa.' And I am pleased, very. She has this air about her, it's hard to describe, but I know that she is someone I will get on with. This happens very rarely to me; in fact, I can't give you an example of when it last did. 'I'm Lottie Morgan.'

'Likewise, Lottie. You asked about my business – I have a small vineyard up near Padstow. I produce a variety of wines and some free-range eggs. Well, I don't produce them of course, my grapes and hens do.' Her laugh is a bit like Peter's, but not quite a chortle. I suppose it's a chuckle – stays more in the throat than out loud. 'We sell the eggs, wine, local cheeses and a few bits of art and pottery in the gift shop, too.'

'That's sounds interesting. Do you have help?' I glance at her ring finger and wish that I hadn't. Why did I need to see if she was married? It's the kind of thing my mother would do. She's wearing a thick band that looks like it's made of wood.

'Oh yes. Even though it's not a large concern, I couldn't manage it on my own, especially not at my age. I have my two grown nephews, my sister and brother-in-law that help run the gift shop, and a local man to lend a hand at harvest time. It can be hard work, but I do love it.'

'You're having a break then, at the moment?'

Louisa nods. 'Just for a few days. I've always wanted to see this cove.' She sweeps her hand across the scene and then tips her face to the sun and closes her eyes. 'I've never been able to resist stories of mysteries and legend.'

'Me too. Didn't a man fall in love with a mermaid here?'

Louisa opens her eyes and looks at me. 'Indeed. Apparently, the mermaid used to go to the little church not far from here in Zennor because she was enchanted by the voice of a young man named Matthew, I think he was called. He had such a beautiful voice that she hid her tail under a long dress and struggled up to the church to listen to him singing. When she saw him, she fell in love with him and he with her. He asked her to stay but she revealed that she could not, as she needed to return to the sea. They couldn't bear to be parted so he went out to sea with her, never to be seen again. And it is said his song can still sometimes be heard at sunset, on still summer's evenings.'

I don't like the sound of the ending. It's too unbearably sad. I say, 'Do you think he drowned?'

Louisa laughs. 'I think there's a chance that it's just a lovely story passed down the ages – it didn't really happen. You do know there are no such things as mermaids?' She winks at me.

I wink back and say, 'There might be, we can't know absolutely. And Matthew might have become a merman and not drowned at all. Yes, that's what happened – I've decided.'

'I have decided, too. I like your version and shall believe it.' Louisa smiles at me and opens her rucksack. 'Would you like an orange? Or I have liquorice.'

'Ooh, yes please, I've not had liquorice for years.'

I put a piece in my mouth and I'm back in my gran's conservatory watching her quick needles knit something fabulous out of scraps of wool. She always had a bag of liquorice to hand – it helped her concentrate, she said.

Sadness tries to form a lump in my throat, but I swallow it down with a bit of liquorice. Memories of Gwendoline should be happy – something to celebrate. I mentally tell her how much I still love her and allow myself to relax into the quiet. We chew our liquorice and look at the view, then after a few moments I say, 'The olive tree on your hand. Does it have any particular significance?'

'Yes.' Louisa's smiley mouth becomes small and tight and she twists the liquorice bag as if she's trying to tear it in half.

'I hope that hasn't upset you. It's none of my business.'

'No, that's okay. I should expect questions, it's in a prominent place after all, and people do ask. I suppose I haven't come to terms with my loss yet. I think I have, and then there it is, banging at my door, accusing me of forgetting all about it and demanding to be let in.'

Louisa looks at me and there are clouds in her eyes. I wish I hadn't asked, and that I could say something to push the clouds out over the ocean. But then, as she said, the tattoo is there for all to see; perhaps she needs people to ask about it, so she's reminded of her loss. I expect she'll tell me what her loss is, though I'm not sure I want to know. We've had such a nice time so far.

'That must be hard for you. Let's change the subject shall we, I—'

'No, I'm fine really. I'd like to tell you.' Louisa puts the bag down and places her hands on her knees. She looks at the tattoo and says, 'We lost the old olive tree to the storms of 2011. It was just a sapling when Jagger planted it forty years ago, we never thought it would last for long, but it did. Over the years it grew thicker, fatter, twistier, crouching over the land like an old druid protecting our vineyard from ruin. Least that's what Jagger used to say.'

Louisa looks at the sky, takes a deep breath and let it out slowly. I can feel her emotion charge the air as if it's another person squeezing in next to us. 'We lost Jagger the day after the tree. Once he saw it broken, uprooted, I think it broke him too. He gave up trying to hold on any longer – he was tired, so very tired.'

A silence wraps around my vocal cords and I cough to make it let go. 'Jagger was your husband?' I say, hoping I'm right. I never know what to say at times like this, or if I should say anything at all.

'Yes, he was. Everyone called him Jagger because he looked a bit like Mick, though more handsome in my opinion, but his real name was John. Cancer stole him. We were together for fifty years, married for forty-five and he was my right hand.' Louisa looks at the back of her hand and splays the branches of the tree.

The reason for the tattoo is now so obvious in its poignancy that I can hardly breathe. 'Oh, I'm so sorry,' I say and hear a wobble in my voice, but I don't care.

'Thank you. It does get easier with each passing year, but sometimes grief just grabs you by the heart, you know?'

I did know. 'Yes, I lost my gran, Gwendoline, about eighteen months ago now. That was cancer, too. I know it isn't like losing a life partner but—' I stop and realise don't know if it is or not. 'Well, I assume it isn't, but as I've never lost one, not to death anyway...' I stop again, shocked at what my words imply, and wonder if Caleb was, or could have been a life partner. The jury is out as usual and anyway, I'm talking about Louisa's loss, not mine.

'You sound as if you have lost a lover – tell me about it.'

Bloody hell – and people say I'm direct. 'Do you mind if we don't? It only happened the day before yesterday and I'm not sure what to make of it all, yet.'

'Of course, not – totally understand,' Louisa says, absently turning the wooden ring around her finger.

My directness feels like it's building a wall between us and I don't want it to. I say the first thing that comes into my head to knock it down a few bricks. 'That ring looks like it's made of wood.' Yes, a bit lame but at least it's something.

'It is.' She holds it up, so I can see the beautiful wood markings more clearly. 'I had it made from the olive tree. I've still got the old wedding ring, which I wear on a chain around my neck, but I just felt I needed something more organic, from the earth. The tree meant so much to Jagger, it seemed appropriate to ensure a little bit of it would be with me forever.'

This is far too sad, so I say, 'I see, that's nice. So how far are you walking along the path?' My words are far too karaoke bouncy and the emotional atmosphere around us recoils from them. The change of subject is too awkward and obvious, but subtlety is not one of my strong points.

Louisa seems glad though and her big smile comes back. 'I was kind of planning to go as far as Lamorna, away past Land's End, but I think I'll be too tired. I'll head home the day after tomorrow when I reach Sennen. I'm staying in Pendeen tonight.'

'I'm heading to Lamorna, too. That will mark the end of the first week. Lamorna was our… my aim and then we… I, was going to decide whether to go home or go on. Like you, I'm staying at Pendeen overnight.' My mouth curses my brain for slipping Caleb's ghost into my sentences without permission.

Louisa must have noticed my slip-ups, but graciously ignores them. 'And do you think you will go on?'

'Possibly, I haven't given it much thought.' As I say that, I make the decision to go home after Lamorna. It feels right.

Louisa nods and stands to a stretch. 'Well, it's been great chatting, but I'd better get going. It's another two hours or so to Pendeen and I have to find a B&B.'

I look up at her olive tree fingers twisting her steel-grey streamers into a tortoiseshell clip and something pushes me to say, 'We could walk together if you like. Of course, if you'd rather not, I would totally understand.' This is very unlike me and I busy myself putting the sketch pad in the rucksack to avoid looking at her face.

'That would be lovely, thank you. I was going to say the same but wasn't brave enough.'

A light feeling lifts the corners of my mouth and I look at her sunlit eyes. 'That's great. Shall we see if we can see Matthew and the mermaid before we leave?'

'Of course, that's why I came, after all,' she says, striding off to the edge of the land and peering over it.

I join her and scan the turquoise-blue for signs of life. There is none apart from a few seagulls bobbing on the waves and the bark of an invisible dog somewhere along the path. 'Oh well, perhaps they're being shy today. I'll come back one evening at sunset and surprise them.'

A chuckle in her voice, Louisa says, 'Good idea. If you see them, let me know.'

I follow her long strides along the path towards Pendeen and wonder if I have met in her what is known as a kindred spirit. I think I believe the spirit of a person is like their essence, or a nucleus, and everything they are derives from it. As I said to you a while ago, social conditions play a huge part in shaping an individual, but perhaps the spirit is where it all starts? Don't ask me to explain it, though, because I've only just thought of it and I would need more time to give you a more comprehensive answer.

Anyway, perhaps she and I have similar spirits and mine recognises hers. Whatever the truth, I am enjoying being with Louisa, and walking together feels much better than walking alone.

Chapter Fifteen

Home Truths

James Vincent looks at his knuckles growing white as his grip increases on the mobile phone, and for a brief moment he wishes the phone was Caleb Walker's neck. The call had lasted about five minutes and James wonders how he'd kept from yelling a string of expletives into the mouthpiece. He throws the phone at a sofa cushion and yells at the ceiling, 'For fuck's sake!' He picks up the cushion and drop kicks it at the door, while allowing the expletives he'd kept reined in during the call to riddle the air as if they were bullets.

'James?' Beth's voice dodges a few as it comes in from the kitchen. 'James, what's wrong?'

James doesn't answer his wife. If he does, she'll want to know all about it, and he doesn't want to talk about the bloody mess that moron Caleb has made of any chance of James at last having some kind of relationship with his sister. God, he is fuming. He can feel the pulse in his neck and his heart is beating too fast.

He sends his voice back across no man's land. 'Ignore me, it's nothing!'

'James?'

Now she's standing in the doorway, her dark eyes full of worry, her hand in the small of her back. She's been on her feet all day and she doesn't need him behaving like a hormonal teenager. He shoves his hands through his hair and pulls his tie off. Why anyone thinks wearing a tie is a good idea he will never know. A bit of material wrapped over the top of a tightly buttoned collar makes no sense. A shirt and tie make him feel like a trussed chicken ready for the oven. He looks at Beth again and says, 'I'm okay. Just had a phone call I could do without.'

'Work?' she sits on the arm of the sofa and takes her shoes off.

'No. A guy called Caleb who is... was, the boyfriend of Charlotte, or Lottie as she now seems to prefer.'

Beth's eyes grow round. 'Lottie? You mean your sister?'

'Of course. How many other Lotties do I know?' James hears an edge in his tone and is sorry. None of this is Beth's fault. She does the single eyebrow raising thing and begins massaging her feet. He knows he's in trouble now.

'I have no clue how many Lotties you know, that's why I asked. If you'd rather not talk to me about it, then don't. I have food to prepare and I am knackered.'

'Yes, I know. Let me help.' He kisses the top of her hair and smells a combination of hospital disinfectant and cheese and onion crisps. Obviously not had time for lunch again; that's no good, no good at all. 'In fact, you sit here, put your feet up and I'll cook,' he says.

Beth's eyes light with humour. 'You, cook? You hate it.'

'Yeah, but I'll have to learn. When you're at home all day with our baby you'll be even busier than you are now.' James likes saying 'our baby'; he says it whenever he can fit it into a conversation.

'That is hard to believe. Do you know how many we had in outpatients today?'

James shakes his head and picks up her shoes.

Beth frowns. 'Actually, I lost count. But it feels like thousands. Dressings, smears, ear-syringing. God, I'll be so glad to go on maternity leave.'

'I think you should go sooner rather than later. You're just over three months now, what will you be like at six? We can afford it. We can afford for you never to go back if that's what you'd like.' James takes her shoes out into the hallway and then puts the kettle on. Boiling kettles always come in handy when cooking and it makes him feel like he knows what he's doing.

'Not sure about packing in work altogether, might go stir-crazy.' Beth folds her arms and leans against the door jamb while she watches him look for something in the fridge.

'We'll see. Shall we have something with eggs?'

'Something with eggs,' she says in a flat tone. 'I think not. No. I had planned spag bol.' She peers over his shoulder and pulls out onions, peppers and garlic. 'Look, just sit down while I cook and tell me all about that phone call. If you don't, you'll just churn it around in your chest and get indigestion.'

James tries to hide his relief both at being let off chef duty and the chance to get his feelings out. He tries not to do that too often, hadn't wanted to talk about it five minutes ago, but there are some things that are better out than in. He makes them tea and tells her all about Caleb visiting the hospital, Lottie's story and more recent events, too.

Beth puts the bolognaise sauce in the oven and joins him at the table. 'So, it's taken you over two weeks to tell me all about Caleb's visit? I knew there was something bothering you.' She crosses her arms over her chest as if she's trying to keep her emotions in lockdown.

'Sorry, I guess I blamed myself for the problems Lottie had when she was a teenager – you know, just appearing in her life like that? Then when Caleb told me Lottie's story recently, it made me feel physically sick. I still felt partly to blame in a way…'

'Bloody hell – I knew your mum was a bit of a prima donna and it's no secret that we don't like each other, but I never expected that of her. What a bitch! And you are not to blame at all, do you hear me?'

James hears the venom in her voice and the surprise must show on his face.

'Sorry if that offends, but how could she behave like that to her own daughter, say those vicious things? I'd have shaved all her fucking hair off and put her in the shed too, if I'd been Lottie!'

Even though his wife is furious, James has to laugh. That's what first attracted him to Nurse Lloyd. A fierce Welsh firecracker and not afraid of speaking her mind. Beth isn't amused though, and she has more for him.

'And then this bloody Caleb goes and tells your sister all about the meeting with you after you'd expressly asked him not to? Idiot! She might never meet you, now. The girl must feel terribly hurt and betrayed. I want to meet her more than I ever did now, poor love.' Beth stands up and walks to the cooker.

'Yes, I know. I really don't know what to do next. I was thinking I'd confront Mum, make her tell me why she was so cruel. Tell the truth for once.'

'Tell the truth? I don't think that's very likely, do you?' Beth feeds spaghetti into a pan of boiling water.

James doesn't, but he'd like to hear why his wife thinks this. 'I think she might be ashamed, so probably not.'

'She might well be, but I think she'll try and wriggle out of it. Remember when she first saw me, saw the colour of my skin?'

'Yes,' James says, trying not to think of the way his mum's mouth had dropped open and how she'd used a beaming smile to quickly cover her shock. Beth had brought this up a few times over the years and it looked like today was going to be no exception.

'The expression on her face...' Beth points a wooden spoon across the kitchen, a distant look in her eye, reliving the moment. 'And then when I said, "Hello, pleased to meet you," she said, "Oh, I had no idea that you were... Welsh." We all knew that she really meant she'd no idea I was mixed race.'

James says what he always says. 'Possibly, but she's never said anything to me to that effect.'

Beth says what she always says. 'No, well she wouldn't dare, would she? She's too frightened of losing you again. Her handsome, successful, precious son – her salvation, I think she said once.' She sighs and shakes her head. 'But I've caught the disdain on her face from time to time when she thought I wasn't looking. She had the same look when she saw my dad at the wedding. I'm not good enough for her angel boy. Nobody would be – black, white or sky-blue-pink.'

'I think you're right, in light of what Lottie revealed to Caleb. What do you think I should do?'

Beth chews the inside of her lip for a moment. 'I think we should go round there in the next few days and announce our pregnancy. Then we should talk to her about Lottie, tell her a few home truths, too. Beyond that I don't know, as far as she's concerned. But as far as Lottie's concerned, I think she needs some TLC from her estranged brother and sister-in-law.'

'And how is that going to work, exactly?' James asks. 'She doesn't seem the kind who would be open to that kind of thing, to say the least.'

She shrugs and turns back to the hob. 'One step at a time, husband. One at a time.'

James watches his wife move around the kitchen, grating parmesan, taking bowls from the cupboard and putting them to warm, her quiet confidence apparent in everything she is doing, and he thinks that she is the wisest, most wonderful woman he knows. One step at a time, she said. He wonders where Lottie is on her walk. Has she abandoned the South Coast Path and gone home, or is she going it alone? He guesses the latter, given her stubborn streak.

He also wonders why he'd just believed his mum's story without question back then. The tale of the jealous sibling dislodged from her only-child pedestal, wayward, spoiled, spiteful, selfish and destructive. If he was honest, it was easier. He was far too busy at the time to allow room for anything else. And the guilt, he'd not wanted to make room for that. He'd tried to put himself in Lottie's position and he'd not liked how it had felt.

James had tried to make contact later of course, but Lottie had point blank refused. Once again, he'd been busy with his career, his life. Too busy to try very hard to make things right. Then he'd managed to speak to her that once, when she'd said she'd felt like broken crockery. Lottie's words had been too painful to bear so he'd just shoved them in a drawer in the back of his mind, covered them over with important thoughts about medicine, about his patients, making the lives of strangers better.

Caleb had texted him a picture of his sister he'd taken on their walk last week and he very much needs to see it again. James walks into the sitting room, retrieves his phone from the sofa and scrolls to the photo of Lottie leaning against the wall of an old tin mine, her long brown hair lifting on the breeze, green eyes sparkling with mischief, yet her whole demeanour said assured, confident, determined.

James makes her a silent promise that he will make up for his shortcomings, will try to forge some kind of relationship with her, and if that fails, he'll bloody well try harder. He looks through the French windows across the sweep of his lawn and over the surrounding fields, and again he thinks of Lottie out there on the path. He hopes she's not miserable and lonely because of what Caleb did. James looks back at the photo and something tells him that if she is, she won't be for long.

Chapter Sixteen

A Change of Plan

Seriously, I never thought grape growing could be so interesting. By the time we get to Pendeen, having stopped to look at seals and cormorants on the way at Portheras Cove, I feel like I could almost do the job myself. Louisa has told me lots about what the business involves and right at this moment I wish myself in her life. Have you ever done that? No matter how much you're enjoying your own life, when finding out about someone else's, you unexpectedly feel like theirs is more interesting.

It could be a case of the grass is greener, but if you had asked me yesterday on a scale of one to ten how interested I was in finding out about the business of vineyards, I would have said two, possibly three, given that I do like drinking wine quite a lot. But then I would have assumed that you meant vineyards outside this country, of course. I think the fact that it quite unusual to grow grapes here adds to the interest factor.

We stop just a little way inland from the cove and Louisa says, 'There's Pendeen Lighthouse just up round the headland if you fancy a look? We'll be able to see the coast all the way towards Sennen now the clouds have gone, I shouldn't wonder.'

'That sounds like a good idea, but I worry that you won't find a bed for the night given it's the height of the tourist season.'

I have an idea that came to me not long ago, but I'm not sure it should be voiced. I'm getting too trusting of late, Caleb proved that, and it's not like me to go out of my way to be so sociable. I do rely on my instincts though, and logic of course. Logic is very useful, I find.

I watch Louisa's mouth twist to the side. 'Yeah, I think you're right,' she says and looks at her watch. 'It's going up for six now, and by the time we've been up to the lighthouse and wandered round, I don't fancy my chances. Pendeen isn't the largest place in the world after all. Still, I have slept out under the stars before now. Quite like it really.'

Instinct prods me. 'Look, say no if you like, but as you know, I have accommodation for tonight. Since my friend and I have parted company, there is a spare room booked at the place I'm staying. I keep forgetting to phone ahead and cancel these rooms,' I finish, hoping that I haven't made her feel uncomfortable.

She doesn't look at all uncomfortable, in fact the opposite. 'Oh, I assumed that you would have just the one double room given that you and he were... Sorry, please forgive my direct manner. It does get me into trouble, sometimes.' Now she does look uncomfortable.

If I wasn't sure about kindred spirits before, I am now. A burst of laughter builds in my chest and I allow it freedom. Louisa's face turns red, so I say, 'Oh, don't be embarrassed. It's so refreshing to find someone else similar to me. However, I must admit I don't often apologise for my directness. I pride myself on it – try to be different from everyone else. I hate convention and rules.'

Louisa laughs. 'You would have loved Jagger, then. He was the one that helped me to be who I wanted to be. He encouraged me to rebel against things I didn't like, you know, gave me the courage to say no, when the expectation was to say yes. But I think that was forged against the backdrop of the sixties, the times were a-changing. Not enough though, as it turned out, sadly.'

'I'd love to have the time to talk to you about your life. It sounds fascinating,' I say and surprise myself once again.

'Then we shall. I'll stay at your B&B tonight and then we'll walk on to Sennen together tomorrow. That should give us plenty of time to chat!' Louisa's smile falters. 'Unless you think that's a bit too much. We have only just met, after all.'

Ordinarily I would have thought it a bit too much. In fact, I would have thought it a huge imposition. Ordinary hasn't been part of my life lately, though, and I am certainly very pleased about that. I tell her it is a wonderful idea and we walk on to the lighthouse. I think I am so lucky to have met so many interesting people lately. I might even go so far as to say I have met more interesting people in the space of a few days than I have in my entire lifetime.

Having checked in to our accommodation and had a quick shower we are now in a very quaint, typically Cornish village pub. My growly stomach is competing against the low hum of conversation and at the moment my stomach's winning. A couple on the next table to us actually stop talking and look in my direction, so I study the menu more closely and pretend not to notice.

My cover is blown though when Louisa says with smile, 'Bloody hell, your stomach sounds like an angry lion.'

The couple look across again and I am caught. But then what does it matter? It's a natural bodily function. I mean, it's not as if I'm farting for England or anything, is it? Even though that is a natural bodily function also, I don't think it's appropriate in this setting. I certainly wouldn't like it if someone else did that while I was eating. But why is stomach growling a potentially embarrassing social situation? I wonder if other cultures would find it so. I know that in certain countries you are supposed to belch to show the host of a dinner party that you've enjoyed their food.

I return Louisa's smile. 'Yes, it is an angry *and* hungry lion. The last thing I tossed it was a bit of liquorice this afternoon.'

She frowns. 'So it was. No wonder I'm so hungry. That settles it – I'm going to have the steak and ale pie and chips.' She closes her menu and laughs as her stomach copies mine.

I decide on the pie too, and then take a thirsty gulp of lager. Isn't it great, that first sip after a long day in the sun and on a fairly empty stomach? You really can feel it trickle all the way down your gullet and then a little sugar and alcohol rush sends fire to your cheeks and puts a giggle in your chest. Well, it does with me this evening. I think it's because I'm in good company and relaxed.

'Shall I tell you about how me and Jagger met?' Louisa says into the thoughtful air between us.

I nod and settle back into my comfy chair. I watch Louisa's face light from within and can see her in her youth. Not that she looks her age, she's a very youthful sixty-seven-year-old, but it's as if thoughts of the past have stripped the lines from her face and put an extra sparkle in her eyes.

'We met, believe it or not, when the Beatles came to Newquay in 1967. It was the day before my eighteenth birthday and a friend of a friend had spied the fab four up near the Atlantic Hotel. We later found they were staying there and were here filming part of their Magical Mystery Tour. Anyway, word got round the youngsters like wildfire and we all swarmed down there.'

'My goodness, how exciting,' I say because it must have been, and I could see in her eyes that she remembers how she felt back then.

'Oh, it was. And even more exciting was meeting Jagger. He was a couple of years older and very charismatic. He was a friend of that friend of a friend I told you about and after we were introduced, he grabbed my hand and threaded me through the crowd, so I could have a great view of the band. He seemed to know everything about what they were doing and where they were going next, and later, four of us went off to Holywell Bay on motorbikes to wait for the Beatles to turn up in their Mystery Tour bus. They did, of course, and we were amongst the first to see them.' Louisa takes a breath, her face flushed with excitement, and she nods at me. 'Still got the autographs safe at home.'

'And then you started going out?'

'Yes, but it was in secret for a bit. My dad was very strict and kept me practically under lock and key. Mum worked on him a bit and Jagger was on his best behaviour when I introduced him to my folks. Dad was a third-generation no-nonsense farmer, so Jagger's ideas about turning the world upside down wouldn't have gone down well. Dad wanted me to marry a farmer and follow in tradition.'

Our food arrives, and my lion demands full attention. Louisa digs in too and for a few minutes we just stuff our faces. Remember that day I stuffed my face when Caleb first came round? Louisa looks just like I did. Two spherical hamster cheeks and a fork poised ready to load more in. I must have mirrored her, because she catches my eye and says through a small gap at the side of her mouth. 'Great to see someone enjoy their food as much as me.'

I choke back a giggle and swallow my mouthful. 'No point in affecting table manners when you're bloody starving.' I dive into my lager again – not literally, the glass isn't big enough – and say, 'So did they give you their blessing to marry Jagger in the end?'

'Grudgingly. By then Jagger had spoken his mind on world politics, tradition, gender issues, race issues, you name it. He and Dad were chalk and cheese on every single one of them. In the end, though, it didn't really matter, because they still had my little sister at home and my older brother would be the one to take over the farm, anyway. Dad just wanted me married to someone like him, someone who'd take care of me and have nothing in his head apart from land and cows.'

'What about Jagger's parents?'

'His dad was a lecturer at Plymouth uni and his mum was an art teacher. Hence my dabbling over the years.'

This prompts me to tell Louisa all about my gran and I don't realise that I have taken over the whole conversation until I glance at the clock above the bar and discover it's an hour later. I haven't touched on my parents or Caleb either – just Gwendoline, how she was with me when I was little, how she inspired me, and then I went off at a tangent, told her all about my degree and teaching career.

'Oops. I've been rambling a bit, Louisa. This was supposed to be about your life. You're just so easy to talk to.'

'Don't be daft. I'm interested in your story, too. Shall we have another drink and chat some more, or do you want to get an early night before our walk in the morning?'

Now that's a tough one. Does she mean she wants to get an early night? I'm not great at reading people. 'I think you should decide.'

'Well, I'd like another, but I don't want to impose.'

'Great. And you really aren't.'

It's nearly another hour later. We've moved out into the beer garden to watch the sunset and I wish I'd not asked her about children. I expect it all would have come out eventually anyway, but at least I wouldn't have been the one to force heart-wrenching memories out into the open, exposing their pain and fragility to a gabble of chatter and clinking glasses.

'I'm sorry. You don't want to hear all this. Let's change the subject,' she says.

Another difficult one. Does she really want to change the subject, or does she think I'm finding it all a bit too sad? I *am* finding it all a bit sad, but I asked and therefore should be tough enough to hear the answer. 'Louisa. If you'd rather not go on I totally understand—'

'No. I think if we are to know each other properly then I'd like to tell you. Pain and sorrow make up a person's character, not just the happiness and laughter. Guess who always said that?' She puts her head on one side and fiddles with the steel-grey hair that has been brushed free of streamers and tided into a ponytail.

'Jagger?'

'The very same. So yes, I had five miscarriages in all. The last one nearly made it. We lost her almost six months in. I suspect nowadays with the new technology and whatnot, they might have been able to save her. There were complications after her birth and I had to have a hysterectomy.'

Louisa stops, and I notice her hand is shaking as she picks up her glass of cyder. She takes a sip and continues. 'We called her Celandine after my favourite flower.' Louisa looks at me and I try not to flinch at the depth of suffering in her eyes. 'She was perfect, Lottie. Just needed to grow a bit more... she'd have been thirty-five this year.'

Not that much older than me, I think. I also think that I would have liked it if Louisa was my mother. I could have called her Mum and we'd have laughed and talked and shared things. I take a drink and say, 'Had you thought of adoption?' That's right, Lottie – lead her away from those memories, the image of perfect little Celandine, the missing womb, because if you don't, you'll both end up crying into your glasses.

'We considered it for a while, but it kind of fizzled out. I was in a bad place for some time afterwards. I was cruel to everyone I loved – Jagger bore the brunt, of course. It was a case of why me? Why us? Why couldn't we have children when we craved them so badly, yet those who didn't want them fell pregnant by accident? I couldn't understand why life was so cruel and senseless sometimes. But as I grew older, I accepted that shit happens, and you have to accept it and move on.'

Louisa finishes her drink and shrugs her arms into a lightweight jacket. I realise a chill is coming in from the ocean and pull my cardigan on. 'And what happens if you don't accept things and move on?' I say, though I had no idea I was going to.

Louisa sighs and fixes me with a cool stare. 'Then life takes huge bites out of you, chews you up, spits you out and watches you slowly bleed to death by the wayside.'

This imagery is very scary and, as we walk back to our bed for the night under a firmament of day-bright stars, I wonder if I have to do a bit more of the accepting and moving-on stuff. As I said before, I think I'm okay with it all – Gwendoline helped me to 'heal' the past. But perhaps I'll tell Louisa all about my life tomorrow. It wouldn't hurt to get another opinion, would it?

Chapter Seventeen

A Few Days More

Everyone loves the feeling they get in their belly at the beginning of a holiday, don't they? And if it's been a good one, they have the opposite feeling at the end of it. I have that now. I am awake and looking at the ceiling and have just realised that it's the end of a lovely holiday, it's Monday morning and I have work. It's not Monday or work really, but I've that sinking heavy feeling you get when it is.

On top of that, there's another layer of something even heavier spreading thick through my system. It has lots of strands and twisty thoughts leading different places, some of which I don't want to pursue, but if I had to give it a name I'd say it was melancholy. You see, two of us started out on this journey and now there's just me. Yes, objectively there are still two if you count Louisa, but I can't pretend it's the same thing – a success. Meeting her was a very happy accident. We crossed each other's paths, but she wasn't part of the original plan.

One of the things I pride myself on is setting an aim and following through. Perhaps it stems from my need to be in control of things, but I really don't like failure – or perceived failure. I have failed at keeping a relationship with Caleb, and the painting, or at least sketching I had planned to do hasn't really happened either, has it? I have a drawing pad a quarter full of bits of this and bits of that. I don't like bits of things. They make my mind feel cluttered and untidy.

I'm in the shower now, still thinking about failure and Caleb and my immediate future, but mostly about Caleb. Have I been too harsh on him? He was only doing what he did because he cared about me, after all. But was he? Could it be that he thought he knew best, let his judgement override what he knew deep down I would hate, just because he wanted to control me, sort my life out for me? Has he been so influenced by what this society expects a man to be like that he's forgotten to fight against it, become consumed by it?

Now I have soap in my eye and it stings. Is that my answer? Is the soap-sting saying don't be silly, Caleb isn't a macho posturing ape intent on ruling his female, he's kind, sensitive and you should have given him another chance? Or is it actually just soap in my eye? I don't know, but I do know that I'm unused to this line of thought. Like clutter, my mind doesn't do well with jumbled thoughts and unanswered questions.

I haven't mentioned it to you, but I have actually thought about Caleb often through the days we've been apart. I'm looking at a view or chatting to Louisa and there he is stepping in on the act like one of those people on a live news item when the reporter is talking to camera. You know the type – they leap on from the side and behind, pulling faces, or waving and shouting something unintelligible and the reporter tries to keep a straight face, carries on stoically. My thoughts of Caleb don't show him leaping or yelling, he's just there in the middle of a view or a conversation, silent, sad and alone.

After a lovely and leisurely full English, the last one for the foreseeable, I find that Louisa has an idea for the day planned if I'm happy to agree. I am. I have too many thoughts in my head and no room for any plans.

We are to make for the ruins of Botallack Mine and another that she says too quickly for me to catch the name of, then we are to go on to Cape Cornwall and just have a look out to sea from one of the most westerly points in England. Perhaps we'll have elevenses there and then walk on to Whitesand Bay, which is only a spit from Sennen, our final destination. She knows a lovely café there that does a wonderful cream tea, which seems a fitting end to the short break in her case, and the holiday in mine.

We set off into the perfect summer morning and my feet carry me to the springy grass along the path. I'm going to miss the fresh smell of that grass, the carpets of wildflowers, the azure sky, wide and vast, this morning adorned with a few white unhurried clouds. I shall miss too the rugged landscape as surprising as its wildlife, and, of course, the ocean singing its ancient song to the wind, or whispering a lullaby in hidden coves along the way.

I can imagine you're thinking that I do actually live opposite the ocean, so what's all the drama about? Yes, I do, but you see this is all new, it's like an adventure. When I'm at home I know what my immediate surroundings are, it's familiar, day to day. I agree it is a wonderful day to day and I wouldn't live anywhere else, but there's something about my feet taking me to new places every day that makes me feel energised, alive. Or perhaps it's only really a state of mind. If your mind is open to the idea of adventure, then you see it in every blade of grass, every turn of a wave. If on the other hand your mind is closed, dull, decaying, then you see only darkness, woe... misery. Yes, that seems to make sense to me. How about you?

The Botallack Mine is perched on a breathtakingly steep cliff side next to the Atlantic which is presently hurling itself at its feet and I am reminded of a scene or two in Poldark. Louisa confirms that this is indeed one of the many areas of outstanding natural beauty used in the programme. I am also reminded of Wheal Coates Mine and that reminds me of Peter, which is good, and, of course, Caleb, which isn't, so I switch my mind back to today and something Louisa is saying about the mine.

'This would make a fantastic painting, you know.'

'Yes, it would,' I say but have no desire to draw it.

'How about a quick sketch?'

'Not really in the mood,' I say in the manner of a moody teenager. My insides feel twisty and grumpy and I don't really know why. Not something specific I can put my finger on anyway.

'Okay, then let's press on to Cape Cornwall, shall we? I'm looking forward to having a look at the Ballowall Barrow I read about in the guide book this morning.'

'A burial chamber?'

'Yes, Bronze Age by all accounts.'

I don't know what I was expecting, but it wasn't something that looks like the remains of a little hut. It is built of dry stone wall and set in two concentric rings. I reach out to the stone and I feel as if I'm reaching back four thousand years. I close my eyes and try to imagine what it must have been like to live here then. I can't, of course, but I try. I open my eyes and face the ocean, just a little way off over the edge of the cliff and Louisa voices what I am thinking. 'What a fascinating place and a wonderful burial site.' She turns in a circle and then puts her head back, closes her eyes. 'It said in the guide book that it's thought they put it here for an important person, so they could face the setting sun over the ocean.'

'Just stunning,' I say, and feel a catch in my chest. I think it's because I recognise the humanity that created such a place. I know it was to do with superstition and a god or gods, but for me that's not what is important. For me it's the fact that people built this tomb out of respect and love for a fellow human being. In a time when life was short and brutal, they bothered to try and create something beautiful for the spirit of the deceased, and in doing so would remember that person's life every time they looked at it. Even though four thousand years separate our civilisations, I feel like we're not that different.

'You look lost in thought,' Louisa says as she leads the way back up towards the end of the cape.

'Yes. I am a bit.' I could have told her exactly what I just told you, but I want to keep it between us. I think sometimes the more people you tell about a deep feeling, the shallower it becomes.

Though the view from Cape Cornwall is breathtaking, the wind has got up and is trying its very best to blow us off our feet. I guess it has to find its fun where it can. Louisa suggests that coffee and cake up here is perhaps not wise, so we head down to the nearest beach instead. This 'beach' turns out to be just a little spit of landfall made of sand and boulder called Porth Nanven. It is quite beautiful though and provides the shelter from the wind that we need.

'How come after a full English this morning I'm ready for coffee and cake?' Louisa says, handing me one of two huge slices of coffee cake we bought from the Pendeen bakery before we set out.

'I think it's to do with the sea air and the trillions of calories we're burning without even realising it.' I grin at her and she nods solemnly back, though the twinkle in her eye gives her away. 'It's true. I think we'll need at least three scones each to make up for it all by the time we get to Sennen.'

A sugar tsunami whirls in my head so I settle back with my coffee and take in my surroundings. I remark on the many boulders on the beach. Louisa says that the guide book said it is sometimes called Dinosaur Egg beach because of them. I balance my flask cup on one and smooth both my hands around another. It's warm but I can tell that just below the surface it's cool and full of moisture. I wonder how many thousands of years old it is and touch my nose to its surface. A deep breath gives me a mixture of salt, seaweed and dried sand and I wonder if it's the first time in all its life that someone has taken the time to touch and sniff it.

I say as much to Louisa and she smiles and says she expects it is. That's the thing about her: she gets me. Halfway through me asking, my brain panicked because it is a fairly 'out there' thing to say. I wouldn't have ordinarily spoken a thought like that out loud; well, perhaps I would have to Caleb because I've known him longer. But I needn't have worried.

And she wasn't just humouring me, because she turns to me and says, 'People don't take the time to get in touch with their environment enough. It's so important to physically connect with nature sometimes like you just did, because it grounds you, makes you feel part of the world.'

Now that was exactly something I might have said – kindred spirits indeed. Right at that moment I knew that she was a central part of this third turning point. You know the one I mentioned the other day when I set out alone after Caleb had gone? It's as if Louisa and me we were supposed to meet, become friends, and share our stories. I'm not a huge believer in fate and destiny, but this kind of feels part of a bigger plan – and it's not mine.

And it's not lost on me that so far, I haven't shared my story. Still, that's going to be sorted when we get to Sennen. Perhaps not all of it, I can't do big uploads of my life all at once. It makes me feel light-headed, anchorless, as if the sharing of important emotional information hollows me out, somehow.

And all too quickly, here we are a few hours later in beautiful Sennen Cove. I came here when I was a teenager with a friend and her family for a weekend. They had a caravan not far away. I don't remember much about it because I didn't enjoy myself. I felt awkward and suffocated by other people's rules and expectations. At least when I was at home I could hide away in my bedroom and shut out the world.

I can see her now in my mind's eye, this friend: Kelsey Edwards – a mass of unruly yellow hair, green eyes, large gravestone front teeth and freckles. She was nice and patient and kind, but I did wonder sometimes if she was my friend because she could see my loneliness. I think she admired me too, me being a bit wild, different and outspoken in class. She was quiet and mousy and perhaps I gave her a bit of street cred. Who knows? Whatever the truth, the friendship didn't last for long. My fault, probably.

'I know the perfect place for the cream tea, come on,' Louisa says, hurrying along the promenade as if she's not eaten for days.

Little Bo Café is certainly in a perfect setting opposite the beach and has a row of outside tables across the road, continental style. I sit down and wait while Louisa orders and feel something in my chest – a cross between nerves and melancholy again. I sometimes talk to myself when I'm feeling unsure, don't you? If

I'm on my own I talk out loud, but internal talking is best for a busy seafront, I've found. People tend to stare and nudge each other. Those people ought to try it because it does help.

I ask myself why I feel like this and the answer comes back that I'm nervous about what Louisa's response to Caleb's story will be, and sad because I know that once we part today, I might never see her again. Yes, of course we'll swap numbers and promise to call and arrange a time to meet up again, but it rarely happens. Life takes over and rushes past and then a few years down the line you think, oh, I never did get to meet Louisa again. Shame, I must look out her number. But when you do, you find it isn't in the hideous coffee pot that Aunt Hilary gave you, nor is it in the jar of keys that don't work, or in the drawer where important things are placed and then forgotten about. It's not on the fridge amongst the Post-its, edged with jam smears and toast crumbs; it's not anywhere.

I watch Louisa walk back across the road, with a huge smile on her lovely face, her steel-grey streamers for hair, her easy stride carrying her tall elegance, and can't bear the thought of her being lost from me. I turn my face back to the ocean and let the breeze do a grand job of whipping the moisture from my eyes before they can even think about forming anything more substantial.

This holiday has been full of surprises, not least the realisation that maybe I'm not just best on my own all of the time. Yes, there's been the upset over Caleb, but Louisa has shown me that I can trust others; it's not just me against the world. Having said that, after today it will be for a while. How could it not?

'The deed is done!' Louisa says with a chuckle and slips off her cardigan to reveal a green T-shirt with a huge rainbow front and centre. How very Louisa.

'Deed?'

'Cream tea and an extra pot of cream just because we can.'

I think I'm going to tell her about Caleb now. It feels right but it feels a bit disjointed just shoving him into a conversation about extra cream. So, I say, 'It won't hurt us. We've walked nine miles today.' We both look out to sea in companionable silence and then suddenly Caleb's out in the open. 'I wonder where my walking partner is now? Probably at home, sulking.'

'This is the lover you split from on this holiday?'

'Yes.' I tell her how we met – him coming to my flat and about me leaving school just like that because it felt like the right thing to do. I told her that we were just friends for ages because I was worried that if it was allowed to be something else it would change everything.'

'It looks like you were right, then?'

'Yes and no. We argued, and I made him leave because he betrayed me. Betrayed my trust and went behind my back to a family member about something that happened to me when I was thirteen. He thought he was helping, but he was actually making things much worse because he had no right to think he knew best – knew better than me about how to run my own life.'

The tea arrives as I'm wondering where to go next and we talk about the size of the scones and laugh with the waitress about the fact that we'd have to be rolled away at the end of it. The waitress leaves and it feels as if we're in a book or a play and I wait for my next line. I can't remember it and there's no cue, so I look at Louisa for help.

'Do you want to tell me what happened when you were thirteen?'

That's not what I was hoping for but at least I expected it. 'Not at the moment. I'm not good with just splurging everything at once.'

'That's fine. Okay, let's see what we have here…' Louisa takes a big bite of jam-and-cream-laden scone and closes her eyes to savour it. A big blob of cream is wiggling about on the end of her nose and I laugh. 'I have cream on the end of my nose, don't I?' she asks, and laughs too.

I wonder if she did it on purpose to lighten the conversation and make me smile again. I take a bite of mine and watch her face. I can practically hear her weighing up the information I gave her inside her head, sorting through a collection of words, measuring the right response. 'How honest do you want me to be?' She dabs at her nose and takes a drink of tea. 'In fact, do you want my opinion at all? You could have told me all that just to get it off your chest.'

'No, I would like your opinion. Your honest opinion.'

'Okay then. Reading between the lines of what you've told me and reaching for the things you haven't, I'd say that Caleb is a good egg. He cares about you.' She lifts another half of scone and then puts it back down again. 'I'd also say that whatever happened to you was huge, has shaped your personality and how you see the world and receive people into yours. You tell me you set out to be different and have maintained it, which is good, we need more people unafraid to be individual. You also say you won't be bossed about, controlled, but I think you may have been too hasty where Caleb is concerned.'

Louisa tucks into the other half of her scone and looks at me thoughtfully. I add more cream to the tower I have been building on my scone and do the same. She's obviously not finished her opinion because she holds up a finger just as I'm going to say something.

'If you don't mind me asking, how many other men have you been involved with?'

I tell her about the one-night stands and my disinterest in making anything long lasting out of relationships. 'Why, is that relevant?'

'Oh, absolutely. Now, I'm no psychologist, but I have met lots of people in my time, listened to their stories, put myself in their shoes, and I'm going to guess that whatever happened when you were thirteen involved betrayal by a family member, possibly a parent.'

I nearly choke on my scone.

'I'm also going to guess that because of this you have learned to rely on nobody but yourself and so when you let your guard down and Caleb in, you rejected him because of your fear, not just because of what he did really.'

'Fear? What am I frightened of?' My heart is beating too fast and the cream curdles in my throat. Her accuracy is like a pointy barb in my ribs.

'You were frightened that you'd exposed yourself, told him your secrets, become vulnerable. You don't like feeling like that because that's what you were like when you were thirteen – when all that hurt came crashing down on top of you. You've built your armour well over the years, and then Caleb's betrayal started to chip away at it, managed to peel it back, leave you naked.'

I take a gulp of tea to wash away that vile vomity taste of cream and see that my hand is shaking. Is Louisa's assessment correct? It feels like it's pretty close and she doesn't even know the big fat secret. It's at once scary and comforting that a person can be so wise about somebody else's hopes and fears. 'I'm not sure what to say.'

'Then wait until you are.' She gives a brief smile and then puts her head on one side and watches me over the rim of her teacup like a bird watches for a worm in the lawn. I look at the silver dash of a boat moving fast over the water and say nothing. I don't have the words. Then she says, 'Can I ask if you love Caleb?'

If it had been anyone else apart from Louisa I would have told them to mind their own bloody business, but to her I say, 'I don't know. I have deep feelings for him and miss him now he's gone. But I couldn't say if it's love, because I don't know what that is. I know what I feel isn't the crap my mother reads in those chick-lit novels. Romantic love is just a social construct if you ask me.'

Louisa puts her elbows on the table and rests her chin on her hands. 'Yes, those books can give us high and sometimes false expectations, but I think you might love him. It's hard to tell because you're not being honest with yourself, I feel.' She holds up a finger again when I go to protest. 'But that is perfectly understandable, and you sensibly know how much story you can cope with sharing at a time. So I think we should talk about something else now.'

On the one hand I agree, on the other I worry that I have nothing else to talk about – and because we have almost come to the end of our time together. It's nearly four o'clock and she's told me that her nephew is coming to pick her up at around five.

The little silver dash of a boat is just a speck in the distance now and before I can stop myself I hear myself say, 'I'll miss you so much, Louisa. When you were telling me how you lost your daughter yesterday, I thought how unbearably sad it was and I did think how wonderful it would be if you were my mother. I know you can't be, but... I wish you were...' I run out of words and feel a hot fire under the skin of my cheeks.

Then the long slender fingers of the olive tree close over mine on the table and I look up into her face. Her turquoise eyes are shimmering with emotion. 'That's a wonderful thing to wish for. And why shouldn't it happen? I can't think of a better young woman to have as my daughter.'

I can only nod because my chest is too full of words and emotion to let anything past my lips. I eventually say, 'Thank you.'

She pats my hand and releases it. 'Look, say no, if you like, but how about you extend your holiday for a few days more? I've a few spare rooms at my place and I'm sure you'll love to have a wander around the vineyard. You might even be inspired to do a painting or two and it's only about twenty-five minutes or so away from where you live.'

Would I like to go? I can't think of anything I would like more. 'What a brilliant idea. I'd love to come!'

She hugs me and for the first time since Gwendoline died I feel like I have an older woman to learn from, relate to and care about. I wouldn't have thought it possible to grow so fond of a stranger in such a short time, but it is, and I have. Isn't it funny that sometimes when you think you're coming to the end of something it turns out that it's another beginning? I'm very pleased by this, because as you know, the end of a holiday is not my favourite thing.

Chapter Eighteen

New Beginnings

James remembers that day fifteen years ago when aged twenty-three he stepped up to this very same front door. Behind it were people who looked like him, news of his extended family, aunts, uncles, cousins, grandparents – in short, his missing history. Lost pieces of a jigsaw puzzle that he thought he'd never wanted to find until looking at the incomplete picture had begun to irritate the hell out of him. He remembers an elfin-faced girl with eyes like his in the kitchen doorway, hesitant, unsure. He also remembers the sharp words she received from his mum and he wished he'd said something – done something.

Never mind. James is here to do something today. A little late, but life is not a neat package to be posted down the years. It's sometimes messy, battered, and often not what you ordered. Beth tightens the grip on his right hand and he lifts the left and knocks on the door.

'James, darling!' His mum pulls him into a hug on the doorstep and ushers them both inside. 'Beth, you look lovely,' she says through a stretched smile and kisses the air at each side of his wife's cheeks.

'Thanks, Jenny. So do you. And have you done something new with your hair?'

His mum looks in the mirror, a puzzled but pleased expression on her face. 'No, just the same old.'

'Really? Well, I think it takes years off you.'

James glances at his wife and realises that she's about as sincere as a fox babysitting a chicken coop. As they follow his mother into the sitting room he pulls a face at Beth and then gestures at his mum's hair. She whispers, 'Well, we do want her in a good mood today, don't we?'

'Dad, how's it going?' His dad gives a broad smile, puts his paper down and then they do the half-hug back-slapping thing that men do when they are pleased to see each other.

'All the better for seeing you two.' He steps forward and envelops Beth in a genuine hug. 'Must be, what – three months or so?'

'I expect it is, yes. Life is just always so busy, isn't it?' Beth says.

'Yes, but we need to make time,' his mum says, handing round canapés. There's a definite edge to her voice. 'Family is important. Work should take a back seat sometimes.'

James feels his wife bridle and jumps in first. 'Of course, but Beth and I do have very pressurised jobs, you know.'

'And two more families to see,' Beth says sweetly.

'Two more?'

'Yes, James's adoptive parents and mine, of course.'

His mum has drawn her mouth into a disapproving button so James jumps in again, 'Anyway, enough talk about work and families, let's sit down and have a catch-up.'

She makes as if she's going to sit next to James on the sofa, but Beth beats her to it. The button grows tighter and his mum's hand holding the canapé tray starts to shake. 'Drinks, Keith,' she says.

'What can I get you both? We have a nice chardonnay in the fridge or we've beer, lager.' Keith rolls his eyes up to the left. 'Oh, and a lovely Chianti that our friends brought back from Italy last week.'

'Just an orange juice for me, Keith, thanks,' Beth says.

'Probably wise, save the booze for the roast, eh?' Keith laughs in that polite way people do when they don't know what to say next and everyone is looking at them.

Beth looks at James and gives an almost imperceptible nod.

'Yeah, thing is, Beth won't be drinking today and for the next six months or so.'

Keith puts his lips together and furrows his brow. Not the quickest on the uptake. James looks at his mum who shoves the canapé tray on the coffee table and slumps into an armchair as if her legs have given up. He tries a tentative smile.

'You're… you're…' His mum looks over at Beth, her hand hovering over her mouth as if she wants to stop the words.

'Pregnant, yes,' Beth says with a big grin.

'Pregnant!' his dad says and laughs again. This time it's big and hearty and full of joy.

'Oh, my goodness,' his mum says and James notices that her smile is fixed, doesn't reach her eyes.

'Well, that's the best news we've heard in bloody ages isn't it, Jen?' His dad slaps his thigh and laughs again.

There is a bit of lull and then his mum recovers from whatever is keeping her happy face from showing itself and she flaps her hand at her eyes. 'Oh my, I'm filling up here. I can't believe it – we're to be grandparents at last!'

James can't see any sign of her filling up, but at least she looks the part of the happy gran now. 'So, you're pleased, then?'

'Pleased? We're over the bloody moon.' His dad's eyes must have stolen the moisture from his mum's when she wasn't looking.

'I thought we might never see a grandchild, you being on the way to forty and all,' his mum says.

'Charmin', I'm only thirty-eight. Besides, the average age for a professional couple to have their first child is thirty-two and Beth's only thirty.'

'I expect Lottie might give you some, too,' Beth says, and takes the orange juice from James's dad. 'She's only twenty-eight, isn't she?'

James thinks that if his wife wants his mum in a good mood, she's a funny way of showing it today.

His mum's button mouth is back. 'Lottie? You mean Charlotte? I doubt that very much. She seems hell-bent on shunning any suitable man we try to find for her and the ones she finds for herself only last five minutes.' She throws her hands up dismissively. 'Charlotte's an odd one, always has been, and I guess always will be. No point in hoping for a normal life for her now.' She looks at her husband. 'We have tried, haven't we, love?'

Dad shrugs and says he'll get James a beer.

'Her latest art shop venture looks to end in disaster, too.'

'Oh, why's that?' James asks.

'Well, she won't take advice. There was a perfectly lovely place just down the road from us I told her about, but she refused point blank. Says a friend of hers from school is going to help her with one she's seen at Mawgan Porth.' Mum takes the glass of wine Dad hands her. 'I mean, have you seen the size of that place? Yes, it's busy in summer, but out of season, who'll go in the shop, let alone buy anything?'

'Perhaps it's not the money she's doing it for,' Beth says and gives a little smirk.

His mum snorts. 'No, that's what she says. Says she has enough of her gran's money to see her right for some time.' She smooths her skirt over her knees. 'My mother did her no favours leaving her everything in the will.'

'Really? How so?' Beth asks.

'Because she thinks she can do whatever she bloody well likes, that's why. Did you know she's chucked her job in at school, just like that?'

'I did, yes. James told me.'

'There you are, then.' James notes that his mum's eyes are hardening into sparky diamonds and the skirt smoothing is becoming more forceful, repetitive. He looks at Beth to try and send her some kind of message with his eyes that hopefully says, 'leave off for a bit.' Beth looks at it and turns her mouth into a button shape similar to the one his mother had earlier. Oh God.

'I don't see what the problem is. If Lottie wants to pack her job in and do something else with her life, then good on her, I say. We only get one of them and we should try to do what makes us happy. That's what's important, isn't it?'

'Dear me, you sound just like her. And she wouldn't thank you for calling her Lottie, I can tell you.' His mum stands up and takes a big gulp of wine.

James tries to catch Beth's eye, but she deliberately ignores him. 'I think she prefers it nowadays, actually.'

His mum nearly chokes. 'Why? What on earth makes you say that?'

James flashes his eyes at Beth and says, 'It's just something a friend of hers told me. Look, shall we eat and then we can talk more about it then? I'm starved.' He does a big cheesy grin and hopes his mum listens.

'Hmm, okay. I'll just pop the Yorkshire puddings in.' She glares at Beth and stalks to the kitchen.

James is glad that the conversation has turned to babies – much safer ground for now. Hopefully they can broach the Lottie question when everyone has full bellies and a few drinks inside them. 'So will you find out the gender at twenty weeks?' his mum asks, offering the plate of extra Yorkshire puddings round the table.

'No. I think we'd like a surprise,' Beth says.

'Quite right too,' Dad says through a mouthful of roast beef.

'Oh, I don't know. It could be useful to know regarding clothes and decorating the nursery, etcetera,' Mum says and pours herself more wine.

'Only if you believe in gender specific clothes and such like. We hate gender stereotypes and will actively fight against the barrage of pink and blue, won't we, James?'

James nods and wonders what his mother will say to that.

'Hmm, I see. Well, it's hard not to buy pink or blue though, these days. The shops are full of both.' His mum stabs a roast potato with more force than is necessary and James can see the conversation taking another nose dive before very long.

'Yes, but we must try to find some. If you want to buy something for the baby and can't find neutral colours, please don't bother. I'd hate to see them go to waste,' Beth says in a polite but firm manner.

His mum opens her mouth to reply and then just shakes her head in disbelief.

James looks at his dad for help and is grateful that he takes the initiative. 'So, what about names? Have you thought of any yet?'

'One or two,' James says. 'Nothing definite yet.'

'We had thought of some traditional Nigerian names, hadn't we, love?' Beth says to James but is looking at her mother-in-law.

James feels his heart sink. They had discussed that possibility in passing but they hadn't liked any so far. Beth is obviously hell-bent on winding up his mother. 'Yes, we have looked at a few.'

'Or perhaps Welsh ones,' Beth says and crunches into a pudding.

'What's wrong with good old English names?' his mum says quietly.

'Nothing, Mum. We're really just thinking of lots of names at the moment.'

'And we thought it might be nice to be a bit different, too,' Beth says.

His mum sets her chin and looks at Beth. 'I think you and Charlotte would get on. She's always banging on about being different.'

'I take it you don't approve?' Beth counters, pushing her plate to one side so hard the cutlery rattles.

'I can't see the point in being different just for the sake of it.' His mum nods at Beth's midriff. 'And I'm sure your little one won't like a name that's so odd, he or she will get bullied at school.'

'What's for pud?' James says kicking Beth's foot under the table. 'I bet it's treacle sponge and custard.'

'He's a mind reader isn't he, Jen?' his dad says, jumping up and clearing the plates. 'Come on, love, I'll give you a hand with it.'

His wife stays seated for a few moments staring at Beth. Beth folds her arms and opens her mouth to say something.

'Home-made custard too, is it?' James says, before she can.

His mum gives a brief smile, picks up some crockery and follows his dad into the kitchen.

'What's wrong with you?' Beth hisses as soon as they're out of earshot. 'Why do you always pander to her nasty little swipes at my heritage?'

'I'm not. I just don't want a full-scale row at the dinner table. We're here for Lottie, remember?'

'Yes, but that was before it was so obvious that she didn't relish the thought of a grandchild that would be part black. She covered it well, but it was there in her eyes alright.'

James had to admit to himself that thought had crossed his mind when his mum's smile hadn't quite met her eyes earlier. In the end they wouldn't know for sure unless they asked her outright and even then, she'd not tell the truth. 'I can't see the point in guessing at what goes on in her head. Let's just do what we set out to do.'

'We don't have to guess.' Beth affects his mum's manner and accent and says, 'What's wrong with English names, the poor child will be bullied if you give it a smelly old Nigerian one.'

'Shh, they'll hear you,' James says and tries to keep a straight face. Beth had really got his mum off to a T.

'So how are we going to bring Lottie's situation up?' Beth says.

'Leave it to me.'

James has three helpings of treacle sponge to avoid bringing up his sister, but then Beth kicks him under the table and he knows he has to go for it. 'So the thing is, Lottie has – had – a boyfriend who told me some stuff that she'd told him about what happened when I came back into all of your lives.'

His dad comes in at that moment carrying a tray full of rattling cups and a coffee pot, which gives James time to weigh up the expression on his mum's face. He guesses at a cross between shock and anger. His dad sets the tray on the table and begins to pour out coffee.

'I'm sorry. Can you repeat that? I'm not sure I heard it all because of your dad rattling the cups.'

James knows full well that she heard every word but repeats it anyway.

James's dad frowns and sits down.

'So this boyfriend—' his mum begins.

'Ex-boyfriend, his name's Caleb.'

'Right,' she says slowly. 'This Caleb tells you that Charlotte has told him things about our family?'

'Yes. Things I didn't know. Things that explain Lottie's behaviour around the time she had counselling and was expelled from school.'

His mum crosses her arms over her chest and narrows her eyes. 'What's she told him?'

James feels on the spot and wonders how to proceed. He predicts that whatever he says won't be met with a good response. 'Er, that you didn't handle my reappearance very well.'

'In what way?'

'Well, Lottie says—'

'Why Lottie? I used to want to call her that and she would never allow it – wouldn't let anyone call her that.'

'As I said earlier, she prefers it now,' Beth says in a chirpy manner and smiles into her coffee.

James ignores this and ploughs on. 'She told Caleb that you were cruel to her, said vile things about her to her face.' James tells her word for word what Caleb told him.

There is a very uncomfortable silence and then into it his mum says, 'Well, she would say something like that, wouldn't she? If she's landed herself a man, or had for a while at least, she might have opened up a bit about her past. She'd have to have made stuff up to justify what she did to me, wouldn't she?'

'You mean when she cut off all your hair and set the shed on fire?' Beth asks in a quiet voice.

'She didn't cut all my hair off, just one side... but yes.'

'So, you didn't say all those terrible things?' James asks.

'Of course not. She was just spoiled rotten because we were making up for losing you, I suppose... our fault to an extent. But there's something selfish in her, reckless, wayward, and she was insanely jealous. I told you all this at the time when she refused to meet you, James.'

James looks at his mother's trembling lips and pink face and can tell that the colour is blooming from lies and guilt. He looks at his dad, but his eyes are anywhere but on his son. 'Dad?'

'Hmm?'

'Is that how it was?'

'I've just told you how it was—' his mum snaps.

'I'm asking Dad.'

His dad looks at the ceiling and sighs. Then he looks at his wife and shakes his head twice. 'No. This Caleb has it right.'

'Keith!'

'Well, it's true. I'm not going to sit here and lie to our son's face. You've done that for too many years.'

James hears Beth's sharp intake of breath and watches his mum's face crumple and morph into a Greek tragedy mask. She draws in a breath through the stretch of her downturned mouth and lets it out with a big sob; her shoulders heave and two mascara teardrops trickle down her cheeks.

'Don't get upset, Mum.'

'Don't get upset!' she yells, a bubble of snot popping out of her right nostril. 'How can I not?'

'Come on, love…' James's dad begins and puts his hand on his wife's.

She flings her hand in the air as if his hand had an electric current passing through it. 'Don't *come on love* me! Why did you have to go against me, Keith?'

'I just told the truth, that's all…'

'Nobody is going against you, Jenny,' Beth says in a soothing tone. 'We just want the best for Lottie, for everyone, and in order to get that we have to admit what actually happened all those years ago, so we can move on.'

'What's all this "we" business?' The woeful tragedy mask is quickly replaced by a hard-edged, sharp-eyed expression. 'You weren't even on the scene back then, so what the hell do you know about it?'

James is sick of his mother's nasty attitude to his wife and says, 'Beth wasn't there then but she is very much part of my family now and you'd better get used to it.' He doesn't hide the cold anger in his voice.

'Yes, well you can't know what it was like back then when I was sixteen. None of you can, well apart from Keith, but he didn't go through the nine months of carrying you, giving birth to you, only to have you wrenched from his arms.' The tragedy mask was back. So were the tears.

'I bet it was awful, but then you had Charlotte. Surely you were happy when she came into your lives?' James says and looks to Beth or his dad for help. They are both staring at the table.

'But she was always so wilful, stubborn. I didn't feel like she was part of me somehow… not like you were, love.'

James says nothing. He has no words. But his mum has plenty.

'I felt like she'd been sent to punish us somehow for giving you away. Nothing we ever did was right for her, she wouldn't do as she was told, always fought us, didn't she, Keith?'

His dad gives a heavy sigh. 'I don't know. I think you provoked her, to be honest, Jenny. You never cut her any slack.'

His mum throws her hands up. 'Oh, I see. It's all coming out now, isn't it? Big bad Jenny was to blame for us having an evil little witch for a daughter!'

'For God's sake, Mum, she was a child! Just a child.'

'Like I was when I had you, people forget that! People forget what all that did to me!'

'Seems like it was you who needed the counselling, not Lottie,' Beth says.

'How dare you!' His mum bangs her fist on the table.

'Beth's right, she's not being unkind, Mum. It was awful what you were pressured into doing by your dad and Dad's parents too. It would have helped to talk to a professional.'

'That's as may be, but you think that Lottie didn't need counselling for creeping into my room and cutting my hair off and then setting fire to our bloody shed?' She addresses Beth.

Beth puts her head on one side and looks at the ceiling, 'That's a tough call. I think it could have helped if she wasn't trying to contend with your rejection at home all the time, I'm not sure. But I don't think her actions were quite so out there, given what you said to her, how you treated her. It's a good job your mother was there for her, that's all I can say.'

His mother opens and closes her mouth a few times and more mascara tears poised in the well of her eyes chase each other down her face. She looks at her son. 'Don't you understand how much I was hurting after they took you away, and how much joy you brought into my life when you returned?'

'Yes, of course. Well, not really, but I can try to imagine what it must have been like for you back when it all happened. But having me back in your life shouldn't have meant that Lottie lost out. There should have been room for both of us.'

'I know you're not keen on me, Jenny, but I honestly think you would do well to have counselling. It isn't too late, and it might help to heal the terrible damage that was undoubtedly done to you all those years ago.' Beth smiles at his mum. James can tell it is her professional smile, but he knows she's trying her best to make things better.

His mum puts a shaking hand to her mouth. 'You think I was damaged by it all?' She looks at James and Beth.

'Of course you were, Mum. And now we need a new beginning. What needs to be done now is for you to apologise to Lottie, to acknowledge that you were wrong, and for us all to try and build a family from these bitter fragments.' James surprises himself with that. He thinks he can see his mum soften.

'Not sure I can – not sure where to begin.' She looks at her husband. 'We have spent the past few years trying to put it all behind us. Me and Lottie are fine now…' Her words run out and she starts the silent sobbing he remembers from their reunion.

'Things are not fine at all. Caleb told me how she feels about you, about all of it. You have done so much damage and need to put it right. The whole mess has damaged a brother and sister too. If you had handled it properly from the beginning, Lottie and I could be great friends by now.' James stops and draws his hands down his face. 'Oh, I'm not blameless. I could have tried harder, a damn sight harder.' He looks at his dad. 'And so could you, Dad. Yes, Mum is a strong character, but you should have stood your ground.'

His dad sighs. 'Yes. You're absolutely right, lad. I was all for wanting a quiet life, pushed things to the back of my mind. And nowadays Lottie keeps in contact, we see her fairly often and, well, I thought everything was okay.'

'Yes, well it's time to make things right now. We have a new life coming into this family and we'd like it to have an auntie on the scene,' Beth says, squeezing James's knee under the table.

There's a round of smiles – even his mum manages a watery one. 'This Caleb. Why have he and Char... Lottie fallen out, then?' his mum asks.

'Because he came to see me behind her back and tried to make an effort to get us together. They went on holiday last week and became closer. He told her that he'd come to see me and—'

'She went bloody nuts and sent him packing,' his mum says.

'Yes.'

'I know my daughter. That's why I'm not hopeful that an apology will work.' The button mouth is back.

'You will have to try bloody hard to make it work, then. Because I'll tell you this,' James says, jabbing a finger across the table at his parents, 'I'm not giving up on my sister this time, and I'm damned if I'll let you two, either.'

Beth squeezes his hand and both parents look at him with respectful eyes. James thinks that the whole thing went as well as it could have done, and he makes a wish that he'll be reunited with his sister very soon.

Chapter Nineteen

Days of Wine and Roses

I have been at Little Petherick Vineyard for only one day, but it feels like I've always been here. The vineyard sits on the south-facing slopes above the tiny picturesque village of the same name and looks over the Camel estuary. The views are stunning, and when I stand on the brow of the hill outside Louisa's cottage and look at the sweep of regimented vines down towards the river, I feel like I've somehow been transported to France. I never imagined a vineyard in England, and although this one is very small, it produces the most delicious sparkling wines and rosé. I know this because I had a wine tasting session last night. It can kick out a few bottles of red too, but Louisa says that the climate in England isn't good at producing the rich full-bodied ones that some people prefer.

Everyone is so friendly, too, and Louisa's nephews, Jack and Ronan, have given me the grand tour of the crushing shed, as she calls it, where the wine making is done. There's nothing in there at the moment though, because harvest time won't be until the autumn. For now, all the vines are in flower, so delicate and pretty, and the scent as you wander through the rows is just heavenly. Louisa says I can come back and lend a hand at harvest time if I want to. It's great that she wants to make me part of her life. I haven't mentioned the big fat secret though, but I think I will tonight.

I'm going to have a little look round the gift shop now before the tourists arrive. There aren't coach loads, but Louisa says they get fifteen to twenty couples or so each day through the main season. That's due to the leaflets in the guest houses round Padstow and the surrounding area, plus some of the shops in Padstow have little posters in their establishments advertising local wine. Ronan does a tasting tour, too, and that proves popular.

Louisa's sister Suzie is in the shop today as her husband Paul is off delivering wine to Padstow and around. They are similar to look at, though Suzie is nine years younger, has raven hair and is plumper around her core. I guess that's because she's had children.

'Morning, Lottie. Sleep well?'

'I did, thank you. It's so quiet and peaceful here it would be hard not to – plus the wine tasting helped to send me on my way.'

'Ah yes, lovely stuff.' Suzie picks up a brightly coloured bowl, dusts it and sets it back on display.

I pick it up and turn it round in my hands. The sun angling in through the window highlights the smudges of russet and yellow as the colours run into each other. Suzie says the artist got his inspiration from the autumn hues of the vine leaves. I can see that now. As I look more closely I can make out the subtle blended edges of leaves and this makes me want to paint. I don't know what exactly; I only feel the physical need to do it.

'You've certainly made a good impression on my sister. I haven't seen her as enthusiastic about a person since… well, I can't remember.' Suzie's cheeks dimple in a smile.

'I'm glad. I feel the same about her. We just gelled, I think you'd say. I'm so lucky to have met her.' I place the bowl carefully back on the shelf. 'And I can't remember feeling at home so quickly anywhere, either.' I turn around and draw in a breath of lavender, cheese and warm eggs on straw. 'Everything here is just so… so…' I look at Suzie and shrug.

'Comforting?'

'Yes, that's it exactly. And Louisa is so strong and cheerful all the time – that adds to it, of course.'

'It is indeed comforting. I'm glad we only live down in the village or I'd get withdrawal symptoms.' She grins, and the dimples deepen. 'And yes, Louisa is strong and generally happy. There was a time after Jagger died that I thought she'd crumble, though.' The dimples flatten, and Suzie rearranges the eggs in the basket.

'Not surprised, he was her soulmate, wasn't he?' I hope this sounds okay as I have no idea what that really means.

'He was. I have never met a couple before or since so right for each other.'

'They must have had a rare and beautiful thing.'

What the hell am I on about? I sound like a line from one of my mother's pink-covered novel creations. Not that she created the cover, of course. She hasn't an artistic bone in her body. But then thinking about some of the covers, neither did the person who designed them. Why are women attracted to pink covers with girls in high-heeled shoes swooning against burly male chests? Or women in silhouette drinking wine and eating chocolate with lots of hearts swirling about? I can only surmise its pure escapism with a smattering of hope that their life will soon follow suit.

'Yes, they were a match made in heaven, alright,' Suzie says.

Before I feel the desire to answer in flowery verse or a similar a cliché, I tell her I'm off to paint and hurry back to the cottage.

Louisa is in the kitchen making lunch and asks me to finish making the salad while she goes off to collect some acrylics for me. She thinks they're in one of the spare bedrooms. I look through the big kitchen window out over the valley and chop some tomatoes. We will have smoked mackerel with it and some hard-boiled eggs collected this morning from the chickens that roam about the place. Then, without warning or invite, into the little warm place in my chest that's been getting larger ever since I arrived here, a cold wisp of a memory snakes...

Me chopping tomatoes, making a surprise sandwich for mother because I thought she looked tired, her taking the knife away telling me I was doing it all wrong, making a mess – a mess that she'd no doubt have to clean up when I got bored of playing the good daughter...

Me upstairs under the duvet with a pin raking my arms until they bled. Worthless, that's what I am, no good... superfluous to requirement. I'd read that in a book somewhere and looked up what it meant. 'More than is needed, required, or desired.' It described me very well.

Damn my mother. Why has she got to come poking her venom into my head when I'm happy? I chop cucumber and decide it's do with the fact that I wish Louisa was my mother and my real one has to make her presence felt to remind me that she's not.

Remember when I had trouble painting a few months ago because of all the crap happening in my life – even the calico cat had to wait ages for its second eye? And then more recently the odds and ends of sketches from my walk incomplete, half-hearted? Well, I am pleased to announce my painting muse is alive and well and living in a box of acrylics.

After lunch I took two-fold-up chairs, one to serve as an easel, and painted the view from the top of the slope I mentioned earlier. I didn't stop for four hours, though I was so engrossed in my work I didn't know that so much time had passed, and do you know, it's the best painting I have ever done. Yes, I like the calico cat, but it isn't complete yet, and this painting shows… well, it shows my true style, I think.

Hitherto (I love that word), I didn't really have a style because I was just learning, experimenting. But this afternoon I just let go, let my intuition guide my hand. It was as if I was being led by something inside that I didn't know was there. Don't ask me to tell you what it was, because I can't put it into words. If I try, it will be flowery and clichéd, I expect, and I don't want that. Whatever it was it just flowed out of me and onto the canvas until something told me it was finished, complete, and pretty bloody awesome.

Louisa came to find me just after I'd put my brush down and she gasped, she actually gasped. She had moist eyes, too, and she pulled me into a hug. She said that the painting was breathtaking, and she'd like to buy it. I said I wouldn't hear of it and made her accept it as a thank you for everything she's done for me. At first, she said no, but then I convinced her that she should put it up in the shop but not for sale. In that way it might help me get known and she'd remember me every time she went in there. She said that would be perfect and why didn't I paint some more for sale?

Louisa also said that she wouldn't have to look at the painting to remember me either, because we'd see each other often. I liked the idea of that more than the painting, and as you know, I liked that a lot.

It's after supper now and I'm sitting on the terrace at a white wrought-iron table with a cluster of scented candles in the centre of it. It isn't dark yet, but the last few pink fingers of sunset are reaching into the navy blue and peace is settling across the valley. I can't remember the last time I felt so content. I think I felt something a bit like this after me and Caleb had slept together the first time but pushing at the edges of that was always the worry about what our relationship would become.

I think I can see a bat swooping through the vines a little way off and perhaps hear the faint call of an owl somewhere in the far distance. There's no wind, the warmth of the day is imprinted on the evening, and once again I can imagine I'm somewhere in the Mediterranean. Not that I wish I was, because as I've said, Cornwall is my favourite place in the world, but it's nice to be transported elsewhere for a while, even though you're not.

By 'eck, as Gwendoline used to say, this sparkling wine has a nice kick. I could get very used to this way of life. Painting by day, sitting on balmy terraces by night, sipping wine made from the vines all around me and eating cashew nuts. The thing is, I can't, can I? Because I will have to return to my flat sooner or later, but right now my old life seems distant and ephemeral. When I reach my mind out to remember the way it looks, smells, feels, it's as if the memory is just out of focus, you know? It's like when you've woken from a dream and try to relive it a few moments later.

It isn't my old life either, is it, really? It's my new old life. My old life would be my teaching days. The second turning point day ended that, and I'm still very pleased about it. It was totally the right decision. And I do want to return to my new old life because it's exciting and holds lots of possibilities, the art shop being the most exciting, I think. I've had a third turning point since then, though, haven't I? After me and Caleb finished. I'm still sad about that, more than sad if I'm honest, which I try not to be too often because what's the point? I just get sadder and confused and there's never a solution, anyway. Better not to think about it too often.

The third turning point set me off on my own to cross paths with Louisa. I have learned lots about life and people since I did and somehow, I feel stronger inside because of it. More grown up, if that makes sense. She's coming back across the terrace now with more nibbles and what looks like a shawl over her arm. It's two shawls, actually, and she puts one over her shoulders and hands the other to me. I'm not chilly yet but thank her for her kindness.

'I've just been chatting to Suzie on the phone,' she says, topping up my glass. 'Apparently four people asked if your painting was for sale and it only was on display for an hour.'

Warm pride fills my belly. 'I had no idea you'd put it in there, yet.'

'Yes, I got Ronan to put it up on the top shelf out of reach as it's still damp. Needs a frame, too.'

'That's fantastic. It's encouraging to know that strangers think it's good.'

'It's more than good. You have a unique style, but if I had to say, I'd liken it to impressionism.'

I feel a little tickle of excitement in my chest. 'Oh yes, a regular Monet, that's me.' I can't quite carry off the flippant tone.

'You may scoff, but that's the artist I was thinking of, but I didn't say it in case you thought I was just flattering you. Your painting today reminds me of his wonderful landscapes. He captures the shifting light so well, and so do you, Lottie.'

An embarrassed chortle conceals my delight and I take too big a mouthful of wine. The bubbles go up my nose and the next minute wine shoots out of my nostrils and I double over in a coughing fit. That's one way of avoiding saying the wrong thing, I suppose. Louisa laughs so much I think she'll cry and I join in after I've got my breath back.

Night bleeds into the scene and softens the edges of the world. Louisa lights the candles and the heady scent of roses idles into the air through the flickering flames. I say that the scent is very relaxing, and she says roses are her favourite flower, yellow ones in particular because they're so cheerful. I make a mental note to buy her some before I leave. We sip wine and eat the spicy Japanese crackers she's just brought out, and the moment feels right for me to tell her about what happened when I was thirteen.

I need to be sure though, so I say, 'You know I told you that Caleb had betrayed my trust by going to a family member behind my back?'

'Yes, about something that happened when you were thirteen.'

'Yes… well, I think I'd like to tell you what that was, if you want to hear it of course.'

She says she does if I'm ready and I decide I am and tell her. The whole thing takes about ten minutes and Louisa sits with her eyes closed and is silent throughout. I'm beginning to wonder if she's fallen asleep and feel a little foolish, so I slip the shawl around my shoulders and shift about in my chair.

Louisa opened her eyes and exhales as if she's been holding her breath for the ten minutes I've been talking; she hasn't, of course, that's impossible, for a human anyway. 'My poor Lottie,' she says, and her voice catches on Lottie.

I can't look at her face because I'm worried that her expression would encourage my eyes to allow tears. I look at a moth crawling along the chair opposite instead and wonder how something that flimsy and papery thinks it can fly to the moon. When I'm sure my voice will come out sounding like mine I say to the moth, 'Yes, it was a tough few years. Luckily, I had Gwendoline, or…' I let the rest hang unspoken in the delicate air.

'It's a good job you had someone, because your bloody mother is a disgrace!'

The fury in her voice snaps my head to her face and I hardly recognised the calm, wise Louisa that I've grown so fond of. Her eyes burn brighter than the candles but without the warmth and she grips the arms of her chair so tightly that each knuckle is plain to see.

'That's something we can agree on,' I say, and give little laugh. I don't like to see her so upset.

'Your dad seems a bit of a wimp, too, why the hell didn't he *do* anything?'

I shrug because I don't have an answer.

'When I think of how much I... how much Jagger and I wanted a child and couldn't have one and then your mother makes you feel worthless, drives you to do what you did... and the self-harming, too.' Louisa sighs again and shakes her head in bewilderment. 'My God, I wish I could have been there, taken you away from them.'

'Me too. I would have loved growing up here, such fun!' There's a flippant tone in my voice again; why am I trying to make light of it all?

Louisa pours the last of the wine and downs hers in one. Then she tucks her hands under her armpits and shivers, though I know that it's not because of the temperature. Neither of us says anything for a while and I wonder if I should suggest that we go inside, then I nearly jump out of my seat when Louisa slaps her hand on the table.

'Damn it all! I don't see why she should get away with this. James obviously wants to meet you, from what Caleb told you, and I think you bloody well should. I imagine your mother would hate it if you two got on – be worried that you'd discuss her and find her wanting. Well, he would, you already do.'

'Oh no,' I hold my palm up to her and say what I said to Caleb. 'I couldn't meet him. It would dredge all the old feelings up and remind me how my parents feel about him and how they feel about me. Besides, it was her that wanted us to meet, don't forget.'

'Yes, but that was then, before you... did what you did to her. You said she was reluctant to let James have your number about ten years ago – no wonder. I can't imagine that James would condone what they did back then.'

'No, I don't suppose he would, but I think it's a bit late to try and play happy families.'

Louisa is silent for a few moments and then she says, 'I was wrong just now. I let anger get the better of me. You should meet James, give him a chance, but not because it will annoy your mother. You should do it because it will make you feel better – make him feel better. You have to swallow down the bitter taste of traumas in your past, let it go… because if you don't, it will swallow you. Consume everything that you are. Remember I said a similar thing to you about accepting things and moving on after I told you about losing Celandine?'

I nod.

'Then trust me. I know about these things… in fact when I lost Jagger – well, I wasn't sure if I could carry on for a while there.'

'If only it was that simple—'

'Oh, my dear. I didn't say it was simple, far from it.' She lifts her glass and then realises it's empty. 'Look, let's go inside and have another drink and we'll talk no more about it tonight. Just promise me that you'll at least consider meeting your brother.'

Can I promise that? I don't see why not. It isn't as if I'm committing to doing anything, is it? No. I'm just considering it. 'Okay, I promise,' I say, and am rewarded with one of her huge smiles.

As I follow her into the bright warmth of the cottage I wonder if my brother still wants to meet me. I shouldn't think so. He's probably decided it will be far more trouble than it's worth.

Chapter Twenty

Desperado

Louisa wonders if carrying a tray of coffee and biscuits down to the river is one of her better ideas. There is a wash of hot coffee in one corner, and if she doesn't keep it tilted away from her it will spill over and make a mess on her white trousers. Why she decided to wear white trousers she has no idea. She found them at the back of the wardrobe the other day when she was looking for the acrylics for Lottie. They'd slipped off the hanger – she'd completely forgotten that she owned them. They are silky and impractical, but Jagger used to love her in them, and so there's the answer to why she put them on after all.

Lottie's wearing one of Louisa's big floppy floral-print hats from the seventies and she looks like a painting herself as she sits engrossed in her work in the sun-dappled clearing at the end of the vines. As Louisa gets nearer she looks up from her easel, smiles and waves, her eyes in her heart-shaped face almost feline. She thinks of Celandine, tries to imagine what she would look like now, and feels the familiar kick of loss in her gut, but as she smiles back she is comforted by the idea that Lottie is now her borrowed daughter.

Borrowed was not a word that Lottie appreciated when Louisa said it in that context last night, so for now she'll just use it in her head. Louisa can't allow herself to imagine that she really is her daughter, even though that is her heart's desire. She can't allow it because Lottie has a biological mother, and who knows? They might eventually bury the past, which would be a good thing for them, but would be very bad for Louisa. Her heart couldn't cope with another loss, so Lottie will remain borrowed and she will make the most of the time they have together.

'You brought coffee and biscuits all the way down here? That's so kind.'

'It's either kindness or madness. Half the coffee is on the tray, and – oh dear. I think we have at least one soggy biscuit.'

Louisa hands a half-full mug to Lottie and takes a peep at her work. My God, this girl is good. When she saw her sketch of Mermaid Cove she'd been impressed, but this is… masterly. 'I feel like I could just step into that river, it's so realistic, Lottie.'

Lottie looks up and wrinkles her nose, which makes her look much younger than her years. 'Do you think so? Oh, I am pleased, because everything else just flowed, apart from the river – which was the whole point, really,' she says with a self-conscious laugh.

'You must be seeing it with typical artist's critical eyes because it is stunning, truly.'

The peaceful scene is interrupted by Lottie's phone ringing. Lottie frowns and pulls it out of her pocket. 'Oh, hi, Anna. This is a surprise.' She mouths 'a friend from school' at Louisa.

Louisa sips her coffee and tries to tune into the buzz of bees on the clover and the trickle of the river, rather than Lottie's conversation, because she doesn't want to eavesdrop. She thinks that might be easier said than done.

Lottie ends the call and pushes the floppy hat back on her head. 'I expect you heard that?'

'Only bits, I tried not to listen.'

'She rang out of the blue to see if I'd go for a drink with her tonight. I haven't even heard from Anna since I left teaching… most odd.'

'I heard you say no to her. You don't have to worry about me, you know, if you want to go out.'

'I know, but I really don't. She sounded a bit weird, asked me what I'd been doing lately and was I on holiday? I told her I'd had a little walking holiday and that I was staying here with you for a while. As soon as I'd said that, she said she must go as she'd just remembered that she had to meet her sister in town, and that was it.'

'Hm, oh well. There's no accounting for some folk.'

Lottie agrees and looks back to her painting. The inclusion of a person from Lottie's life outside theirs makes Louisa think that she has to broach the subject of her leaving. Much as she loves having her here, she would hate to think Lottie's spending her days with her because she thinks she's lonely or something. Besides, she's been here nearly a week and Louisa knows she wants to get on with the business of buying her art studio and filling it with her lovely work.

'Lottie, if you think it's time for you to go I won't be upset, you know. I know you can't stay here forever and it won't be long before I see you again…' Her voice mustn't have noticed the bit when it just said, 'I won't be upset'. She swallows and thinks of cheerful things.

Lottie's mouth twists to the side and she nods. Louisa can tell she's having similar feelings to hers. 'I know. I've been thinking that it's probably time, but I have so loved being here. You're so good for me.'

'And you me.'

'I think I'll finish up here and then pop into Padstow for an hour. I'll get some nice food and I'll cook. Then tomorrow, I'll be on my way home.'

She says all this to her coffee mug and Louisa takes a big sup from hers. 'I'll take you, if you like? Then I'll be able to see you in your own environment and picture you in it.'

Lottie does the loud and carefree laugh that Louisa likes so much. 'My own environment – I'm not a bloody wild animal, you know.'

This nearly makes Louisa snort her coffee out of her nose and she and Lottie laugh together. They look at each other solemnly for a moment and then Lottie turns back to the painting. Louisa wants to say something sloppy like she isn't a borrowed daughter but her true one, but that would ruin the moment and cause Lottie to respond in kind. Then if she didn't mean it, that would be rubbish. It would put a dampener on things and Louisa would remember it more than she would all the nice times. People tend to do that.

The phone rings a few hours later. Lottie is in Padstow and Louisa is under the kitchen table scrubbing the red-brick tiles. The thought of Lottie leaving tomorrow has unsettled her; she always cleans when she's unsettled. It makes her feel more in control – Freud would have a field day. She temporarily forgets she's under the table and goes to stand up to answer the phone. She cracks the back of her head on the tabletop as she does so. 'Fuck it!'

'Hello!' she snaps down the phone. Under her hand a lump is forming at the base of her skull. Great.

'Mrs Truscott?'

Louisa doesn't recognise the man's voice. He's probably someone wanting to do a tour but has come through to the home phone instead of the shop. 'Yes, can I help you?'

'I hope so. Your sister put me through to you.'

Not about a tour then, Louisa thinks. He's gone quiet now and she wonders what it's about; he's getting on her nerves because her head aches like a bastard and she needs to get a cold damp cloth on it. 'Okay, I'm listening,' she says in a business-like manner as she runs water into the sink.

'It's about Lottie Morgan. I think she's staying with you?'

She wasn't expecting that. Louisa wonders if it's James as she presses the cloth lightly to her head. 'Depends who's asking.' She walks outside to the terrace and sits down at the table.

'It's her boyfriend, well, ex-boyfriend to be more precise.'

'Caleb?'

'Oh, so she's mentioned me?' His voice sounds ridiculously pleased.

'Yes, she has. How did you know she was here?'

'I got a mutual friend of ours, Anna, to ring her for me this morning. I was getting a bit worried, you see, because the receptionist at the last guest house we'd booked told me she'd never arrived. I've been round to her apartment a few times too and she's never there. She's blocked my number from her phone so… anyway, as I said, I was getting worried and running out of ideas.'

'I see. Well, she's absolutely fine, no need to worry.' Louisa wants to say more, but she'll leave it to him. It isn't her place to offer information.

'Thank God for that,' Caleb says, and Louisa hears a sigh of relief and the scrape of a chair on a hard floor. He's probably sitting down before he falls down. Poor guy must have been out of his mind. 'Um, do you know when she'll be home?'

'I do, but I can't tell you.' Louisa weighs up her next response carefully before tipping it down the line. 'As you know, Lottie is a very private person and doesn't take well to people she trusts discussing her business without her knowledge.'

Another heavy sigh. 'She's told you about why we split up, then?'

'Yes.'

'I only did it because I love her, wanted her to—'

'Yes, I realise that, but I also totally understand her reasons for ending it.' Louisa already feels like she's saying too much. He says he loves her though…

'Yes, I handled it badly. I just miss her so much, Mrs Truscott, could you please ask her to contact me?'

The anguish in his voice races along the line and grabs her by the heart. Poor boy. 'I do understand, Caleb. But I really don't think she'd appreciate me—'

'Please, Mrs Truscott. Your sister told me how you met and that you're really close. That's unusual for Lottie, so I know she'd listen to you.'

Damn it. Suzie had no business telling him stuff. Louisa sighs and dabs at her head a bit more. 'I don't know…'

'Please. Just try. I'm not expecting miracles.'

It's obvious to Louisa that Caleb adores Lottie, and Lottie, if she'd admit it, feels the same. The depth of feeling in his words is loud in his quiet voice.

Before she can change her mind, she says, 'You said you love her. Do you, truly?'

'I do. I never actually told her because I could sense that she didn't want me to… but yes I do, very much.'

'Look, I'm not promising anything, but I'll talk to her.' Louisa ends the call before Caleb can say anything else. 'Right, let's hope I don't get in Lottie's bad books for bloody interfering,' she says out loud to a sparrow perched a little way off on the handrail that runs around the terrace.

After a few moments the sparrow tilts his head this way and that, then hops onto the table to eat a bit of Japanese cracker from last night; Louisa stills her body, so she can admire its fragile beauty. Something about it reminds her of Lottie. She thinks it's the bird's watchfulness, so wary of danger that must be real and huge in its little life. A sudden gust of wind blows a strand of her long hair towards the sparrow and it's off and away over the vineyard so fast that by the time she's tucked her hair behind her ear it's just a dark smudge on a brown fence post.

Louisa makes a mental note to make sure her hair is securely tied back when she mentions Caleb's phone call to Lottie.

A huge bunch of yellow roses with legs walks into the kitchen a little while later. Lottie sticks her face around the petals and says to Louisa in a southern American drawl, 'Thought you might like these, marm. Them being your favourite flower an' all.'

'They are gorgeous, but they must have cost a fortune! You shouldn't have.'

'Why do people always say that?' Lottie says, a half smile on her face.

'I don't know, it's the done thing? Daft really. But it's true – I don't want you spending lots of money…' She sees the disapproving look on Lottie's face and says, 'Thank you, they smell divine.' Louisa takes them over to the sink and pulls out a crystal vase from the cupboard.

'And for madam's dinner I have found a fresh sea bass and some Cornish new potatoes.' She holds one up. 'Look, still got the earth on it. And a variety of vegetables which I will toss in something wonderful and roast in the oven.'

'That sounds delicious. I baked some bread while you were gone – we can have that too if we really want to be greedy.'

'Excellent. I didn't buy wine, though, I thought we might have enough here.'

'Indeed! I know just the bottle, too. This shall be a celebration!'

'Of me going home?' Lottie sticks her bottom lip out.

'No, silly. Of our meeting and becoming firm friends.'

Lottie smiles and begins unpacking her shopping. Louisa wonders whether to wait until morning to tell her about Caleb or drop it in after dinner. She's not sure if she could sleep soundly if she waits until morning, though. There's your answer then, Louisa.

They are back on the terrace and Louisa is patting the round of her stomach. 'My goodness, that was a feast. You can certainly cook.'

'Gwendoline taught me. She was the bee's knees.' Lottie grins. 'Do bees really have knees? I must look into it.'

Louisa laughs. Lottie really is a tonic with her forthright tone and the way she speaks her mind in such a confident manner. Jagger was the same and taught her to be, to an extent. She doesn't think she's as confident as Lottie, though. Louisa looks at the moon rising in the velvet sky and decides that she must 'go for it', as the young ones say nowadays.

She tops up both their glasses and says, 'Lottie, I had a phone call not long before you came back from shopping.' Good. Her voice sounds calm, measured, despite the tight anxiety building in her chest.

Lottie looks at her over the rim of her glass. 'Oh, yes?'

'It was Caleb.'

All of a sudden everything about Lottie reminds her of the sparrow from earlier and Louisa pats her hair to check it's still tidy.

Lottie's eyes dart here and there, she shifts in her seat, looks ready to fly away. 'How on earth did he find me?'

Louisa watches Lottie's face closely for signs of panic and tells her everything, including the fact that she said she'd ask her to contact him.

'He actually *told* you he loves me?' Lottie says, cocking her head to the side, fixing her sharp green eyes on Louisa's.

'Yes. And that he's been worried to death. I told him that you wouldn't thank me for interfering after what he did with James and everything. He realises that, and I told him I'd make him no promises.'

Lottie nods her head but says nothing.

Into the silence Louisa says, 'I hope you don't think I betrayed you, love. I would never do that. I told you almost immediately and—'

'No, of course not.' She reaches for Louisa's hand across the table. 'You're only really passing on a message, after all. I can see now that he would be worried about me. Just never thought about it.'

'He did sound like a very nice man.' Louisa is pleased to see that Lottie looks less sparrow-like now, so pushes a bit further. 'And it might not hurt to meet and talk it through.'

Lottie shakes her head. 'Let's not go mad here. I agreed to think about meeting James. Caleb will have to take a back seat in my thoughts for now. I can't cope with too many swirling about in there.' She taps the side of her head with her forefinger.

'Okay, I can see that.' Louisa takes a sip of wine and then a snatch of an old song drifts across the terrace from the CD player in the kitchen. One of Jagger's favourites. ' Fences...rainbow above you...somebody to love you before it's too late,' she sings softly.

'Great song,' Lottie says and wraps a shawl around her shoulders.

'Yes, and wise words.' Louisa looks at Lottie and Lottie gives her a half smile.

'You're about as subtle as a brick, Louisa.'

'How very dare you, young woman. Subtle is my middle name.'

The two of them sit and listen to the rest of the song and the sounds of the night. Louisa thinks about Jagger and how wonderful it would be for him to be here now, to have met Lottie. She thinks about lots of things, mostly about the past as she traces the olive tree on her hand. Louisa hopes that tomorrow will be sunny, because saying goodbye in the rain will be far too sad.

Chapter Twenty-One

Plans Are Afoot

Louisa in my sunny apartment feels totally surreal. Isn't it funny when you're used to seeing a person in one type of environment, in Louisa's case out on the South West Coast Path or at her vineyard, and then they're in a place totally familiar to you, but the opposite to them? She doesn't *look* awkward or out of place, but it's as if her life has been superimposed over mine. I feel like I could flick the edge of the room like a page and we'd be back on the path. Yes, I agree, that idea is totally 'out there'. Maybe it's my mind's way of rebelling against all these serious things I'm meant to be considering.

'I know I live in a lovely spot, Lottie, but this is just wonderful!' Louisa says, turning in a circle and taking the place in all at once just as Caleb did not that long ago.

I have to agree. Of course, the vineyard was one of the most relaxing, beautiful and peaceful places I have ever visited, but I was missing the proximity to the ocean. I think I'll go and paint Dragon's Breath Cave when Louisa has gone.

'Yes, I am very lucky. But the great thing is, we're only twenty-five minutes apart so you can pop over here any time and vice versa. You could even come and stay for a few days if you like. I have a sofa bed.'

'That would be wonderful.' Louisa perches on the arm of the sofa and picks Algernon out of the biggest rucksack ever made. 'Such a cute little rabbit. I bet he'll be glad to be in his own bed tonight.' She jiggles him about by his ears.

What's wrong with people? Caleb, now Louisa? 'Isn't it obvious he's a bear?' I say, scooping him up and holding him close. He smells like the rucksack and chocolate biscuits, and there's a hint of bergamot cologne. Odd. Then I remember that Caleb cuddled him one evening when we were getting ready for bed, pretended that he wanted Algernon for his own. I don't want to think about Caleb and bed.

'No. His ears are too long for a bear,' Louisa says.

I hold Algernon at arm's length and give him a hard stare. No. He couldn't possibly be a rabbit... could he? Before Algernon has the time to turn into one I shove him back in the rucksack. I really cannot cope with that. 'Shall I put the kettle on?'

'Not sure it would suit you.' Louisa gives me one of her best dimply smiles.

'Oh, hardy har.' I look away because I realise she's about to leave and all of a sudden, I'm not sure how I will be when she does.

'No thanks. I have a few bits and bobs I should be getting on with.' She stands up and pulls me into a warm hug. 'Right, I must be off. Let me know what the estate agent says when you ring him later about the studio, won't you?' Her tone is brisk and business-like, and she releases me and moves to the door.

'I will. Plans are afoot. And perhaps we can get together in the next few weeks some time?' My tone is equally no-nonsense, and I realise it's not like me to follow convention – hiding emotion behind a safe screen of organisation and cool beans. Well, it is sometimes, like when I was with Caleb for example... Now I think about it, it is like me in situations where people matter to me. I don't hide angry emotion though; an example is when I went bananas at the tabloid man in the pub. What does that say about me, I wonder?

'I'd like that,' Louisa says, her olive tree fingers around my door handle.

A memory of the day she'd explained that tattoo rushed into my consciousness as if it were a wave on the ocean and I abandon convention – come out from behind my screen. As she opens the door and turns to face me I say, 'Thank you so much for everything. I have learned so much about life and myself from you. I know you think that our mum and daughter status is just borrowed, and I think I know why you do. But you are more of a mum to me than mine ever was… or could be… I think.'

Bloody hell, that was a speech and a half. The only other person I have been open and honest with my caring-type emotions is Gwendoline, and my parents when I was very little, I suppose. But as you know, I like to be open and honest – speak my mind when I can. And even though I've made Louisa cry and my eyes are trying their best to copy hers, I'm relieved I said it all, dared to be different.

I get another hug – a bone-crushing one this time, and then Louisa's gone.

There's always one missing sock, isn't there? I did my walking holiday laundry at Louisa's, but the last few days' worth is in the machine waiting for detergent and the lost sock. I am sure there were two dirty socks this morning, but now there's just one. Perhaps it's been whisked away by the sock fairy to a land of one-legged people. It's a mystery and no mistake. Other people have reported the same problem. Socks make me think of feet and feet make me think of the word 'afoot'. I said it to Louisa earlier, yet another of my favourite words. I have no idea why people say it in this context, though, or any other, come to think of it.

I make coffee and Google it. Not the coffee, the word.

Afoot: in preparation or progress; happening or beginning to happen.

I do like the sound of that. It means that my new studio-shop venture is actually going to become a reality. This makes a few butterflies do a quick flight round my belly. I'm excited because it's probably going to happen soon, and nervous because I'll be doing it all by myself. If you remember, Caleb said he'd help with the business side, but now he's off the scene it's just me. I know I might have said a while ago that I should rely on nobody but me, but Louisa has taught me that some people are kind, caring and can be trusted. Peter taught me that too, and certainly Leo and Neave.

No time like the present; I'll phone Mr Laurence at Laurence Swift and Jones right now to tell him that I want to rent the property and go around and sign everything tomorrow. I can't do it this afternoon because I promised my artistic and in-touch-with-nature eyes that we'd paint the Dragon Cave again – the first attempt looks flat to me, now. I could do it another day, but since the first painting day at Louisa's I have learned to listen to my inspiration voice. It's quite insistent and always right.

Thanks to the heat of the August sun, the wind, though brisk, is warm. At the moment it's having great fun picking up huge waves and chucking them at Dragon Cave. The dragon's breath is heavy with spray today and you'd think it'd be difficult to paint. It isn't, though, and I worry that the voice of artistic intuition might be getting too big for its boots. Boots? No, I think flip-flops would be more appropriate, because it's a bit laid back and surfer-dude in its appreciation of my handiwork. It's telling me that this painting is, well, awesome, man – so cool – and that I'm a truly gifted artist.

I stand back and try to be more objective, but do you know, it is pretty bloody marvellous. Louisa told me I had to be less critical and more honest about my work on the drive back this morning, so I'm trying to be. Gwendoline would be so proud if she could see me sitting on top of this headland covered in paint daubs with a big daft grin on my face. There's sunshine in my heart, and a warm glow of satisfaction and pride is spreading through me, as if I'm one of those kids in the old advert going to school on a winter's morning having just eaten a bowl of porridge substitute.

The reason for this is because I'm pleased with the painting, of course, but also because I just let myself go, allowed myself to get lost, submerged in my work. Any uncertainty that I was born to do this I might have had before I set out on the walk has gone.

It's hard to put into words how I feel because they keep moving about, refusing to be ordered into coherent sentences, but I suppose you could say I feel centred. Rooted. I'm comfortable with the immediate prospect of starting the next bit of my new life, because I will be starting it as a proper artist, something I have always wanted to be deep down, but didn't really know it until the day in the vineyard – and today's painting has strengthened that conviction.

Why it's happened I couldn't say with any clarity, but it has to do with who I am now, and, as I said before, the people I met recently. Louisa has played a big part in it all and so has Caleb, of course. He let me down in the end, but… I don't like the way these thoughts are heading, so I cut them off.

There are lots of people around today because we are now in the height of the summer holidays. Lots of people are on the beach or wandering past me, either playing at happy families or they actually are that happy. It's hard to tell, isn't it, when people are on holiday? They think they should be having fun and enjoying themselves because they've paid out lots of their hard-earned cash that they've worked all year for, and because they have invested lots of 'so looking forward to it' time in this week or fortnight.

Some of them have peered over my shoulder and said very complimentary things; I smiled politely but made it clear I didn't want to engage in conversation. Some have given me a wide berth because they obviously didn't want to disturb me, but all who passed have sounded jolly, seemingly having a good time.

So, what to do about my not-so-happy family? I have kind of been thinking that I might be open to speaking to James. It could be better to go that way instead of jumping into a meeting. I didn't throw away the card with his number on that Caleb gave me. It's still in the Velcro pocket at the side of the rucksack. That must have meant that on some subconscious level I thought I might need it in the future, mustn't it? There's a nagging worry about whether he still wants to have contact, though, as I've said. But I won't know until I make the effort, will I?

A strand of hair has come loose from its clip and I tuck it behind my ear. That's what me contacting James is like too, really, isn't it? Making the strands of my life secure, neat, tucked – instead of blowing about in my mind making everything a jumble. Most of what's in my mind is fairly ordered now, what with the confidence in my work and the plans being afoot, so I know I should probably give James a ring in the near future. The Dragon Cave snorts at this, so I decide I will do it this evening, after dinner, or perhaps even before.

The calico cat is still in the position on the easel where I left her staring out to sea. She wouldn't have moved though, would she? She is a painting of a cat, not a real one, and she can't really stare, as I said when I gave her the second eye and a cat in a tree nearby to keep her company just before I set out on holiday. Over two weeks of facing the sun has faded her coat, though, and she looks a bit dry and dusty. The outline of the second cat is downright ghostly, and I make a decision to finish the painting tomorrow. It's only fair, really; they have been waiting ages, after all.

I set the Dragon's Cave painting on a spare easel next to it and immediately notice the difference in brush application. Yes, they are very different subjects, but the latest has been painted with a more confident hand. A definite style is present in each sweep of the brush too. The calico cat is one of my better pre-holiday attempts, but it is a bit flat, hesitant, and wishy-washy. Tomorrow I'll bring it to life, complete it – make it real.

The smell of the chicken casserole and jacket potato I have in the oven causes a bit of a rumble in my stomach, so I open some pistachio nuts and a bottle of Louisa's wine. It would be daft to have too much wine on an empty stomach, though, particularly because I have that all-important phone call to make. 'All important' is another newish phrase people use nowadays, isn't it? How can anything be *all* important? Things can be more important than others, like making a decision to cut my toenails wouldn't be as important to my existence as making a call to my estranged brother, for example, but it isn't *all* important, is it? How can it be?

I realise that procrastination is something people do when they have important things to do that might not be a success.

Even though I'm just pondering on 'all importance' it's still putting things off. Then I wonder if I actually ought to cut my toenails and paint them because it's over two weeks since I gave them a second thought. That would be procrastination, though, and my nails aren't that bad anyway. The fact that I'm even considering doing such a thing is a result of the socialisation process. I mean, who decided that painting toenails different colours, so you have 'holiday ready' feet when wearing sandals, for example, is a good thing?

The whole fashion and beauty industry stinks, if you ask me. I could go on and on, but I won't because then my food will be ready, and I'll have to eat it and then I won't have made that very important call that I promised myself I'd make before dinner. Procrastination extraordinaire. I shell a few nuts onto a saucer, then pick up my drink and my phone.

'Hello?'

This is the first time I've heard my brother's voice for ten years and I think it sounds more cultured, mature than last time. 'Hello, this is Charlotte, your sister. I use Lottie nowadays, though.'

'Lottie! Oh, I'm so glad you've called.'

This is encouraging. 'I thought I should really – see what we can work out.' I sound much more relaxed than I am, and I hear a few muted voices on the line. James is probably doing that holding the phone to his chest thing that Mother does while he talks to someone in the room. He's probably telling his wife that I'm on the line.

'Great! I thought that you wouldn't after Caleb told me that you weren't best pleased… um… upset…' His voice falters and stops.

'Well, yes. I wasn't best pleased that he'd gone behind my back to you, betrayed my trust. But it wasn't to do with you, really.'

James's words come out in a rush, run into each other as if he's worried that I'd not want to hear them or something.

'No, no, of course not, I totally understand. I told Caleb that you'd be pissed off if he did what he did when we first met. Oh, that sounds bad, doesn't it? I'm not trying to get him into more trouble, he does genuinely care about you and I think he's a good guy.'

'Yes, well, I didn't ring to talk about Caleb,' I say a bit too stabbily. I had only meant to aim for my 'in control of the conversation' voice. I sigh and pop a few nuts into my mouth. I then wish I hadn't – I imagine that someone crunching nuts down the phone into your ear is very annoying.

'No, of course you didn't. Look, can we meet tomorrow? I have a few days' holiday and face to face is better than the phone, isn't it?'

I shove the crunched nuts to the side of my mouth and pin my tongue against them, which of course isn't the best idea when you are expected to answer a question, but there's a panicky feeling in my chest and my heart is beating fast. Tomorrow? Crikey, that's a bit soon, isn't it? I wasn't expecting that. I'd expected time to mull over the conversation, eating chicken and potatoes with my feet up watching some drivel on the box, while not really watching it at all. Hell. Now, as you have no doubt noticed, my thoughts are turning themselves into a big pile of nonsense and I fear my tongue is permanently stuck in this position.

'Lottie? You okay?'

I grab my glass and wash down the nuts, but the fizz makes me cough a little. I take a breath. 'Yes, just eating nuts and got one stuck momentarily.' Momentarily? Who uses that in normal conversation?

'Oh, I see,' James says, and I think I can hear a suppressed chuckle. 'So, are you free tomorrow?'

Am I? I have the calico cat to finish and I suppose I should get some shopping in. Then I hear Louisa's voice in my ear. *Go for it, Lottie. Make peace with the past before it swallows you whole.* 'Yes, okay. Late afternoon for coffee somewhere?'

'Fantastic! I'll come to you. How about Mawgan Porth? Our mum said you were thinking of renting a studio and shop there.'

'Mother would.' I emphasise the word *mother*. 'I seem to be quite the topic of conversation with a few people, don't I? Unbeknownst to me, of course.' Unbeknownst and momentarily... I shake my head and take another drink.

'You do. And Lottie, just so you know, I went to see our mother a few days ago with the express purpose of talking about the way forward for our family. My wife came, too. I'm telling you now because you might think it sounds like some sort of betrayal again if I just spring it on you tomorrow.'

I really don't like the sound of this. My 'family' getting together to talk about me behind my back. 'Right. More behind the scenes plotting,' I say in a pondering type of way. I don't know what else to say, though. I don't want to tell James that I don't like the sound of it because I'm supposed to be making peace, not starting battles, aren't I?

'Hopefully it will make sense tomorrow. And Lottie, this isn't plotting or a betrayal, it's a way forward… I hope. Closure, if you like.'

I say I hate that word and he laughs, says he's not too fond of it either. We agree to meet at three at the Merrymoor Inn and then end the call.

The calico cat watches me as I set the table and take out the casserole. I ask her why Mother always has to fuck everything up for me. I was sort of looking forward to making contact with James, you know, just me and him? I was getting used to the thought of talking things through with him, getting his perspective, and now I find that everyone in the family has recently met up together apart from me, and why? So, they can talk about me.

The calico cat listens to my ramblings for the next while but says nothing. Neither does the ghost of her companion in the tree. The casserole could have been cotton wool for all the enjoyment it gave me, yet I appear to have finished it all. I push my empty plate to one side and realise that's how I feel now. Empty. Is there really any point to meeting James tomorrow, raking over how I feel, how he feels, as if we're in some bloody therapy session? I have a cat to finish and other stuff to do. In the end I decide to sleep on it and see what tomorrow morning tells me to do. Hopefully it will have a better idea than I do right now.

Chapter Twenty-Two

Naming the Future

It's afternoon and I'm putting the shopping away. I have bought enough to sustain the population of Leningrad through their entire siege period. Okay, that's a lie, but there is far too much. The freezer is full to busting and so is my head. Of thoughts, I hasten to add, not food. That would be very uncomfortable and quite surreal.

The calico cat rolls her eyes and huffs at me. Well, I imagine she does because I haven't finished her as I promised. When I woke this morning, it seemed like a good idea to get out and do something that I didn't have to concentrate on too much. Something day to day like shopping. Turns out that I perhaps should have concentrated just a teensy bit more, because in my hand is a packet of nappy sacks. Must have picked them up instead of bin liners.

I turn my back on the calico cat and run water into the kettle. Taking up the majority of space in my full to busting head is thoughts of the meeting I'm having with James later. The shopping trip has seen me change my mind about meeting him several times. Each time I thought I'd put forward valid reasons for not going, a trickle of counter reasons seeped through them as if they were acid on litmus.

The idea of ringing Mother even made an appearance, because I thought it might be a good idea to get a picture of what happened at this closed meeting, so I can be prepared when I meet James. Mother, as we know, can embroider the truth, or just plain lie, however, so that scenario had been sloughed off into the frozen fish section and shoved under some fish fingers.

The clock tells me I have only about an hour and a half to eat lunch, do a bit to the calico cat, and then get ready before I leave for the meeting. I tell it to mind its own bloody business because I haven't decided if I'm going or not yet. The phone sits quietly on the counter trying its best to make me ignore it, but my eyes flick over to it every few minutes. I manage to pull them back to my ham sandwich each time, because it would be the easy way out, wouldn't it? Pick up the phone, make up some excuse to James about why I couldn't meet him, and then I could get on with my life.

Eventually the same dilemma would barge its way into the business of getting on with my life though, wouldn't it? James won't just dissolve into the ether, will he? No. Louisa's advice whisper in my ears again and I consider ringing her. There's no point, though, because she'll just tell me to meet him and get it over with. Damn it. I ought to just do it and stop piddling about. My eyes meet those of the calico cat over the top of my coffee cup and I know that there's not really enough time to do her justice. Not when my head is all over the place. I tell her I'm sorry and I imagine that she yawns as if she's trying to pretend she couldn't give a shit.

So here I am in the beer garden, looking out over the ocean. I got here half an hour early because I didn't want him to be the one to pick a table, watch me walk towards him, control everything from the off. No. I want to be the one to do that. It's very busy and I'm lucky to have a table nearest the beach. I only secured it because I did the hovering vulture act. As an elderly couple stood up to leave I swooped in and slid along the still warm bench even before the woman had picked up her bag. I nearly spilled my tea over her in the process, but she didn't look too put out. Or at least that's what I told myself.

A thought occurs to me. How will I recognise him? I've seen photos of him at my parents' house, but photos aren't always a reflection of reality, are they? Besides, I don't look at them if I can avoid it. I draw my disinterested filter blinds across my eyes mostly and Mother knows not to deliberately draw my attention to them. I even refused to look at his wedding pictures.

I do know that Mother doesn't like his wife, but then nobody would be good enough for her precious son. When I found out that her father was from Nigeria I did wonder if that was another reason Mother didn't like her, because I'd noticed her nasty small-minded prejudices over the years. Not just against black people, but people who lived on council estates, who had children outside wedlock (yes, really), same-sex marriages, the people who took advantage of the welfare system, the list goes on.

Upon a challenge, she would argue that she wasn't prejudiced, just remarking on the fact that they weren't the same as us, lived in a totally different way, and that it wouldn't do for her, but she guessed it took all sorts. I told her that as she knew, I liked difference and not to rope me into the 'us' bit, thank you very much. I asked her if the dislike of her son's wife had anything to do with her colour and she said that was ridiculous. Her cheeks went pink and her mouth tight, so then I knew my suspicions were correct.

I think I hear someone call my name and my stomach flips. I turn to see a man hurrying up the steps towards me: James, of course, he has my eyes. Before you say it, they aren't actually mine, they just look like them. I think what a good memory he must have for faces, because he hasn't seen mine for fifteen years, unless Mother makes him look at my photos, of course. I stand. My heart is thumping, and it looks like he's going to hug me, so I stick my hand out – I'm not ready for hugs.

'Lottie! So fantastic to meet you,' he says, pumping my hand. 'You are even more beautiful than your photo.'

Annoyingly my skin decides to set itself on fire and my voice comes out a little too loud. 'You're very kind, but beautiful is pushing it. I'm not bad, of course – well I don't think I am, though it's hard to be objective when looking in the mirror, isn't it?' I was about to say something else but realised this was more than enough.

'Yes, I suppose it is. Nobody wants to think they're ugly, do they?' James grins and then stops. 'Not that you are, of course.' His skin is copying mine and I watch his Adam's apple bob. 'No, as I said, you're beautiful.'

His vulnerability has put me at ease, or at least a little bit. The fact that he's a consultant and obviously very clever has been quietly whispering in my head on the way here; in fact, it has popped up now and again even before I agreed to meet him. Not that I don't think I'm clever, but it's the white coat syndrome thing, I suppose. Plus, the fact that he's always been held up as a beacon of success that everyone should aspire to (especially me) by my mother hasn't helped.

'Well, thank you. And you're very handsome,' I say, because he is. 'Have a seat – I got us a good one.'

'You have, it's lovely.' He looks at the ocean and pushes his hand through his hair. I think he could be nervous. I also think he's considering what to say next. James looks at me and his smile is warm. 'I'll go and get us a drink, shall I?'

I nod at my cup. 'Another tea would be nice, thanks.'

'I was thinking of a bottle of champagne – this is a celebration, after all.'

This is not what I'm expecting. We've a bloody long way to go before we can decide that meeting again is a good thing. What if it all goes tits up? I opt for the obvious response instead of speaking my mind, which annoys me. 'No thanks. That wouldn't be a good idea with both of us driving.'

'No. But I'm staying here at the inn overnight and I thought I'd arrange a taxi for you home and one back again in the morning to collect your car.' James grins and looks very pleased with himself.

It's a good job he is, because I'm certainly not. This is a man who likes being in control, getting his own way. I hear a scornful little voice in my head that says we're well matched, then. But this time I'm not going to pull my punches.

'No thanks. I don't really like people arranging things for me and I don't think it's appropriate to be celebrating yet. Of course it's a good thing that we've met after so long, but tea is just fine for now.' I allow a polite smile and then look away from the disappointment in his eyes and at my hands on the table. Tough, but had to be done.

'Of course. I did wonder if...' He clears his throat. 'Okay, back in a tick.'

So that was a marvellous start to the reunion, wasn't it? When I saw the disappointment I felt a little twist of regret, but it wasn't big enough to change my mind. Champagne was a bad idea; it would loosen tongues and allow emotions to wriggle out into the world. I don't want any wriggling emotions, thank you very much. I want clarity, honesty and, for now, a little detachment.

James is back with tea and a selection of cakes. A wasp has decided it's joining us and dips its abdomen up and down as it buzzes atop a slice of carrot cake. Wasps seem permanently angry, don't they, even though they aren't? We know what they're capable of, so we perhaps project our anger onto them. I'm already mildly irritated because of the way the meeting has gone so far, but the sight of that buzzing black and yellow creature thinking it can stick its germ-laden feet and proboscis into our cake makes me jab at it with a fork. Of course with that approach I achieve precisely nothing, apart from to make it properly angry and it does a frustrated little dance on the table.

James takes a napkin and flicks it so quickly at the wasp that I hear the snap. The wasp is no more, and peace is resumed. I listen to James talk about the journey down, the weather; we make small talk while we eat cake. All the time I'm comparing our approaches to the wasp nuisance and can't help getting the beacon image out of my head that Mother placed in it so carefully many years ago. I jab at my problems ineffectually; he executes his – sharp, swift, deadly. Then I tell myself that's not true now. It's how I used to be in my old life. I have a new one now, and so far, it's going in the right direction.

The small talk becomes so small it's in danger of disappearing, so I decide to take control. 'Tell me, James. How did the meeting go – the one you all had recently to talk about me?'

James's face struggles between smile and a frown. It settles for the former with an added twist of his mouth. 'It wasn't quite like that, Lottie.'

'What was it like then?'

He leans back and folds his arms. Classic defence position – I thought he would have known that and altered accordingly.

'Beth and I…' James unfolds his arms and leans his elbows on the table. 'Beth's my wife. We decided that we needed to set the past right after what Caleb had told me. I had no idea how it was and was appalled at her behaviour towards you.'

I watch his frown deepening and his face cloud with anger on my behalf. I like that he cares. 'So, you went round to our parents' house and confronted Mother?' I say, imagining how she would have reacted to that.

'Sort of. In the end it got a bit awkward. Our mother became upset.'

I bet she bloody did.

'But initially we went around for Sunday lunch and hoped to make it more of a discussion rather than a confrontation.'

James then tells me that he told her all the stuff that Caleb had told him about the way she'd behaved and how it had affected me. His wife, Beth, had apparently said it was Mother who needed counselling! My God, what I wouldn't have given to have seen her face. I like this Beth already, she sounds honest and fearless. And can you believe Dad stuck up for me too – stood his ground for once and told the truth? Miracles do happen after all. James also says he's not blameless and should have tried harder to meet me and make a relationship, and that he reckons Mother was psychologically damaged by being made to give him away.

He has stopped talking and I can hear my heartbeat competing with the babble around us. It's almost too much to take in. 'So, what happened in the end?' I say and pour more tea for us.

'The thing is, Lottie, I'd hoped our mother would have done what we all agreed on at the end of the discussion before I met you. But you contacted me out of the blue before she had a chance.' He looks at my frown and quickly adds, 'Don't get me wrong, I'm so glad you did. But I'll have to tell you what happened. We agreed that she should apologise to you for the vile way she behaved back then. We need to make things right before we can move on as a family.' He reaches for my hand and I am so shocked I don't pull away. 'And I have to give you my deepest apology, too. I'm so sorry, Lottie. Please forgive me.'

James blinks his eyes a few times and swallows hard. This whole thing is crazy. Mother, apologise? As if. And even if she did I'm not sure I'd believe her. She might do it just to keep in favour with James. He's still looking at me, waiting for an answer. I don't know what to say, but words somehow order themselves and leave my mouth.

'I haven't really considered that you were to blame for anything. I was the one to reject you each time you tried to contact me.'

'But I only tried a few times and I should have known better, but I was too busy with my career. I was the cuckoo in the nest, the one that pushed you out in the cold.' He squeezes my hand and I take strength from it. 'Of course, having said that, the majority of the blame lies with our parents. If Mother had handled it all differently, and Dad too, then it wouldn't have been like that, shouldn't have been like that.'

'I guess so.' I remove my hand because it's beginning to feel uncomfortable. If I'm honest I have blamed James at times for not trying harder, particularly when Caleb pointed out that he should have when I talked about being the broken crockery. But in the main I haven't tried to let him into my mind very much at all. I have always kept him distant – at arm's length. And that's because of the way my parents feel about me and the way they feel about him. 'In that case I accept your apology,' I say.

'Thank you. I'm not expecting instant forgiveness either – that's something I will work on in the future, if you'll let me.'

He looks like a vulnerable young boy now and I can see something that looks like shame in his eyes. This isn't what I want. 'Please don't feel bad. In the end the person to blame is Mother. And to be frank, even if she does apologise, I'm not sure it will be for the right reasons.'

James shrugs. 'That thought had crossed my mind too – she might do it to please the rest of us. But we have to give her a chance.' His face brightens as if something nice just occurred to him. 'Another reason why we think now is the right time for fresh start is because you are soon to be an auntie and we'd really love you to be involved in our child's life.'

Hell's bells. Not sure I can take any more shocks today. An auntie. Me? How does that feel? In fact, how does being a sister feel, having a sister-in-law? A muddle of thoughts swill about my brain and I need to drain them. James scans my face and bites the edge of his thumbnail.

'Sorry, Lottie. That came out wrong. It sounded selfish, as if just because we are having a baby we want everything to be neat and tidy, our family made whole – happy. It's not like that at all. We do want those things, but our main concern is you. You have had a shitty time of it all and we want to help make that better – eventually. No easy quick fixes.'

I'm glad he said that about the selfish part, because I had started to think it. For something to do because I need to think before I speak, I drink my tea and look at the ocean and let my thoughts free-fall. The idea of being an auntie is very appealing, which surprises me. I picture myself bouncing a big-eyed brown baby on my lap and teaching it to paint. That's the teacher in me, I expect. Children are the future, after all. Who doesn't like to feel that they have a part in shaping it?

'Lottie, what's on your mind?' James has his arms folded again. I tell him almost exactly what I have been thinking apart from the bit about bouncing his baby on my knee. That's too private and I need to get used to that a bit more before I share it.

'Children are indeed our future.' He grins and unfolds his arms. 'I'm overjoyed that you're considering being involved.'

'Any names yet?' I ask because it seems like a good idea.

'One or two, but nothing definite.' He tells me about Mother's reaction to Welsh and Nigerian suggestions. I tell him I think she's a narrow-minded prejudiced snob. He laughs humourlessly and says, 'Beth's instincts are spot on, then.'

I'm about to say that I'd like to meet Beth, but don't. That sort of thing should come from them, because if none of it works out,

I can't be blamed for pushing things along. James's phone rings and he says it's Beth and would I mind if he answers it. I say of course not, and he wanders off, chatting to her.

James is in the car park just in front of me and I watch him pace up and down. He stops, closes his eyes and tilts his head to the sun, a big smile on his face. Then he ends the call and comes quickly back up the steps and to our table.

'Beth is chuffed to death that we've met, and I told her what we've been talking about. And… I'm not sure how you'll take this, but she asked that you think of a few names for our baby for us to choose from.' He holds his hands up. 'Of course, we would totally understand if you weren't happy with that.'

'What?' My skin's on fire again but I realise I'm honoured to be asked. 'Why does she want me to do that?'

'Because regardless of what happens with our parents, she said it would show you how much we want you in our lives, our child's life. You will feel like you're really part of our little family if you name him or her.'

My throat seems to have developed a lump. Perhaps I'll ask James to have a look, him being a doctor and all. This thought makes me smile and the lump is dislodged. 'I would be honoured to name the future, James. Thank you.'

James does the blinking and swallowing thing and puts his hand on my shoulder. 'No. Thank you.'

'You might change your mind when I tell you the names I have lined up,' I say in a serious voice, but I know he can't fail to see the humour in my eyes. 'Favourites are…' I screw my face up and pretend to concentrate. 'Algernon, Confucius and Salvador, for a boy – Ethel, Betty and Edna for a girl.'

'Ah, right. I'll try and remember those,' he says and grins again. Then he looks out over the ocean and says quietly. 'I'm so glad you came today, Lottie.'

I don't have to take time to consider my response. 'So am I, James. So am I.'

Chapter Twenty-Three

The Next Step

The calico cat is looking so much better two days on. Her coat is shiny and glossy as if she's just been groomed and her green eyes have more life and depth. I'm not sure if it's a good thing as I can feel them on me wherever I'm in the room. Sometimes I think she's looking fondly at me, sometimes I'm found wanting. This is obviously a ridiculous idea, but one that I can't shake. The companion in the tree turns out to be called Bella – and is a beautiful tabby. She is finished and so is the tree. Bella's eyes follow me too, on occasion, but I can tell that she's never anything but happy with what I've done for her.

I'm folding towels still warm from the dryer and I catch the calico cat's eye as I take them to the bathroom. I can tell she's fed up again and realise it's probably because her foreground – a garden of spring flowers – isn't finished and nor is she. She has missing whiskers and those tufty bits some cats have sticking out of their ears. I think she'll be happier when the whole painting is finished so she can walk through those flowers and nose about the garden.

And surprise, surprise, Mother has phoned and informed me that James had told her we'd met. She said she'd phoned to apologise as agreed, because she couldn't do it face to face as she would get too emotional. She used a voice I'd not heard before. Not stabby, karaoke, wheedly, or snotty. The closest to it would be the ironed-out flat one. It sounded as if she was reciting lines in a play – in fact I did wonder if she was reading it at one point – then she broke down. So much for not getting emotional.

She cried and cried. In the lull between sobs I asked her to please stop, said that I accepted her apology, and can we just put it all behind us now? Mother said no, she had to finish, had to get it all off her chest, and she sobbed and hiccupped through the rest of the script. I held the phone away from my ear at one point, because her words became intelligible and the snot bubbling sounds were most unpleasant.

Areas covered were her extreme youth upon giving birth, her overbearing father forcing her to give James up, the fact that she was psychologically damaged, the guilt – oh, the guilt, I had no idea – and also the fact that at the time she was so worried that something would happen to me – that I would also be taken away from her somehow – made her keep an emotional distance from me.

This bit did make me wonder if she'd looked it up on the internet, but I gave her the benefit of the doubt. She repeatedly apologised for the vile things she'd said and snivelled most horribly – but then immediately qualified her actions by reminding me that she was damaged and so forth. She told me her heart was breaking, but I remained unmoved. In the end her words amounted to excuses for her behaviour, really. Still, I would never have believed she would even consider saying half of what she had. Just before we ended the call, Mother asked if we could start afresh, look to the future. I said we could and that we'll see what happens.

Will it ever be okay between us? I have no idea. I will try though. If it's true she was damaged then I have to give her a chance, don't I? Before my walking holiday I wouldn't have considered it, but I think I have changed so much, learned so much en route and after. Having said that, I'm not sure that I will ever trust her completely. Of course I need to swallow the past, but I need to take small mouthfuls at a time to ensure against indigestion. She put me through too much to just let my guard down and go skipping through the tulips with her.

Tulips… I look over to the painting again. I will definitely put some of those amongst the spring flowers – red and yellow should complement the calico cat's fur. Have I got time to make a start now? No. I'm meeting Louisa at my new studio. I can't get over how wonderful that sounds and keep saying it over and over in my head. I picked up the keys yesterday and then just pottered about there for ages thinking about decor and how to display my work to the best effect. I need to think of a name for it. I also need to think of a selection of names for my niece or nephew.

Who would have thought I would ever have had such a task? Certainly not me. Am I glad I have it? Yes and no. Mostly yes, because, as I said before, I like the idea of being an auntie, teaching, having fun with a little one. The no part is just apprehension, I think. I have never been used to being part of a wider family and, as you know, after the age of thirteen, I struggled with the narrower one I had. Narrower as in the opposite to wider, but I suppose you could apply it to Mother's mind, too.

Involvement with a wider family isn't necessarily something to be apprehensive about, but because of our history, it is a bit daunting. If James and I had grown up together it wouldn't be a problem, would it? We didn't, though, so that leaves me unsure of how to behave when I meet Beth and so forth. However, I am determined to try my best. The new me won't allow anything less.

I tend to think of myself as a new me after the third turning point when Caleb and I parted company. This is tricky, though, because I was already a new me after the second turning point when I walked out of the classroom. Now I think about it, before we parted company, I had learned such a lot from people we'd met on the journey too... so now I'm confused about whether I am in fact newer after the third turning point or not.

I'm in the bathroom now, putting make-up on and thinking that this is one of those times where I need to stop thinking about things, analysing everything to within an inch of its life. In the end what does it matter about measuring newness, and anyway, can it be measured? There I go again – thinking too much. Too much thinking is sometimes bad for you. Don't worry, I haven't turned into a *Daily Mail* reader, it's just that sometimes my brain can't cope with itself.

It's one of those humid August afternoons that have skies heavy with pregnant clouds. They are full-term and desperate to give birth, but for now they just hang suspended over the ocean in hopeful anticipation of a storm's release. Once out of my car I hear a grumble over the hills and expect they won't have to wait too much longer.

Louisa is already here, and she turns and waves as I approach. We hug and although it's only just over a week since I saw her, I feel like it's been forever. Well, not forever, obviously, but a long time. Isn't that the way of things? When you really like a person it seems like ages, when you don't, it seems like minutes. Mother's face looms so I push her away. Things have to be different now.

'You look lovely, my dear,' Louisa says, holding me at arm's length.

'Do I?' I say, wondering what was lovely about black jeans and a red T-shirt.

'Yes. You look fresh, happy, as if excitement is bubbling up inside you.'

'Really? That's good, then.' I think about what she said and guess she's right. 'I think it might be the fact that I have this place, and also that I've started swallowing more of the past and keeping it down.'

Louisa gives me a puzzled look but laughs. 'Do tell.'

I put my key in the door. 'I will when we're inside. I have cake.'

An hour later we have eaten half a chocolate cake and are on our second cup of tea. I have told Louisa all my news and she is very pleased that I took her advice.

'I knew you would feel better for meeting James. And you have come to an understanding with your mother, too. So much in a short time.' Louisa leans forward and pecks my cheek. 'I'm so proud of you, love.'

'I should hope you are. She's my mother but you're my mum, after all.'

You know, quite near the beginning of my story, I said words to the effect that sometimes what I mean to say and what comes out are poles apart? In fact, more than sometimes? What I said to Louisa might be right at the top of those occasions. I can't believe what just came out of my mouth. But having said that, I realise I *did* mean to say it. I wonder if I really am a new me. Not just metaphorically, but in reality. Do you think I have been actually replaced by a clone that has no issues whatsoever with showing deep emotion so easily? No, I think you're right. That would be impossible.

Louisa looks in shock but it's a nice shock. She has her hugest dimpliest smile and her eyes are swimming a bit. 'Oh, what an absolutely lovely thing to say,' she says, dabbing at her mouth with a bit of kitchen roll.

'Yes, it is, rather. But I meant every word.'

She flaps her hand at me which I decide to ignore on this occasion. 'Stop it. I'll be in bits soon.'

'I have never understood that saying. I mean a person can't really break up into bits, can they? You know, like an ornament that's fallen from the shelf?' I chortle, which makes her do the same. Good, she's unlikely to cry now. I don't like seeing people cry, even if they are happy tears.

We wander round the studio chatting about the right colours to use on the walls. Louisa says that she thinks blues and greens with perhaps a bit of lemon here and there. In that way it will reflect our surroundings – the main window faces the beach. I have been thinking along similar lines but not the lemon. She's so clever – lemon is perfect, it's like the sun.

'When do you think you'll open?' Louisa perches on the windowsill and frowns at the darkening sky. The cloud's waters have broken now, and the birth is well underway.

'When I have enough paintings to sell. I only have three really good ones, and *The Calico Cat*, of course… though she has still whiskers to find and a few flowers in the garden. I intend to do some more over the next few months or so, perhaps even come to the vineyard again and paint there?'

'Of course. You know you're welcome any time, think of it as your second home.'

'Thank you.' I smile and then our conversation halts while we listen to a grumble turn into a growl over the sea, and a few moments later we watch a sheet of lightning flash itself at a line of clouds. 'Perhaps October half term might be a good idea. It gets quite busy again around that time here.'

'Excellent.' Louisa claps her hands. 'Isn't it exciting? Will you have an opening launch party?'

This had crossed my mind but very fleetingly. 'I think it might be a good idea, yes. I will have to advertise it properly, of course. I don't have that many friends.' An image of Caleb surfaces wearing a dog smile and I block him with one of a dragon. Don't ask. I find it's best.

'Well, you have me, your parents, James and his wife, my sister will come and perhaps one of the boys, Anna from school? And—'

The look on her face encourages Caleb to shove past the dragon so I cut in. 'Peter the lottery man I told you about that we met on the walk said he wanted to be told when I'd opened, and perhaps even some ex-pupils might want to come.'

'There you are then, and if everyone brings a friend.' Louisa stares into my eyes and says, 'There *is* another person that would—'

I know who she means, and I don't want to hear it. 'Oh, and I can't think of a name for this place. Nothing feels right.' Then I tell her about me being asked to name my niece or nephew.

'How wonderful! Have you any ideas?'

I hadn't until that very moment. 'Yes, Louisa for a girl. No idea about a boy yet.'

'Oh. I don't think I can cope with you today – you'll have me in—' She stops, looks at me and grins. 'You'll make me cry.'

Louisa is backlit by a flash of lightning and we both give a nervous laugh. 'Let's count down the thunder to see how near it is,' I say, and we turn to face the ocean. In unison we say 'One, two, three…' The sky yells at us so loud that we clutch each other's arms and laugh again. Isn't it funny that thunder makes you nervous? We all understand that it's a natural phenomenon, but it feels other-worldly somehow. Leastways it does to me.

'It won't be long passing now – it's obviously directly overhead,' Louisa says, pulling her cardigan closely about her. The humidity has gone off somewhere and left us with a little chill breeze, so I shut the door.

We talk about baby names for a while and possible names for the shop, until a light comes on in the corner of the sky. Slowly it pushes back the darkness until the sky and clouds agree on an uneasy truce between blue and grey. I ask if Louisa wants to come back to my place for a spot of supper and a look at my latest paintings. She does. Just as we're leaving the shop she says, 'You know, I'm not going to pretend that Caleb doesn't exist, even though you might want me to.'

I shrug and mumble something like 'hmm' into my bag as I search for keys.

'It's just wonderful what you've done to this cat and her friend since I last saw them.' Louisa takes a sip of wine, stoops her shoulders and peers into the eyes of the calico cat. She glances at me and then stares into the distance, trancelike. 'You have come so far, Lottie. You have taken little steps back into your past, and because of that, you're now able to take big steps forward into the future. It's wonderful to watch you.'

'Thank you. That's a lovely thing to say.' Warmth rushes to my cheeks and I want to hug her.

'The next big step, though, is one you might not want to take.' Her turquoise eyes turn serious, hold mine, and I look down into my wine glass. I know what's coming, I think. 'It's time you spoke to Caleb. He phoned me again a few days back and I told him that I couldn't do more than I have.'

I sigh and take a mouthful of wine. I don't need this right now. Not when we're having such a nice day. 'I don't think I can be faffed with all that, Louisa. Everyone seems obsessed with happy ever afters, don't they? Life doesn't always have them, you know.'

'Yes. I do know.' Louisa gives a sad smile and looks back to the painting.

Fuck, of course she does. Images of dying olive trees overgrown with celandine flash in my head. What a bloody jackass I am at times. 'That was a thoughtless thing to say, forgive me.'

'Easy done. And I'm not suggesting that you go looking for wedding dresses, I'm just suggesting you at least phone him – even if it's to tell him there's nothing left to say,' she says to the cat.

I think about this and decide it seems like a fair idea. Otherwise he'll keep bothering Louisa, and it's not her problem, is it? 'I'll do it tomorrow.' I pat her shoulder and go to check on the curry in the oven, which is currently spreading aromas of spice and piquancy around the whole apartment.

Louisa follows me and perches on a high stool next to the kitchen counter. 'Good. So what will you tell him? Is there anything left to say – to salvage?'

I know her keen eyes are on me, so I look in a cupboard for nothing in particular. I don't know the answer; I keep blocking any discussion of it when one part of my mind presents it to the other. 'The truth is, Louisa, I don't know.'

'Well, that's encouraging.' I look at her face for a trace of sarcasm. 'No. I'm serious. When we were in Sennen you said you didn't know if you loved Caleb and I said I didn't think you were being honest with yourself.'

'Yes, and I said that romantic love is a social construct. How am I to know what love really is when all we get as reference points are pink glittery hearts, heroes and happy ever afters?'

'Look. Caleb hurt you – he knows that as well as you do. But you need to sort your head out. If you can't be honest with yourself, stop hiding behind social constructs and tell *me* how you feel.'

'As I've said, I don't know. I haven't allowed myself to think about it with everything else that's been on my mind lately.' I take the curry out of the oven and give it a stir. Louisa is obviously trying to help, but I'm feeling bossed about and that's something I'm not good with.

'Did you love Gwendoline?' she says, swallowing the last of her wine, her eyes sweeping the ocean view.

'Of course, but that's not the same thing, is it?'

'I don't know. How do you tell?'

'Well, romantic love and love that you have for a grandparent are different types, aren't they?'

'How do you know, if romantic love is just a social construct?'

She's irritating me now. What is she trying to say? 'Well, you have a bond when you have sex with someone you care about, don't you? Sexual love feels different to the love you have for a grandparent.'

'So, the love for a grandparent isn't as strong as the love you feel for a sexual partner?'

'That's not what I'm saying. Not just any old sexual partner, someone that you really care about. I'm also saying that that kind of love is just different – not necessarily stronger or weaker.'

'So how did you know you loved your grandmother? Isn't that a social construction too?'

This was a possibility I'd not considered. A very quick assessment prompts, 'To an extent, I suppose. You are taught to respect and learn from your elders and so forth, they give their grandchildren treats, are presented in a cosy way on film and in stories... but I don't need that reference. I felt the love in here.' I thump my chest. 'It was real... still is.' I chew the inside of my cheek and focus on pouring rice into a pan.

Louisa nods enthusiastically. 'Of course, you do. But I bet you can't define *exactly* what that love feels like, can you?'

My eyes flick to hers and away. I replace the rice jar on the counter a little too hard. If I thought about it for long enough I expect I'd come up with something, but all these questions are making me uncomfortable. 'Not really, can we just change the subject now?'

'Can you feel anything at all in your heart for Caleb resembling some of what you felt for your gran?'

'I don't want to talk about it.' I pick up the wine bottle and fill both our glasses.

'Okay. I think you should because we're getting somewhere, but I don't want to upset you.'

While she sets the table, and I attend to the food, we chat about nothing in particular, though my thoughts are allowed free rein. If I'm honest I feel like we're getting somewhere too, and it would be a shame to slam the anchors on.

Steam is rising from the strained rice in the colander and I stare through it at a memory of how I felt after I had slept with Caleb for the first time. I told you about it, remember? It was about our connection deepening; it was no longer a connection, we almost became the same person – more than just physically – it was as if our hearts and souls were one, too.

I give the rice a shake and tip it into a warmed serving bowl. Louisa takes the curry over to the table and crunches into a poppadum. She's talking about the first time she and Jagger ever had a curry, and, quite unexpectedly I cut across her with, 'I think I did love him… as far as I can tell. But that was before he betrayed me. I don't feel as strongly now… although I do miss him. Quite a lot, really.' I bite into a poppadum before my mouth has chance to say anything else.

Louisa gives me one of her dimply smiles and raises her glass. 'Good. At last it's out in the open. Please ring him.' She holds up her forefinger before I can say anything. 'I don't mean to tell him that you probably did and still do love him, just ring him and arrange to have a talk. If it doesn't work out, then at least you tried, eh?'

I ignore what she said about me loving him. 'I suppose so. But as I said, happy endings might not be possible… or even good for us, really.'

'How do you arrive at that one? Surely a person having a sad one isn't a desirable option?'

'No, but because it's so important to us, we might be sad if it isn't perfect, doesn't live up to our high expectations of happiness. So, we might pretend that we have a happy ending when in fact we don't.'

'Has anyone ever told you that you can overthink things, Lottie?' Louisa says with a twinkly smile.

'No. But I have told myself it a few times.'

She laughs at this. 'Right, that's settled, then. You'll phone Caleb tomorrow?'

'Yes.'

'Wonderful. And so is this curry – you are a very good cook, my girl.'

We then change the subject and have a lovely evening, but all the time there's a little wriggling worry worm in my head, and I need to stop feeding it before it grows into the Loch Ness monster.

Chapter Twenty-Four

Honesty

Why I feel the need to wear the 'right clothes' is beyond me. I mean clothes are just clothes, aren't they? What on earth does it matter what one wears in the end? Having said that, I do realise that going out in a snowstorm in a bikini isn't a good idea, nor is wearing wellies, thick socks and an Arran sweater in a heatwave. To that extent there is such a thing as the 'right clothes'. The idea about wearing the 'right clothes' to impress or make a statement is wrong, though. People should be more honest about what they're trying to do – why not just say how you feel instead of wearing bits of cloth to try and say it for you?

Apart from the obvious practical necessities to choose the right clothes that I have mentioned, I normally choose clothes for aesthetics. Cost is also a factor, as is where they are made. I avoid clothes that might have possibly been made in the sweatshops of the 'developing' world, but sometimes you just can't be sure, can you? Therefore because walking around naked in public can be an arrestable offence, I have to take a risk.

So far this morning, I have tried on three different sets of clothes and am currently sitting on the edge of my bed in just my underwear. I'm angry with myself because I have allowed the 'right clothes' theory to influence my decisions. As you know, I pride myself on being unconventional, but because Caleb is due here in half an hour I wanted to make sure my clothes didn't 'say' anything to him that could be misconstrued. Bloody ridiculous. It's all just peacockery and flimflammery and I won't be a party to it.

I pick up the green lacy top that I think suits me, having previously discarded it because it's a bit low cut and I thought it gave the 'wrong message', and pull it over my head. Then I slip back into red shorts and reapply the eye make-up that I wiped off a few minutes ago and loose my hair from the clip I strangled it with. Okay, that will do. The discarded clothes are gathered up and rammed back into the wardrobe and I leave the bedroom before my head has time to consider the 'right clothes' theory yet again.

Are you a bit surprised that Caleb is on his way here? I am. I phoned him and before he had time to say very much at all apart from, 'Lottie, thank God!' I said he should come round here at ten thirty, so we could have a chat. He said it was a bit short notice and he'd have to cancel something. I said take it or leave it. He took it.

My bossy attitude isn't because I want to be a puppet master or anything, it's because I can't bear the thought of arranging something with him for tomorrow or the next day, or even later this afternoon, because that will give me time to ponder and fret and the wriggling worry worm is already so fat inside my head that it's pressing against each temple. Perhaps I'll take a couple of paracetamol.

Coffee is on, cherry scones are in the oven and my gut feels as if it's in a lift descending from the thirtieth floor and then immediately going back up again. At least the paracetamol are doing their job. Twenty-eight minutes past – is there enough time to go for a quick wee? I have had four quick wees in the last hour so it's hardly necessary. The human body is a wonderful machine, isn't it? But sometimes it goes a bit mad when it's full of adrenaline. Fight or flight. Why should I need to do either? Calm breaths and a clear mind. I walk to the kitchen. In through the nose, out through… the doorbell.

On the way to the answer the door I tell my mind to stop screeching at me that everything might go wrong and take a deep breath as I open it.

Caleb's face is hidden behind a huge bunch of purple flowers and I'm straight back to the first time he came to my place. Perhaps that's why he's bought them, you know, to fill me full of nostalgic and welcoming thoughts? This idea isn't very charitable, so I push it away and concentrate on Caleb's face as he lowers the flowers to chest height.

'Look, it's me,' he says, and does the dog grin that I've missed so much. 'Bet you wondered who it was at first, eh?'

'I did. I thought you were a flower salesman and was about to give you short shrift.'

'Wonder what that is, short shrift – and is there a tall one?'

That sounds so much like something I'd say that my lips curl of their own free will. Perhaps he's been contaminated by my influence. 'I expect there is a tall one and even a middle-sized one. We just need to find out what the origin of shrift is now.' I stand aside and sweep my arm back towards my hallway.

As he steps inside he holds out the flowers out to me. 'These are called honesty. I wanted to say it with flowers, but I couldn't find any called so-sorry-for-being-a-complete-fucking-idiot.'

My big laugh surprises us both, not least because it is amplified in the small hallway. He laughs too, and I can't help but look into his lovely eyes. A fire is starting under my skin, so I take the flowers and he follows me to the kitchen. I say, 'I don't think you were a complete fucking idiot, you were extremely misguided though and I think honesty is a great choice.' I find a vase and run water into it. 'We need to be perfectly honest with each other for the future, Caleb, if this is to work.'

'Absolutely. That's why I picked them.' He sits on a high stool and drums his fingers on the counter. 'And… and so you're saying that you want us to work?'

I'm about to hedge – I hadn't really thought about what I meant when I said the future bit – but then I look at the flowers and say, 'I think so, yes. But we should definitely have a good discussion about things and I'm certainly not going to rush it.'

'Oh, that is such good news! I haven't really allowed myself to hope that you might take me back—' He stops when he sees my frowny expression. 'Sorry, yes, of course. We shouldn't run before we can walk.'

Despite myself, I have to bite back a giggle when I turn to the oven to take out the scones. He looked like a little kid that had been told he could go to Disneyland or some other horrific fun park when I said I wanted it to work. At least I know what I want now, even if I didn't know it until the words were out of my mouth. I had guessed that's where I was headed after the discussion I'd had last night with Louisa, but it still felt a bit odd hearing it out loud.

'Wow – have you just made those?' Caleb asks, nodding at the scones I'm putting on a cooling rack.

'No, Caleb. I don't know how they got in my oven… must be magic.' I wink at him.

He does the twisty thing with his mouth that tells me he's unsure about what he's going to say. 'Lottie, you look absolutely gorgeous. I can hardly take my eyes off you.'

To add emphasis to his words his eyes sweep up my legs, which I know are toned and tanned from the holiday and come to rest on my breasts. He shakes his head and draws his hands down his face. 'God, I'm sorry,' he groans through his fingers. 'I'm messing it up already. But you said be honest and it's been so long since I saw you, my mind is in overdrive.'

I'm having similar feelings, but I can't tell him that, or I know we'll be in bed before the butter has melted on the scones. I'll have to be the tough one. Talking is crucial if we are to move forward. 'Thanks for the compliment, but let's have coffee and scones and talk things through. Shall we sit on the balcony or is it windy…'

'Out?' he says and pulls a silly face.

It isn't really windy out, just a bit of a puff now and then as if the clouds are doing deep-breathing exercises. I have stopped doing mine now because my adrenaline levels are back to normal and Caleb and I are chatting as easily as if we saw each other only yesterday. I have told him all about the meeting I had with James and my mother's apology, such as it was. I have eaten two scones and Caleb is on his third.

'I'm glad that things seem to be working out. James is a nice guy, isn't he?' Caleb says, though I can tell he is choosing every word very carefully. It must be hard for him not to say that if it hadn't been for Caleb, brother and sister would still be poles apart.

'He is. And I know you meant well by meeting him in secret, but that kind of thing can't happen again. I can't cope with it.'

'Yes, I know, and I promise it won't. I was a bloody fool – thought I knew best, but it was only because I wanted you to be happy.' Caleb looks at me and wipes scone crumbs from his mouth with the back of his hand. 'I do love you, you know, Lottie.'

Oh dear. This wasn't supposed to happen; he isn't supposed to say things like that while we're having a serious talk about everything. I look away and into my cup as if there might be the right response at the bottom of it. I must admit, though, hearing Caleb say those words did make my heart do a bit of a jump. This heart jumping isn't unpleasant either, as it goes.

'There I go again. I've made you feel uncomfortable... sorry.'

'No, I'm not uncomfortable with it. It's quite nice to hear if I'm honest, and that's what we are being, aren't we? I won't say the same back to you though because I'm still not quite certain about all of it. I do have very strong feelings for you, of course.'

Caleb's voice is a bit wobbly as he says, 'That is so much more than I deserve. I didn't mean to, but as you said at the time, I did betray you. And I have thought since about why what I did was such a big thing for you.'

I drain my cup and put my feet up on the balcony rail and wiggle my toes. The nails are almost the same colour as the sky. Cerulean, or is it more cobalt? I realise that this is thought-procrastination and say, 'Okay, I'm listening.'

Caleb clears his throat and puts his feet up next to mine. He's wearing brown trainers and they look like two huge pasties silhouetted against the sky. 'Okay. The betrayal thing runs very deep with you. Before the big fat secret revelation you loved your mother. I know, by the calico cat day she was beginning to get on your nerves a bit, and that prompted a rebellion, but nothing that most kids don't experience with parents.' He looks at me and I give him a quick nod to let him know this is pretty accurate.

'But then after the BFS revelation and the subsequent way she belittled you, made you feel worthless with all the vile things she said, presented you with a brother you had never met, a brother that was held up to be perfect, the chosen one – you felt horribly betrayed. You loved her, and she took that love and stamped all over it.'

I feel his eyes on me but I'm looking at my toenails again and trying hard to focus on whether they are darker or lighter than the ocean, but the light keeps changing making it hard for me to decide… but I'm not trying to decide that at all, really. It's like those thoughts are a trailer for the main film that Caleb is projecting, but I have changed my mind about wanting to watch it.

I can't look at him, say anything, so just nod again, but that action tips a stream of hot tears onto my cheeks so I quickly pull my long hair to the side and comb my fingers through it. I don't think he can see my face at all, now.

'So, when I betrayed you, you couldn't live with it – it brought everything back.' Through a gap in my hair I watch Caleb take his feet down and lean forward, elbows on his knees. 'Of course, my betrayal wasn't the same – I'm not saying you loved me. But you did care about me and I went behind your back involving the same person that had made such a huge impact on your life all those years ago. When I think about it all now I feel so stupid. Unutterably so.'

He's talking as if he's in a period drama again. He does that from time to time and no matter how serious the situation, it makes me want to laugh. I wipe my cheeks behind my hair curtain and flick it back over my shoulders. I say in a breathy little voice, 'Unutterably? Why, Mr Darcy. I am quite undone by the use of such an elegant and unusual word.'

Caleb looks at me from under a deeply furrowed brow. 'I'm being serious. Am I close with my explanations about why you felt so upset at the time?'

Too late, I realise that flippancy has no place here, even if it did help me recover my composure. 'Yes, you are. In fact, it's more or less the conclusion I came to myself.' I want to change the subject, go for a walk or something, anything to stop my deepest emotions bleeding out into the warm afternoon. But then I remember the honesty thing and heave a sigh. 'Okay, Caleb. I'm going to just open my mouth and see what comes out. These thoughts have been milling around in my head for weeks anyway as if they're a wind turbine in a force ten.'

Caleb takes my hand and kisses the back of it. His lips are soft and warm, and I take comfort from the strength of his hand. 'Take your time, Lottie.'

'As I said, you were correct about back then and why what you did hurt so much. However, I have been thinking about feelings and love and what it actually is quite a bit recently. Louisa helped me with it, too. Love is very tricky to define, and, in the end, I guess you could say it's indefinable – it's something you just feel for a person or you don't. It's a bit like faith, isn't it? Believers have said similar things about that to me – it's something they have in their hearts but can't define it – you just believe in God, or you don't. So anyway, I can honestly say now that I don't love Mother. I think the reason is that she's not very important to me anymore. I don't need her approval, advice, help or love.' I pause and give Caleb a little smile. 'I don't need her for anything.'

'That's pretty succinct for you just opening your mouth and seeing what comes out,' he says, and kisses my hand again.

'Yes, I suppose it is.' I must admit talking about it like this is helping to finally pull my scattered thoughts into cohesion. 'Since we set off on the holiday, and after, I've been thinking more than usual – and that's saying a lot for me. I told you about my turning points, remember?' He nods. 'Well, I think I had a third on the walk. That's why I'm able to say what I said about Mother and the way I think about my past now. I worked lots of it out before, with Gwendoline's help of course, and since then with you, the people we met on the walk, and the wonderful Louisa.'

'She certainly has made an impression on you. Seems a lovely lady,' Caleb says.

'Oh, she is. And you must meet her soon – you'll get on so well.' I can hardly believe the two people that I care about most have never met. 'Mind you, she can wax a bit lyrical from time to time. The other day she said that going on the walking holiday was a journey of self-discovery for me, a coming of age. Talk about a cliché – and I'm twenty-eight for goodness sake.'

Caleb bites the inside of his cheek and looks at a seagull hanging in the sky above us. 'I think she's right. Perhaps the definition is too narrow. I don't think it matters how old you are – if you don't feel like a whole person, comfortable with being you until much later in life, then you can come of age at any time. Perhaps some people never do. And the journey of self-discovery on the walk – yes, I can see that, too.'

I think Caleb is almost as wise as Louisa at this moment and I want lean across and kiss him. I know where that will lead though and for now I need to take things slowly. I can't tell you why… okay, I can. It's because I want to be in control of the situation. If we sleep together I will have given in too quickly. I can forgive him but not immediately. I have accepted my past, am less angry about it, come of age or whatever, but that doesn't mean I have completely changed who I am. I still like to be in control, be different, speak my mind, stand up and be counted.

To Caleb I say, 'Now you put it like that I can see it, too. I have some wine in the fridge, would you like some?'

He would, and I stand up and open the sliding door from the balcony to the apartment. Just before I go inside, Caleb says, 'So if you don't love your mother and all the stuff you said about not needing anything from her, why are you considering a family get-together?'

I consider that for a few moments. 'I suppose it's purely for selfish reasons. I do want a relationship with my brother and his family, and if I try to forgive Mother and be nice to her, I suppose it will help me move forward without the resentfulness and hatey bits hanging over my head.'

Caleb smiles. 'Yes, I get that – and you're not selfish.'

'No. I'm a kind, mature, magnanimous person, don't you know?' I say in a voice like the Queen's. He laughs, and I join in, then I say, 'I can rise above the person she was and still is to an extent. She *was* probably damaged by giving up James, but whether she was a Grade A bitch before that, I will never know with absolute certainty. Gwendoline had her reservations, as I told you. Left nothing to her in the will.'

I am just about to bring the wine out when Caleb comes in and stands in front of *The Calico Cat*. 'Hey, this is… just fantastic! You've really changed your style since the holiday, haven't you?' He crouches down to look at the other paintings against the wall: the Dragon Cave and the ones of Louisa's vineyard.

I take a mouthful of wine. 'Are you trying to say my painting was pants before the holiday then, Caleb?'

He whips round, mouth open, and then catches the amusement in my eyes. 'Of course not. But I do have to say that these are nothing short of outstanding.' He holds the vineyard one at arm's length. 'Almost impressionist in style, but then I'm far from an expert.'

I smile. 'That's exactly what Louisa said.' I hand him his glass and he stands up and clinks it against mine.

'Here's to a successful career and may your studio never be empty of admirers.'

'Thank you. I still have to find a name for it. Nothing seems right.' I walk over to the sofa and sit down.

Caleb takes a swallow of wine, pushes his hand through his hair and looks at the ceiling as if it's the most interesting thing he's ever seen. Eventually he says, 'I have a suggestion that would be perfect, I think.'

'Let's hear it, then.'

He sits by me and points his wine glass at the easel. 'The Calico Cat.'

I look at the painting and into the cat's eyes. The cat thinks it's a brilliant idea and strangely so do I. It feels right to me, though I don't know why it should. 'Why is it perfect?'

'Because the cat is you.' He shakes his head when I frown. 'No, of course you're not a cat, or a painting. You chose to paint this cat to remind you of your first turning point, but also to represent who you are. A metaphor if you will. Remember that time in Bustopher Jones when you told me that you liked calico cats because they were different? They were neither one thing or the other. Not black, white, Siamese, and so forth. You said that most people don't choose to have them as pets because they like order – things in boxes, pigeon holes, compartments. They like their cats symmetrical, neat. You don't.'

My goodness, he listened well. I can't even recall saying some of it. 'Yes, I remember most of that. And it's all true. If I were a cat, I'd be calico.'

'There you are, then. The decision to paint and open a studio is intertwined with your second turning point, and the cat is an essential part of your first. The two things should go together.'

A big wave of something is crashing about in my chest. It feels like happiness and certainty and relief all at the same time. Caleb looks into my eyes and I can tell he's unsure that he's said the right thing, so even though I know I shouldn't, I put my glass down and kiss him full on the mouth.

'Wow,' he says when we come up for air. 'You like that suggestion, then?'

'It is totally and unutterably perfect.' I cup his face and give him a few more pecks. 'And you are part of my third turning point, even though I didn't think you were to start with. You influenced my acceptance of the past and were the impetus behind me meeting James.' I slap his cheek playfully. 'Even though you came at *that* from the wrong angle.'

Caleb rubs his cheek and pretends to cry until I lift my hand to do it again, so he stops and does the dog grin. 'Does this mean I have to be painted and put in your studio?'

'Yes, of course.' I look at him, my head on one side. I can picture him in all sorts of settings, but disconcertingly my mind keeps presenting him naked on a secluded beach... He's looking at me with lust in his eyes and I move towards him. 'A nice background for that might be Louisa's vineyard. We could go there soon and kill two birds.' I stand up and take my empty glass to the sink for no other reason than to put some distance between us.

'Suits me. We should go soon, though – there's only a week or so before I start back at school.'

Poor Caleb. He doesn't look overjoyed at that prospect. I think he's overdue for a turning point of his own but decide to keep that idea floating about in the lesser-used parts of my mind. There's enough to think about for now. 'Yes, okay. We'll arrange something soon. And now, my dear man, I must ask you to leave. I have a very important painting to finish.'

He looks a bit disappointed but covers it with a smile. 'Of course. Will I see you soon?'

'Yes. How does tomorrow sound?'

'It sounds pretty good to me.'

I walk him to the door and we kiss. I rest my forehead on the door after he's gone and think that this not getting close too quickly idea of mine isn't going to work beyond the first few minutes of him coming round here in the morning. I then realise that if I'm the one to take the lead, be in control, it will be fine, and I shouldn't worry too much about it. Not now we have a perfect understanding.

At the easel a few minutes later, I give the cat her whiskers and start on the flowers in the foreground. By the end of the day the painting is complete, and I stand back and admire it. It suddenly occurs to me why I haven't finished her until now. It's because if she is me in the way Caleb suggests, I had to feel complete in myself before I could do the same for her. Then I wonder if that might be pushing the idea a bit too far, you know, romanticising everything?

The calico cat says she's not certain, and to be honest it doesn't matter. Her main concern is that she's bloody finished at last. I agree and wander off to clean my brushes. What I need is a quiet evening watching mindless TV to give my brain a rest. Absolutely no over-thinking is going to be allowed.

Chapter Twenty-Five

Friends and Family

Louisa and Caleb took to each other like ducks to water. This wasn't a surprise to me, but nevertheless, there had been a little grain of doubt in my mind trying to grow itself into a wheat field. I always like to have grains of doubt, or perhaps smidgens – because they don't sound as if they can grow into anything very much, do they? Anyway, the reason I do this is if one just breezes through thinking that everything is going to be wonderful and then it isn't, one gets a big kick in the guts, but a smidgen of doubt makes sure that kick has less of an impact.

We had a lovely three days at the vineyard where I spent most of the daylight hours painting and most of the evenings out on the terrace eating, drinking and talking to my two favourite people. Then, later, Caleb and I spent until the early hours in bed, making up for lost time. Before you ask, I was the one to initiate this activity and feel very much in control of how our relationship is developing, so that's just fine.

At the moment we're in the car on the way to stay with James and Beth. This wasn't at all planned, but James happened to ring just as we were about to leave Louisa's and head for home. James said that as our bags were already packed, why didn't we pop up to them for a few days? I wasn't sure how I felt about this, because it was one thing meeting James for a few hours near where I live, and another thing entirely staying in his home, particularly as we hadn't even met his wife yet. What if Beth and I don't get on? That would be most uncomfortable. I said I'd discuss it and get back to him.

After a chat with Louisa and Caleb I was persuaded to go. They quite rightly said that we could leave early if there were any problems, and it was unlikely that Beth and I wouldn't get on, given what I'd told them about her after my meeting with James. I remembered I had almost told James at the time that I'd like to meet her but didn't, because the invite should come from them. So here was the invite.

My brother and sister-in-law certainly live in a lovely part of the world. We are driving through the main street of Topsham, a picturesque and ancient settlement on the river about five miles or so from Exeter. The Vincents live in a fifteenth-century farmhouse in the rolling Devon countryside. As we approach it via the twisty lanes, I'm reminded of an old advert for rice pudding. The whole area is truly idyllic. Perhaps there will be a painting opportunity while we are here.

I have already committed Caleb to canvas as he rested in an old wicker chair of Jagger's in the shade of the vines. Both he and Louisa were delighted with it and I must admit, it is pretty special. It might be nice to paint him under the full sunshine in the hills or around here, or perhaps by the riverside. The trouble with using Caleb as a subject though is that I won't want to put the results up for sale, and I do need more artwork pretty quickly if I am to open in October. The answer might be to paint lots more of him and then at least I can allow some to grace the walls of my studio.

'I think this is it, can you check?' Caleb is saying and I'm aware that the car is stationary. My thoughts of painting float off into the ether and I focus on the low-rise L-shaped structure at the end of the gravel drive on which we are parked. The house is built of stone with slate roof and large deep-set windows, the foreground sprinkled with wild flowers. So beautiful. If I could pick somewhere to live, this house would be it, and I've not even seen inside yet. I'd have to move it to the ocean though, of course. I couldn't be without that.

'The sign said Moonridge Farm, is that what we're after?' Caleb asks, peering at the bit of paper in my hand.

'It is. A lovely name for a lovely house.'

The stable door opens, and James comes out, arms waving like a windmill, followed by a small slight woman with caramel skin and the cheekbones of a fashion model. They're her own cheekbones, obviously – she just looks like a model. She's wearing a multicoloured boho dress and her dark hair is long and in two plaits over her shoulders.

'Welcome, both. You found us okay?' James asks, hugging me briefly, and shakes hands with Caleb. We say we did and then James introduces Beth.

'I am so happy to meet you at last,' she says to me and puts her hand lightly on my arm. Her beautiful face is lit by a huge smile and there is so much warmth in her eyes that I surprise myself by giving her a quick hug.

'Likewise.' I step back and slip my arm through Caleb's. 'This is Caleb,' I say unnecessarily, as James has obviously told her all about him, but I am feeling slightly awkward, despite the warm welcome, so I have to fill any silences. I think it's because I want everything to go smoothly.

Caleb and Beth hug and then James leads the way indoors. It's just as lovely inside as out and we take a seat on a big comfy sofa facing French windows that look across a sweep of yet more fields and rolling hills. On the patio, which is dotted with pots of bright flowers, there's a black-and-white cat stretching itself languidly under the late afternoon sun and a smaller ginger one at the bottom of the lawn sharpening its claws on the fence.

Beth says that the black-and-white is called Pie, the other Marmalade, and both are her pride and joy. 'They might not be in a few months' time,' James says bringing in a tray of nibbles. 'The baby will be number one, then.'

'I guess you're right, but I have room in my heart for all the family, human and non-human,' Beth says and pulls her tongue out at him.

'Even me?' James says, dropping a kiss on her forehead.

'Well, that might be pushing it a bit.' Beth laughs and tosses a few peanuts into her mouth. The fact that they are a perfect match is imprinted on the look they give each other. I then wonder if there actually is such a thing as a perfect match, or if it's just something we are meant to aspire to as a partnership.

But then I take a step back as if I'm in an audience in a theatre and watch their gestures, their eye contact and body language as objectively as is possible while they talk about the house, the cats, what their favourite flowers are, and I conclude that it is blatantly obvious that they are very fond of each other – dare I say it, in love, even. I know without doubt that it isn't an act. Their feelings are almost palpable.

James goes off to get drinks and for the second time today I surprise myself by saying, 'You seem very happy together – I'm glad.'

Beth nods and relaxes back into an easy chair by the windows. 'Thank you, yes we are, ridiculously so.' Her face grows serious and she holds my gaze. 'I do worry that such happiness won't last, you know? It doesn't seem fair sometimes that we have such a lovely life when others live in misery.'

The depth of feeling in her voice is so genuine that I warm to her even more. She is obviously a kind and caring woman and patients must love her. 'I know what you mean, I think. Perhaps there is some mileage in the karma thing – what goes around, comes around. If you are good and kind to others, then you reap the rewards,' I say.

Caleb nods and slips his hand into mine. 'I'd like to think that's true, but sometimes good and kind people have awful lives.'

'Yes.' I sigh. 'Perhaps there is actually no such thing as karma. I try to be good and kind when I can, though. Why be horrid to folk if there's no need?'

'Exactly,' Beth says. 'And I can think of quite a few people who are horrid but have great lives.' She wrinkles her nose at us. 'Doesn't seem fair, really.'

There is a wicked response waiting on my tongue that really oughtn't to be allowed free, given my new outlook, but I can't resist. 'True. Talking of Mother, I hear you visited her recently.'

Beth looks at my deadpan expression, but she must have caught the humour in my eyes and snorts down her nose. 'Do you know, I was just thinking exactly the same but daren't say so, of course!'

Caleb laughs and so do I. Then I say, 'I shouldn't have said it really, because she did apologise after a fashion, and I *am* trying to look to the future in a positive way.'

James comes in with the drinks and he pretends to be offended by us when we explain what we are all laughing at. He folds his arms and says in an excellent imitation of Mother's voice, 'I fail to see the humour in it. All I have ever done is my best for everybody, and this is how you repay me – my own flesh and blood.'

Everyone collapses at that and we go on to have one of the best times ever. Later, after dinner, Caleb and James are in the sitting room playing cards and Beth and I are sitting at the kitchen table over a drink. She has a glass of elderflower pressé, no alcohol of course because of the baby – much to her disgruntlement. 'It's not that bad, really. I don't miss having a drink, you know, I can take it or leave it,' she says, tapping her fingernails along the stem of her glass.

I smile and take a sip of wine.

'Oh my goodness, what's that out there?' Beth says suddenly and points to the window, her eyes wide, her other hand on her chest.

I whip my head in that direction and feel her fingers snake around my glass. I look at her in surprise and she heaves a heavy sigh and folds her arms. 'Damn it, I nearly got away with that...'

We both laugh and then talk about her work, my painting, and eventually fall into a discussion about Mother and it seems so easy and natural to talk about it all to her, I can hardly believe it.

'I do wonder if Mother's behaviour after James came back was due to the fact that she was traumatised after she was forced to give him up, or if she's always been a right cow,' my tone is light-hearted, but I mean every word.

'That's hard to tell, really. I think what makes up someone's personality is very complex. In the early days, parents have a huge influence on our lives, obviously, and wider societal influences and individual life experience helps to shape who we are later on.'

I nod. Beth must have had some sociological theory in her education somewhere. 'Yes. That's what I think, too. There's the ongoing nature versus nurture debate, though, isn't there? How much of an individual's behaviour is guided by nature, in other words innate, and how much is to do with everything else you just outlined.'

'Yes. I don't like to think of anyone being born bad, though, do you? Some people still believe that nowadays. I see it as the easy option. It stops you having to think about societal influence. It's really political, too. Because let's say that if someone is a thief, murderer, rapist etcetera, it's because they were born bad, it's in their genetic make-up and that's it. It has nothing to do with poverty, a violent upbringing or powerlessness for example. The ruling elite and politicians and the like are therefore off the hook.'

Beth and I are so much alike it's uncanny. 'Exactly,' I say. 'It's so refreshing to meet someone that has similar ideas to me. There must be an element of nature, though? Isn't that what makes us all different – even if identical twins grow up under the same conditions they are still likely to act in different ways, sometimes. They aren't clones of each other.'

'Yes. But each twin will have slightly different life experiences, especially as they grow up and away from the family nucleus. So, it's hard to say how much of the difference in personality is nature and nurture. Perhaps we will never know.' Beth shrugs and gives me a smile.

'What was your upbringing like, Beth?' I ask because I am genuinely interested. Sometimes people ask those questions out of politeness or convention. I can't see the point of that, because if the story turns out to be boring you have to pretend interest with a rictus grin stretched across your face.

'The best. Don't get me wrong, having a black dad and white mum wasn't always plain sailing. There were always plenty of bigots and small-minded people ready to have a pop. But we three children had a stable home with parents who loved us and each other. I couldn't want for more.'

I'm happy for her, of course I am, but there is a smidgen of jealousy hanging about my mind and I wish there wasn't. To bury it I say, 'Glad to hear it. James tells me that your dad's family originates from Nigeria.'

'Yes. Dad was born here but Granddad came over here from Nigeria in the nineteen fifties.' Beth shakes her head and looks at her hands splayed out on the table. 'Dad's upbringing was a totally different kettle of fish to mine. He was beaten on a regular basis. Nigerian culture sees that as normal – or did then. Spare the rod, spoil the child and all that crap.'

'Your poor dad. Yet he never raised a hand to you?'

'No. I think Mum's influence helped, but I think he never wanted to inflict pain on his children after the horrible way he and his siblings were treated.'

An uncomfortable thought pushes its way to the front of my mind and brings a few sheepish friends with it. 'Compared to your dad's, my situation wasn't that bad at all, was it?'

Beth's eyes grow wide and she takes my hand. 'Of course, it was. Just because there was no physical abuse, you suffered just as much. Perhaps more. Words can be just as wounding as having a broom across your back or a punch to the head. Words can be lethal weapons.'

I nod and think about that and wonder if I would have preferred beating to being told that I was Mother's penance, a nasty little bitch, hard to love and all the rest of it. A tough call. I read somewhere that a victim of abuse said the bruises heal, but the wounds words leave behind are still open years after. I don't want to think about this anymore and take my glass to the sink. 'Anyway, you'll be pleased to know I made a list of names for the baby,' I say and nod at Beth's tiny bump.

'Ooh, let's see,' she says, a big smile on her face.

'It's not a very long one.' I pull the list from my jeans pocket and push it across the table to her.

Beth taps the bit of paper with her nail as she reads down each of the list of eight names. 'Nice, hmm, no, lovely, perhaps, really nice, no, hmm.' She looks up at me and smiles again. 'Thanks, Lottie. I'll show James and let you know. There are at least two that I really like.'

Though it has become important to me that I help choose the name for my niece or nephew, I would hate it if they went ahead just to please me. 'You know, it's a huge decision, the child will have that name forever, so please say if you don't really want any of them.'

'Oh, believe me, I would, Lottie. I'm a bit like you there. I say what I think even though it might not go down well.'

'Yes, James told me what you said to Mother about counselling.' A chortle rolls in my throat unexpectedly. I sit back down opposite.

Beth wrinkles her nose. 'I wasn't joking, either. I often feel that she's "on the edge".'

'Oh yes, me too. I do wonder if my granddad is partly to blame for the way she is. I mean, besides the fact that he made her give up James. He was very domineering, used to getting his own way... though my gran was one of the most wonderful people to have walked the earth. She had a quiet confidence and didn't take shit from anyone, certainly not her husband. Gran told Mother that they would work something out if she wanted to keep her baby, but I suppose she didn't want to enough, in the end.'

'I'm no psychiatrist, but that could be the kernel of the whole problem.' Beth turns her palms to the ceiling and shrugs. 'The guilt.'

'Yes, Mother said that on the phone. She also blamed it on her father... but now I look at it in the light of our conversation, it could have been down to her in the long run. Yes, Granddad made it hard for her, and my other grandparents too, but with Gwendoline behind her, she could have dug her heels in... I'm sure of it.'

There is a little lull as we sit with our own thoughts for company. What happened feels clearer now, but I mustn't forget that Mother was only sixteen at the time – who am I to judge what she should have done? Dad was probably just as wimpy back then as he is now, in fact more so. He would have just gone along with what everyone else wanted, and if Mother didn't want it enough, then he would have supported her decision.

'You okay?' Beth says, tapping my wrist.

'I will be. And no matter how much I toss it all up and down in my head, it still happened. Then there was the counselling, the suicidal thoughts, the self-harm. I can't change that, and I've already started to deal with it. In a way, there's no point going over and over it, is there?'

'I guess not. But in my experience, things like this do need revisiting from time to time with fresh eyes.' Beth laughs. 'I call it "protracted closure".'

My eyes roll, and I laugh, too. 'Has your husband told you how much I love that word?'

'Indeed.'

'Hmm.' I narrow my eyes and my mouth twists itself to the side.

'I'm going to say something that might be a bit embarrassing for you – it might not, of course.' Beth's expression turns serious and my heart does a bit of a thump. 'All this talk about family and the past has made me realise something connected to that old saying, you can't choose your family, but thank God you can choose your friends.'

She stops and looks at me. I feel uncomfortable. Why doesn't she just finish what she has to say? 'What has it made you realise?'

'That James and I are incredibly lucky to have found a family member that we would also certainly pick as a friend. I'm so pleased you are in our lives, Lottie.'

The kick of pleasure in my gut switches a heater on in my face and Beth says she's sorry she's embarrassed me. I shake my head and say, 'I'm not embarrassed, just very flattered and very pleased… and I'm lucky, too.'

James and Caleb walk in and ask if there's any wine left, which I'm pleased about, because I don't think either of us know what to say next. I watch Beth sorting drinks for everyone, the men chatting about something unimportant in the Vincents' homely kitchen, and I try to commit the moment to memory. It isn't a turning point, or anything of significance really (though the wider context is, of course), but it is real and genuine, you know? One of those times when you realise that you aren't doing anything extraordinary, but that the swell of happiness inside you grows so big that you just have to acknowledge it.

I could ask if I could paint them all tomorrow in here, so I will have a physical aid memoire, but then the moment would be lost, contrived and meaningless. No. My eyes and brain can handle the painting right now and I have a feeling that they will do a much better job for me. James catches my eye and asks if I'm okay.

'I am very okay, James. In fact, I'm bloody marvellous.'

Chapter Twenty-Six

Not for Sale

I t's October and the day before the opening of The Calico Cat. Sorry I've neglected you, but you'll have to forgive me as I have been very busy. Okay, let me catch you up. The stay with the Vincents was lovely and James and I have talked on the phone a few times since. Me and Beth text regularly, too, and at last I have a real friend of around my own age. You know I said before that I didn't really have many friends because they got on my nerves? This isn't true of Beth at all. We have loads of shared ideas and interests and we can speak plainly without worry of offending.

Out of the eight names I picked for the baby, James and Beth have chosen Louisa and Jacob. Obviously, it would depend on the gender of the child as to which one it gets. Louisa was beyond thrilled when I told her. After Caleb returned to school, I stayed with her for a week and painted as if I were a machine. Not literally, of course – the paint would have landed everywhere. I don't think machines have much of an artistic and in-touch-with-nature eye, or hands to paint with, come to think of it, unless they are a robot type of machine.

The result of all my hard work will be on display tomorrow. This thought makes my knees go wobbly and a little organ grinder appear in my insides. Don't get me wrong, I am totally happy with my painting, ecstatic even (Louisa keeps prodding me to be more vocally proud of it), but it's only natural to worry about a new venture, isn't it? Especially when that venture is so personal to you. If the paintings don't sell, then it's a reflection on me. If they aren't deemed good enough, then I'm not a good enough artist. If I'm not a good enough artist, then the launch of the new career is dead in the water and I'm back to the drawing board – except I won't be, will I? Because I can't draw well enough.

I know – I'm jabbering. I can practically hear you sigh and see you rolling your eyes. Louisa and Caleb have given me a good talking to about it all. Caleb asked me what had happened to that confident, couldn't give a toss what other people think girl he knows and loves. I told him that she's still inside me ninety-nine point nine per cent of the time but seems to do a runner when it comes to thoughts of opening day.

Caleb is back on board with the business side of it all, thank goodness. He's going to do the books and other stuff that I'm no good at and have no desire to learn. He did most of the organising, too, while I was being a painting machine. A friend of his knew a signwriter who did a wonderful job. 'The Calico Cat' in orange, black, and white letters now sits over the door. It sounds garish but it's not. You'd have to see it to appreciate it.

Caleb also contacted Peter, Leo and Neave, and to my surprise they are all coming. I thought Peter might, because he doesn't live far away, and he said he would at the time, but the other two live north of Bristol, which is a good three hours from us. There is also the fact that we didn't totally see eye to eye over the charity walk, too. Nevertheless, they said they'd be delighted to come and I will be delighted to have them.

There are also ex-colleagues from school, including Anna, who is very jealous that Caleb and I are together, my parents, his parents and his brother and sister, Beth and James, of course and my lovely Louisa. She will bring her sister Suzie and her husband, and there might be other people that have been persuaded by the very swish leaflets Caleb designed and left around the main tourist haunts. To think I was worried about nobody turning up – now I wonder where we'll put them all in such a tiny space.

Louisa helped organise the nibbles and wine. In fact, she supplied it all, really, which was so generous of her. I made her promise to tell people that it's from her vineyard. Mother came round a few weeks ago to meet Caleb and wanted to stick her beak in over the 'decorations'. She thought it might be nice to have some tasteful party balloons and bunting about the place. I agreed to the bunting but drew the line at balloons. When she complained, I said that if she didn't like it, she could do the other thing. Mother immediately became complacent and overly affectionate, saying how proud she was and so on. I wanted to say that this was too little too late but knew that wasn't a good idea. I need to be the grown up in the relationship, because she finds it so hard to be.

Mother had to sit down when she learned that Beth and I were big mates and that Caleb and I had stayed at Moonridge Farm. I really wish you could have seen her face. It looked as if her eyes didn't belong to the rest of it. The muscles that organised the smile function were working overtime, which pushed her cheeks into little pink pillows, and her eyebrows were arched almost into her hairline in a show of happy surprise. The eyes couldn't hide a kaleidoscope of emotions that flickered back and forth, though, totally at odds with the expression of delight she was trying so hard to pull off.

Afterwards I tried to clarify in my head what the eyes were saying, but that conversation was complicated. Overall, if I had to pick the overarching theme from those of regret, jealousy and hunger, it was mostly hunger. Mother wants what I now have with James; she couldn't give a stuff about Beth, as we know, but she can't bear the fact that we all like each other so much and want to be in each other's company. She's obviously worried that when we meet up we might discuss her and find her wanting, just like Louisa said. There's nothing to be done about that, though, is there? It is what it is.

Caleb, unlike Beth, has apparently found favour. Mother couldn't stop talking about him to me on the phone the next day. She said that he was a good-looking chap, so kind, considerate, intelligent, and that I must try and hold on to him. I said he wasn't a prize trout on the end of a fishing line, for goodness sake. If he didn't want to be held on to, I'd chuck him back over the side. Furthermore, people shouldn't be bullied into liking someone, it made for an unstable relationship. Mother just harrumphed and changed the subject. But then I didn't expect anything else really.

So, it's the day of the opening and I'm in the studio with my immediate family, Caleb, and a Greek tragedy going on in my head. Will they like my work? Will my speech be too speech? Should I just forget the speech? No. Of course they won't like my work, how could they? I'm not ready for this yet. I need more time. I tell myself to shut up and look out of the window at the ocean. We have decided to open the doors in a few minutes, then I say 'a few words' and declare the studio open. Luckily, it's a lovely day because we would never fit everyone inside here at once.

Louisa is outside chatting to guests and handing out glasses of sparkling wine. A playful breeze makes steel-grey streamers of her hair and I am reminded of the first day I saw her. Who would have thought that we'd become such great friends – mum and daughter, even – such a short time later? Not me, but if there are such things as lucky stars I do thank them, very much.

A good-looking couple, possibly in their mid-sixties, wander up and have a chat with Louisa. Caleb whispers to me that they are his parents and hurries out to meet them. In all the excitement I'd almost forgotten that they were coming and now I'm even more nervous. What if they don't like me? What if? What if? This constant negativity is beginning to get tiresome and it's so not like me. Who cares in the end who likes me and who doesn't? Who cares if none of my work gets sold and the day is a disaster? Not me.

In the end it's what I want to do and the main thing is I *am* bloody doing it. I'm not chained to a career that's killing me bit by bit, draining my creativity and spitting me out wrinkled, used up – a husk of a person at the other end of forty years who barely has the energy to wonder where all the time has gone.

Louisa checks her watch and gives me the nod and I'm pleased to find that the last conversation I had with myself has dumped the nerves and I'm ready to enjoy my day. Caleb opens the door and I step out and smile at the assembled guests. I abandon my huge speech that was far too long and a bit grand for such an occasion and just say, 'Good morning, everyone, and thanks so much for coming. I feel so honoured that you did, and I know some of you have come a long way,' I smile at Leo and Neave who are just coming up the path. 'Please help yourself to refreshments, have a browse, ask questions and don't feel obliged to buy anything – it's enough that you are here to help launch my new venture.' I stand to the side of the door, give a huge smile and sweep my arm inside. 'Welcome to The Calico Cat.'

It's an hour later and can you actually believe it – nearly half my work has been sold! This is both overwhelming and terrifying, because how on earth will I paint quickly enough to keep replenishing? Louisa calms me by saying we'll have to make prints and sell other bits and pieces until I have built up my collection. Mother hovers at her shoulder nodding and adding her advice, which is really a repetition of what Louisa says. I noticed her expression when Louisa and I shared a warm hug a little while ago. This time it was unadulterated jealousy. This made me a bit sad for her, but not too much.

Dad appears to have changed, become more decisive, forceful even, so miracles do happen. He told me that I was one of the finest artists he'd come across, which was nice. Then he got me in a corner and tried to have a heart to heart about the past after one too many glasses of wine, but I told him we'd do it another time. And we will, because I think we need to.

A lion's voice behind me says, 'This collection is totally awesome. We just bought this one.' I turn to Leo and Neave and look at the painting he's holding. It's the one I finished from the Holywell Bay sea monster drawing the day we met.

Before I can reply, Neave gives me a huge hug. 'Told you it would look fantastic as a painting,' she says, her open freckle-dusted face just as I remember it.

'Yes, you did! Thank you so much for buying it. How are things going with the walk?' I hope this doesn't lead on to difficult questions about charity again, but I didn't know what else to say.

'Thanks to you we cut it short. It was all getting a bit much, to be honest, now that autumn is here,' Leo says, his darty-about eyes doing just that over my face.

Thanks to me? What on earth did he mean? I hope my argument didn't mean that they abandoned the cause – that would be just awful. 'Not sure I'm with you.'

'You told Peter about us, didn't you, or Caleb did, and he donated more than we could have raised in a thousand walks around Britain,' Neave says and does her tinkly laugh that I like so much.

What a relief. 'Really? I had no idea. How did you know it was him, though, it being anonymous and all?'

Leo slips his arm around Neave and she leans her head on his shoulder. 'It was because he donated so much. Half a million needed proper verification!' When they see my jaw drop they throw back their heads and laugh out loud, his golden curls mingling with her red ones as if they are a sunset.

'Oh, my word! What a wonderful gesture. Have you met him?'

'We've spoken on the phone, of course, but we haven't seen him here, yet,' Neave says.

'Yes, he sent word that he was running late but will definitely be here. I can't wait to see him again. Winning the lottery couldn't happen to a nicer man.'

'Nice of you to say so, Lottie,' Peter's voice says in my ear.

'Peter, you're here!' I turn around and the broad smile on his moon face encourages mine to try and beat it.

'I am indeed, and what a wonderful painter you are, just stunning.' He flings his arm towards my work on the far wall.

Neave's eyes fill and she puts a tentative hand on his arm. 'Peter, it's Neave.' She takes Leo's hand. 'And this is Leo. As I said on the phone, we can't ever find the words to tell you how grateful we are to you for'

Peter's moon turns pink and he pats her shoulder. 'You have thanked me many times. I know you appreciate it – no need to say more.'

Leo dashes at his eyes with the back of his hand and pulls Peter into a huge bear hug. Though it's a poignant moment, I feel a laugh snake into my throat and have to pretend to look for something in my pocket, because Peter looks like a helpless little rag doll in Leo's grip.

At last he's released and after a few minutes chatting, Neave and Leo wander off to talk to Louisa. Peter looks at the wall of paintings and strokes his chin. 'I can't make up my mind which one I like best, so I'll buy them all, how about that?'

Of course, he's being his ever-generous self, but I don't want him to. As I told you before, it's not about the money really; it's about the love of painting. I want people to come in here and fall in love with something. I want my work to speak to them, to their soul. I know we had the discussion about souls before and perhaps having artwork speaking to them might sound a bit 'out there', but it's how I feel right now, so this is what I tell Peter.

'I totally understand, Lottie.' He looks around again. 'All of them are speaking to me, but not as strongly as that one in particular.'

My gaze follows his finger to *The Calico Cat*. She's just come along for the day to oversee proceedings, but she's certainly not for sale. Caleb made a not-for-sale tag that was there earlier but now is missing.

'Sorry, Peter. That one's not for sale.' It occurs to me that he must be beginning to wonder why he bothered coming.

'Why? I adore it.' He goes over and looks into her eyes. 'It's speaking to my soul – and I'm not making that up.'

'It belongs to me. I only brought it because she inspired the name for the studio.' That is only partly true as you know only too well.

'Name your price.' Peter looks from the cat to me, his moon bright with longing. 'I'll give you a million for it.'

My jaw drops for the second time today and for much longer. That kind of money would be life-changing. Then into my stunned thinking process comes clarity. But my life is already changed.

I don't need more money; I have good friends and family, I have Caleb, and I'm doing what I've always dreamed of but never had the courage to try.

'Now that is a most generous offer, Peter, and I thank you... but she isn't for sale.'

It's Peter's turn to drop his jaw. 'My God, you must be very attached to this painting, Lottie.'

I think about that one for a few moments. 'Yes, I am... but you see, it's not the painting but what it represents that isn't for sale, if you know what I mean.'

Peter shrugs and turns one side of his mouth up. 'Not sure that I do.'

No. Why would he when it's a bit tricky to explain it to myself. Caleb did it best the day we got back together, when he talked about the cat being a metaphor for me and turning points and so forth. I couldn't tell Peter all that, though. It would take far too long and I'm not sure he'd really understand.

'In a way the cat represents me – who I am.' I look at the cat. 'I praise the fact that I am individual, different, stubborn... apart to an extent, but not totally. I used to think that I didn't need other people and that I could only rely on just myself. Then I did some learning and discovering during and after my walking holiday and found that I do need some people after all. The right people.'

'And the painting says all that about you?' Peter says, and his eyebrows do a bit of a wiggle.

I knew he wouldn't understand properly. How could he? 'Kind of... but the main thing you have to know is that she will never be for sale.'

'Right. I get that.' Peter rubs his nose and then points to the *Dragon Cave*. 'Now this one really speaks to me even more than the cat! Please tell me it's for sale?'

'Yes, of course,' I say, though each time I see a painting being wrapped, it feels like a part of me is being taken away, a memory lost. Then I tell myself that I have plenty more memories in my paintbox just waiting to be made.

It's early evening and everyone has long gone. Caleb and I are sitting across the road from the studio on the beach watching each new star come out. We have a picnic hamper, Louisa's wine and a warm blanket wrapped around both of us. We're talking about the day and how wonderful it's been, even though the ocean keeps shushing us. The tide is coming in and we'll have to move back up the beach soon.

'Did you know that Peter paid a thousand pounds for the *Dragon Cave*, even though it was priced as two hundred and fifty?' Caleb says.

I swallow a strawberry. 'No, I didn't. But I'm not surprised he gave more, considering what he wanted to give me for *The Calico Cat*.'

Caleb doesn't even flinch when I tell him how much and my jaw drops. I expected at least a few words of incredulity. 'So you're not shocked, disappointed?'

'What, that you turned down a million squid for a painting that is to all intents and purposes a physical representation of your life journey, of who you are? Of course not. I wouldn't expect anything else. That's why you're so special to me. You're extraordinary, beautiful, clever, headstrong, stubborn, sexy, unpredictable'

I place my hand over his mouth. 'Okay, enough! My head will grow bigger than the moon up there if you carry on.' I pull the blanket tighter around us both and kiss him on the cheek. His skin tastes of strawberries and sea salt. In a way I can hardly believe that he just took the news like that. I mean, I could have given him some money to him to help follow his dreams too, whatever they turn out to be. But he did just take it like that, and that's why I'm so fond of him. Okay, I'll admit it to you. I love him, I suppose, but don't tell him or his head will grow bigger than Jupiter.

'What else have we got in that hamper? Any salmon left?' he asks, shoving his hand into the basket and rummaging ineffectually.

'I'll get it.' I hand him a variety of foods while my mind shouts at me to say something nice to him. He needs to know that I want him around for the foreseeable, but the happy ever after conversation I had with Louisa isn't resolved yet. So why not ask him what he thinks?

'Caleb. What do you think about happy ever afters?'

'As opposed to sad ever afters?'

'Kind of.' I shove my hair from my forehead and realise I've put cream cheese in my fringe. 'I mean, do they exist, really?'

'I'd like to think so. Who wouldn't?'

'Yeah, but the thing is, because having one is so important to us, we might be sad if ours isn't perfect, doesn't live up to our high expectations of happiness. So instead we pretend that we do have a happy ending, when in fact we don't.'

'Is that a reason not to aim for one?' His eyes look into mine, the blue in them soft in the fading light, and my heart rattles about a bit.

'No. I suppose not.'

'Good. Because happy or sad, I'd like to be with you on the way there. I mean, everyone needs to know what happens at the end of a good story, don't they?'

The ocean is shushing louder but I need to be heard. 'Okay. I'll let you come with me and we'll see what happens. And I agree… this story is so far, so good.'

A bully of a wind turns up and kicks sand in our faces. It's time we went anyway; the tide is almost in and I can't feel the end of my nose. Caleb slips his arm around me as we walk up the beach and his body feels warm and strong against mine. In my imagination, a picture is forming of a bird's-eye view of us walking like this towards a hopeful future. I think I'll paint it tomorrow.

The End

Lightning Source UK Ltd.
Milton Keynes UK
UKHW01f1127240518
323147UK00001B/23/P